GREEN TO GO

JOHN H. CUNNINGHAM

Other books in the BUCK REILLY ADVENTURE series
by John H. Cunningham

Red Right Return
Crystal Blue

GREEN TO GO

A BUCK REILLY ADVENTURE

JOHN H. CUNNINGHAM

GREEN TO GO

Published by Greene Street, LLC

Book design by Morgana Gallaway
Cover image © MaxB77 / iStockphoto

This edition was prepared for printing by The Editorial Department
7650 E. Broadway, #308
Tucson, Arizona 85710
www.editorialdepartment.com

Print ISBN: 978-0-9854422-1-7
Electronic ISBN: 978-0-9854422-0-0

www.jhcunningham.com

To my ladies,

Holly, Bailey and Cortney

Thanks for your love and support

Acknowledgments

FOR THEIR HELP WITH THIS BOOK, AND FOR SUPPORT, ENCOURAGEMENT, and assistance with the series, the author would like to thank Ross Browne, Renni Browne, Peter Gelfan, Morgana Gallaway, Chris Fisher, Mark Korsak and the entire team at The Editorial Department, Anne-Marie Nieves and Lori Edelman at Get Red PR, Steve Troha, Jita Fumich and Folio Literary Management, John Wojciech at C:straight Media, Pege Wright from Parrot Heads in Paradise, Gloria Garcia for Spanish translation, Jim, Jay, Mary, Beth and my family.

Also, a big thank you to all the readers, reviewers, bloggers, Facebook fans, Twitter followers, Jimmy Buffett fans and my friends, new and old, who have embraced Buck Reilly and my writing. It's been a fun journey that I hope continues into the foreseeable future. The goal is to entertain and share some of the irreverent and crazy things I've seen, done and imagined, so far. More to come. . .

Note: At the time of publication, Fidel and Raul Castro are still alive, but things have already begun to change there, albeit slowly. This book takes place during the immediate vacuum anticipated after their demise.

CONTENTS

Driving While Blind

1

"YOU COULD'VE AT LEAST WORN A SUIT, BUCK."

Ben was wearing one of my old Armani suits. When you owe someone money, a lot of money, nothing's sacred. If my linen pants and aqua green fishing shirt weren't out of place here, my flip-flops were.

On the table was today's *International Herald Tribune.* Typical headlines: RAUL CASTRO'S FUNERAL . . . UNITED NATIONS TROOPS IN DARFUR . . . U.S. WARNS IRAN . . . There's something different, DEMONSTRATIONS IN PERU.

Just the name of that country brought back memories of fast friends and past adventures. The first paragraph stated that Javier Guzman, one of the candidates in the upcoming presidential election, demanded that the European nations who had stolen thousands of tons of silver from Peruvian soil centuries ago provide just compensation now. His rhetoric had launched a wave of frenetic nationalism across the country.

Click-clack. Click-clack.

A tall young woman in a tight blue skirt and starched white blouse marched through the cavernous lobby. Her high heels pounded the granite floor like ball peen hammers. I swallowed but had run dry of saliva. Her blond hair was cropped short and her blue eyes were shielded behind metal-framed glasses. She was a *precise* beauty.

"Mr. Reilly?"

"Yes?" Ben and I said at the same time.

No smile.

"Come with me, please."

No accent, either.

We followed her through a metal gate and into a small waiting room. She directed us toward a computer terminal and instructed us to enter our account numbers. Ben went first, and I noticed a small bald patch on the back of his crew cut. My hair was still as thick as ever. Guess that gene must have skipped me. Ben finished, then moved aside.

Once we were done, a green light lit the screen. So far, so good.

The woman led us down another hallway and into a smaller room with a table and two chairs. We remained standing.

"I'll return momentarily."

Ben turned to me when we were alone.

"I wasn't sure they'd let us in, considering the investigations into your—"

"It's over, Ben. And now's not the time." I motioned around the heavily monitored room.

He shook his head and shifted his focus to the door. With family, the past is always present. Once tagged good or bad, you're forever judged in that light, especially when the media dumps gas on the fire.

Moments later, Ms. Personality reappeared pushing a stainless steel cart with what appeared to be a keg sitting on top. She stopped the cart next to the table.

"Your keys, gentlemen?"

Ben pulled a chain up from inside the open collar of his shirt. His key was a duplicate to the one I'd stored in my waterproof pouch and hidden below the seat in my 1946 Grumman Widgeon. Mine had been stolen by a Key West art dealer cum Cuban spy named Manny Gutierrez and wound up on the bottom of the Florida straits just outside the Cuban territorial line.

The woman and Ben stared at me.

"I don't have my key."

Ben closed his eyes and the woman stood even straighter.

"I'm sorry, but you must have—"

"I'll be using the five-letter code established as an alternate."

"Dad's ciphers? Are you *kidding*?"

The woman opened a narrow drawer on the side of the steel cart and withdrew a small apparatus that resembled a credit card machine used in European restaurants.

"Re-enter your account number, and when prompted, enter the five-space response," she said.

The machine nearly slipped from my glistening palms. I caught Ben's head-shake out of the corner of my eye and his long sigh filled the silence.

All the different five-letter combinations I'd considered tumbled through my head.

"There were what, five ciphers?" Ben said. "I tried to figure them out, just out of curiosity, and got nowhere. How could you—"

"They all led to a last one which was a statement, not a cipher," I said. "'Love of my life.' Guess this is the only way to know for sure."

"That's great, Buck. I financed this trip—you could have told me—this will be the last straw if—"

"Mr. Reilly, please."

I licked my lips and my index finger hovered over the keypad that contained all twenty-six letters of the alphabet, along with the numbers zero through nine.

"While we're young, Buck," Ben said.

I turned away to shield the keyboard. I pressed a "B" and no alarm sounded, so I continued. "E," "T," "T," "Y."

A phrase in what I assumed to be German appeared on the screen. I handed it back to our hostess, who read it and pursed her lips.

Ben and I stared at her with open mouths.

"I'll be back in a moment." She hugged the small machine as she left.

Ben turned to me. "You lost the fucking key? Are you kidding me?"

"Not now, Ben—"

"After everything—"

"Drop it." My gritted teeth stopped him mid-bitch.

The woman reappeared, alone. From her pocket she removed a key.

"I'm sorry, I had to retrieve this from the vault. Normally account holders alert us when a key has been lost."

"There's nothing normal about my brother," Ben said.

She inserted both keys into slots on top of the cylinder and turned them.

A green light pulsed.

"I'll be in the anteroom. When you're finished press the button by the door and I'll return. You may use the briefcase on the cart if you need one." She offered enough of a smile that I could see perfect white teeth peeking out from behind her thin pink lips. She closed the door behind her.

Ben put his hand on the handle next to the keys.

"Let's hope you'll be able to pay me back all the money I've lent you," he said.

My heart leapt and I slapped my hand on top of his.

"Can we take a minute to think of Mom and Dad before opening this?"

He laughed. "Now you want to get sentimental? They would never have had this account—or been in Switzerland at all—if your freaking company hadn't been cooking its books and cratered. And if you hadn't warned them—"

"Then you wouldn't have inherited all their wealth, so let's leave it at that, okay?"

"—There never would have been an accident that killed them, Buck, and I'll never forget that. You're just lucky Dodson took the fall."

"He *was* the one who cooked the books, Ben."

My partner from e-Antiquity, Jack Dodson, was still in jail after being convicted of fraudulent conveyance of assets. The FBI had been unable to prove the same against me, which is why I was able to flee to Key West with the airplane Ben had reluctantly bought me. Once there I started Last Resort Charters and Salvage. The old flying boat allowed me to make use of the copies of the treasure maps I'd squirreled away when e-Antiquity tanked, but they too were stolen by Manny Gutierrez and lost at sea along with my Swiss Bank key.

With a tug Ben opened the vault. I saw his eyes widen.

"Oh, my, God . . ." he said.

"What is it?"

He reached inside. "This can't be . . ."

As he withdrew his hands I recognized the contents. Not cash, not stock certificates, not precious metals.

He pressed his face into the open cylinder.

"That's it?" he said.

I smiled.

"I'll be a son of a bitch," he said. "So much for you paying me back, big brother."

The contents fell from his hands and landed with a thud onto the table. It was a notebook wrapped in plastic and secured with a rubber band.

Our father had been a career Foreign Service officer who at one point was considered as a candidate for Secretary of State, but he was also a dreamer. He encouraged me to start e-Antiquity and was our original venture capitalist, so when I realized e-Antiquity's financial fantasy ride was about to hit the wall—

"Is this what you sent him as you hurtled toward insolvency? All your secret maps?" He paused. "The evidence the Feds need to prove the insider trading?"

"For which you're the sole benefactor, thank you very much."

The notebook contained the originals of all the maps and research information that could lead to many lost treasures.

"I was going to let you have all of what was in here anyway, less what you owe me, but I don't want anything to do with . . ."

"History?"

"Ha! Treasure maps, unauthenticated ones at that? Old letters and miscellaneous ramblings of ne'er-do-wells?" His mouth hardened. "This is what got Mom and Dad killed, you know."

I couldn't meet his eyes.

"Treasure hunting," he said, "the original lottery, but with worse odds."

I peeled back the rubber bands and the notebook sprang open. Each of the archival plastic sleeves contained documents with unique stories, historic relevance, my team's sweat from scouring the globe for them. Not to mention the dregs of our investors' capital. All of it squirreled away to prevent them being sold at the bankruptcy auction with the rest of e-Antiquity's assets—what's this?

A lone envelope stuck out from the middle of the plastic sheaths. Ben saw it at the same time and plucked it out.

Written on the front: "Charles B. Reilly, III."

Ben tore it open.

"Hey, I'm the one—"

"It's a letter from Dad," Ben said.

"Can I—"

"*Son*—"

"Okay, Ben, fine. You read it."

Son,

If you're seeing this for the first time, it's because we never had the chance to discuss it. It never mattered to us, and it shouldn't to you.

Your mother was told early in our marriage that she couldn't have children, so we set out on this course. Your brother was a surprise, a few years later. You have always been our son, even if you weren't born a Reilly. We love you no different than had you been, so don't let this change a thing.

These papers are all we have from the adoption. The laws were very specific back when you were born, and the birth mother's anonymity was always protected. We will not be hurt in the least if you choose to pursue your past, and given that you're now over thirty, we encourage you to do so for medical history purposes, at least.

We are your parents, and you are our son. That will never change.

We love you.

Mom and Dad.

Silence.

I was adopted?

He dropped the letter on the table and I picked it up. It was Dad's handwriting, for sure. Adopted? Really?

"Wow." Ben shook his head. "Must be a shock to the system, huh?"

"You could say that."

"It does explain a lot."

What? I couldn't believe I was adopted and only finding out now.

"Good luck with all your maps, Buck. See you around."

I heard a buzzer, the door opened, then Ben was gone. I slumped into a chair. I felt as if I'd been punched in the stomach, kicked in the nuts, hit over the head with a 2x4.

I was adopted?

2

Key West, Florida. A month later . . .

"KEEP IT ON THE LINE," I HOLLERED. "DAMNIT, LINE . . . QUIT . . . MOVING."
Lights pinwheeled through my fogged vision as I concentrated with all my might on keeping the bike upright on Whitehead Street.

Stay awake . . . concentrate . . . Sing a song . . .

"*Oh say can you see?* Just barely . . ."

The bike swerved right.

"*By the dawn's early light*—almost dawn, anyway . . ."

I swerved back toward the middle. No cars at this hour.

Good thing, too.

The Pier House had been packed for Karen's going away party. She'd rather be in New York than Key West? And I was too . . . what? Chicken? Fucking-a, chicken's right! She told me she wanted to be with me, and what did I say? Ha!

The bike swerved hard—

Too hard.

Everything spun—I hit the curb, tumbled, stars lit the night, but my eyes were closed. I rolled up onto my knees, but felt as if I were still spinning. I gagged once, and suddenly puked on the sidewalk . . . Sorry about that, tourists.

I rolled onto my back and concentrated on breathing.

"Don't fall asleep. You'll wake up in the drunk tank."

A small voice in the center of my alcohol-saturated brain noted that speaking to yourself, out loud, is normally a bad sign. But when you're really, really drunk, it helps get you through.

"Get up, there's not a soul here to help you," I said.

I got up—and stood weaving.

What's that? A man . . . a big man. Hey, it's—

"Truck," I said. "Truck *Lew*-is!"

I veered to the right, looking at my feet to keep from falling. Boxer's feet. Dancing feet. All the while telling the world, "Won't go down . . . stay off the ropes!"

Truck was carrying something, and somebody was helping him.

"What's that, a coffin?" I laughed. "You an undertaker now?"

Truck and the other man lowered the crate. They blurry-walked toward me. My eyes flickered, and then they were in front of me.

"You're drunk," Truck said. "Real drunk."

"What makes you . . . think . . . that?" I swallowed acid reflux.

The other man whispered something to Truck.

"Who's your buddy? Buddy pallbearer?" I giggled

A flash of Truck with his arm cocked back. Hey, what the—

Boom!

I took a blow to the face, and was back on the ground. I saw the other man's shoes. The right leg lifted.

"Hey, what are—"

When my eyes opened I saw light. Not sunlight. Not the light from the windows in my suite at the La Concha. Light from a naked bulb, high in the room. There were bars on the walls . . ..

Crap.

My head pounded, way beyond a bad hangover. I moved my hand over my scalp and winced: my fingers had found a massive lump amidst the matted hair in the back.

Had I been in a fight?

With one eye open I scanned the room. There was another drunk, snoring like an idling chainsaw. With great effort I sat up.

What the hell happened? My mouth was dry-sealed shut, and my throat felt as if I'd swallowed battery acid. A vague recollection of endless shooters with silly names caused a spike of pain behind my eyes. I should have stuck to rum.

My watch was gone. What time was it?

Karen, my quasi-almost-totally-girlfriend, had left. By now she'd be halfway up the Keys. New York awaited, with a management job at a top hotel and a publishing deal pending. Would she have stayed if I'd asked her to? Last night she'd pulled me aside, and her eyes had searched mine, waiting, while the only thing that ran through my head was 'Can't we be happy like we are now?' Bullshit. So I said nothing. I didn't need to. She knew. So I drank, way too much, instead.

Hello, drunk tank.

I saw movement beyond the bars.

I saw a policeman peering into the cell.

"You alive?"

"So it appears." I rubbed the knot on the back of my head. "How'd I get my head smashed in?"

"The officer who brought you in found you lying on Whitehead Street next to your bicycle in a puddle of booze you barfed up. Lucky you didn't puke while you were on your back—you'd be in the morgue instead of here."

Did I smash my head falling off my bike?

"What time is it?" I said.

He checked his watch. "Seven-fifteen. You were brought in at nine past three, so you've been asleep for four hours. I need to keep you until your blood alcohol content is back to legal, and in your case that might take a while."

Oh, God. I just wanted to be in my own bed.

"Has Currito Salazar shown up yet today?"

"Curro? The bail bondsman?" he said. "Client of his?"

"Am now," I said. "He's more of a friend, though."

"There's no bonding process for drunks, Bubba." He twisted his mouth to the side. "But hey, Curro's my cousin. I'll call and see if he's up."

The guard strolled around the corner. He was a large guard, probably too large to be out on patrol. And if he was Curro's cousin, that meant he was an old-time Conch, so maybe the rules were more malleable than if I was just another drunk tourist.

The chainsaw sputtered next to me, then revved again with renewed intensity.

The guard returned and said Curro would be here in a half-hour or so. I settled back against the wall and dozed off. I was awakened soon by another man, in plain clothes, who shook my shoulder. His eyes burned brightly and his motions were quick, determined.

"Come with me, Mr. Reilly."

When I stood I felt a wave of nausea. I again touched the knot on the back of my head. It hadn't subsided but at least it wasn't any bigger.

"Do you work with Curro?" I said.

The man didn't answer but walked me down the hall, where we picked up a uniformed escort. I was led to an interrogation room: small, with a table and two chairs.

The man identified himself as Detective Johnson of the Key West Police Department, then got me to give my name, place of residence (the La Concha Hotel), employment (Last Resort Charters and Salvage), marital status (divorced and freshly dumped), date of birth, etc. etc.

"Are you always this thorough with drunks?" I said.

"What were you doing on Whitehead Street at three o'clock this morning, Mr. Reilly?"

I told him about Karen's going away party at the Pier House, how I had too much to drink and tried to ride my bike home. The rest was a blur, probably as a result of this plum on the back of my head. He asked if he could feel it, which I allowed, then he pressed down, which made me flinch and yip.

"There were around fifty people at the party and several could confirm I was one of the last to leave." I felt silly blurting that out, but this guy was so serious maybe we'd balance each other out.

"You see anything strange as you were traveling on Whitehead this morning?"

I blinked my eyes a few times. "I'm afraid I don't recall *being* on Whitehead."

He studied a file for a moment, and his eyebrow rose.

"You're blood alcohol level was .26. No wonder you don't remember anything."

He was turning pages and reading what I assumed to be my rap sheet. Lovely. His forehead furrowed. No surprise there.

"You have quite the colorful past, Mr. Reilly. e-Antiquity? I remember that company. And you were the *president*?" The long stare spoke volumes. "Says here I'm to notify the Federal Bureau of Investigation if you're arrested, for anything. Agent T. Edward Booth in Miami. Mean anything to you?"

I bit my lip. This day was going downhill, fast.

He asked another few questions but I had nothing more to offer. My curiosity was aroused, though.

"What happened on Whitehead that you're wondering if I saw?"

"What makes you think I'm wondering if you *saw* something, rather than considering you a suspect?"

That made my heart double-clutch. "Do I need a lawyer, or what?"

He stood, stared down at me for a moment, and left me alone in the room.

What the hell happened? Had I run somebody over on my bike? Possibly, but how much damage could that have done?

An image fluttered through my mind. I'd seen someone when I crashed. Someone familiar? Maybe it was just details from the vivid dream that woke me in the cell. I couldn't recall, but whatever Detective Johnson was investigating, it had to be worse than puking on the sidewalk.

3

ANOTHER TWENTY MINUTES ELAPSED BEFORE THE DOOR SUDDENLY OPENED. Someone stood in silhouette thanks to the bright light behind him. He was wearing shorts.

"The hell you done now, cuz?"

Currito Salazar stepped inside the door. Five feet eight inches, beer gut, salt and pepper beard, cargo shorts with chicken legs, flip-flops, and a ratty old T-shirt emblazoned with "Full Moon Saloon."

"I'm guilty of getting drunk, Curro. I don't know what these guys are talking about. What happened on Whitehead, do you know?"

"Let's get out of here before they change their minds," he said.

"You bonded me out?"

"Ain't no bond. I'm to take your ass back to the La Concha where you're to go straight to bed and sleep off the rest of whatever shit you drank last night." He grinned. "Good party?"

"Not exactly."

We went through the release procedures and I was given back my meager possessions: watch, wallet, and a Spanish piece of eight silver coin on a gold chain. Outside, the heat hit me like a bucket of water and got the knot on my head throbbing.

Curro's vintage Cadillac Coupe d'Elegance awaited. The trunk was so voluminous that the lid shut with room to spare after we put my bike in. Maybe I'd be better off in the darkness there myself.

Once in the car, Curro lit a Parliament cigarette, drained what was left of a Michelob pony bottle, and put the car in gear. We swung out onto Simonton, crossed Duval, and took a left on Whitehead.

As soon as we turned the corner my eyes nearly burst from my head. Police cars were everywhere.

"What the hell happened?" I said.

"Treasure Salvors was hit in the middle of the night. Picked clean."

"Holy shit."

"Exactly."

He slowed the car and pointed with his chin. "They found you right out front, too. Lucky you were so fucked up, otherwise they'd still be grilling your ass." He shrugged. "Even so, I'm surprised they let you go, to tell the truth."

Given the gravity of the issue, so was I. An image of my crash popped into my head, and the recollection that I'd seen someone. A couple of people, maybe. I needed to remember what the hell I'd seen and whether it might hold a clue to the robbery.

Yellow tape and barricades were stacked up in front of the Treasure Salvors Museum. A quick count identified a dozen police cars—Monroe County Sheriff's Department, city cops, state cops—along with a bunch of news vans.

Robbed? How much of the half-billion dollars' worth of gold, silver, and jewels harvested from the wreck of the *Atocha* over the past thirty years had been kept at the museum? I wouldn't think much beyond what was in the displays and the gift shop. But considering the price of gold and silver these days, that could still be worth millions.

A pair of antique cannons were perched atop the red brick stairs outside. Standing in the doorway was Donny Pogue, the director of Treasure Salvors. His Midwestern pallor and round frame looked more stooped than usual as he watched the comings and goings of police.

"Let's get you home—"

"Hold on, Curro, there's Donny. Let's ask him—"

"I'm not going anywhere near that place, cuz. Get out and I'll circle around the block. I told my cousin I'd bring your ass back to the La Concha, and that's what I'm doing, but I didn't say we wouldn't make any stops."

I walked around until I was directly in front of the entrance but still thirty feet away thanks to the police barricades. Donny eventually spotted me, and even from that distance I saw him shrug. He came down the steps, between the two cannons, and over to me.

"Robbed?" I said. "I thought this place was like Fort Knox."

"So did I, but whoever planned this knew what they were doing. Took down the alarms, used light explosives to enter the building and vaults. In and out in fifteen minutes. We didn't know shit until I got here this morning. Unbelievable."

I looked around at the various police cruisers and officers that swarmed the property.

"What do these guys think? Any clues?"

Donny shook his head. "They're not telling me anything. The way it went down, so smooth, I'm sure we're all suspects. You know, guilty until proven innocent." He looked back over his shoulder, then leaned in closer to me. "One thing, though—when I got here this morning? I found a note."

"What kind of note?"

"Weird note. It said: 'This was never yours.'"

"That *is* weird. Any idea what it meant?"

He sucked in a deep breath. "Only thing I can think of is some of Mel's original investors, ones that crapped out before the find, or maybe competing treasure hunters from back in the seventies. The cops asked for all those kinds of records, anyway. Guess they'll be checking every possible angle."

"Any previous threats or weird comments like that?"

He rubbed his chin. "I guess you could count those nuts from South America who wanted to repatriate raw materials stolen by the Spanish in the 1500's."

"You mean like the reports out of Peru in the news?"

"Haven't seen any of that. I'm talking about the wackos who were in a few months ago. I thought they were historians, or maybe kidding, to tell you the truth."

An older man in a suit called Donny's name from the door of the museum. I thought for a second it was Detective Johnson.

"Gotta run, Buck."

"Let me know if there's anything I can do to help."

A sardonic smile bent his lips. "I'm sure there'll be a reward of some sort. With all the cops involved, I doubt there'll be any privateers hired, but you never know. Maybe you'll finally get that gold doubloon you've been after."

The suit now stood behind the cannons with his hands on his hips. He called Donny's name again, and Donny jogged back up the steps. But the suit kept his gaze fixed on me. I turned away. Last thing I needed was for him to find out I was the idiot passed out at the scene of the biggest crime in Key West's history. That and my past as an e-Antiquity treasure hunter were bound to make me a person of interest in this case.

I heard the screech of brakes and turned to find Curro's Cadillac by the curb.

"Seen enough of this crazy shit, Buck?"

"Yeah, I'm ready for bed."

My throbbing head hadn't been helped by the sun and flashing police lights. I closed my eyes and tried to remember what I'd seen here six hours ago, but between the headache, dehydration, and exhaustion, I drew a blank.

4

SIRENS CONTINUED TO WAIL UP AND DOWN DUVAL STREET, DRIVING NEEDLES in my aching head. The elevator deposited me on the sixth floor of the La Concha hotel, the highest point on the island, where I hoped the noise wouldn't be as loud. I opened the door, and—what's this?

A letter was halfway under my door.

My name in Karen's handwriting on the envelope. I thought of the last letter I found, from my father informing me that I was adopted. Holding the envelope with both hands. I caught a whiff of Karen's lilac scent and my heart dropped. I placed the envelope on my bookshelf. I wasn't in shape for any more surprises just now.

The message light blinked on my machine but I only wanted water, and after guzzling a quart, I collapsed on my bed. Out instantly, I didn't budge, even though the phone occasionally penetrated my inebriated slumber. Last Resort Charter and Salvage was closed for the day, maybe the week. After an hour and a half and another missed call, I finally turned on the television and lowered the volume to a whisper.

I expected images from the Atocha Museum but found shots of South American rebels instead. Peru was back in the news. The rebels had fanned the flames of nationalism and were gaining credence in Lima as the elections approached. Centuries of Western opportunism had stripped Peru of precious raw materials and left behind a destitute populace. My archeological and commercial activities there a few years ago would have had me strung up in this environment.

Washington and European capitols were increasingly under attack as have-nots around the globe found their voices. Revolution fever has spread from the Middle East to South America, and many places in between. According to the news, Peruvian rebels still demanded repayment from past imperialists, to the tune of billions of dollars.

Maybe we could help them build casinos.

I got out of bed—very slowly—guzzled some more water, and was stopped cold by a picture of Karen laughing in my kayak with Betty in the background. She'd loved flying around in my Widgeon the past few months, accompanying me on fruitless efforts to find ancient shipwrecks in the waters around Fort Jefferson.

The phone rang.

"Reilly, is that you?"

"Who's asking?"

"It's me, Nardi. Got some news for you."

Officer Frank Nardi, from the United States Coast Guard, Officer of the Deck aboard the Mohawk, a 230' cutter, and one of the guys I played basketball with on Tuesdays at Douglas Community Center. What day is this?

"I know, the Atocha Museum—"

"Not that, and not so fast. This'll cost you lunch, but trust me, it'll be worth it."

We agreed to meet at Pepe's in a half-hour, which forced me up to face the day.

Coffee could wait until I got there, but a shower was imperative. Ten minutes later, I was ready for food and starting with a handful of aspirin as an appetizer.

Through the lobby I avoided eye contact with the new day manager, Bruce, who was Karen's replacement. Maybe it was time to find another place to live. I'd been a month-to-month resident at the La Concha since coming to Key West, and having broken my vow not to complicate things here, I now felt like a trespasser in my own residence. Karen had been the first woman I'd opened my heart to since Heather divorced me in the midst of all my other troubles, but I still hadn't been able to give her anything more than a good time. She deserved more and she knew it. I was back to the mantra that relationships weren't for me. La Concha employees gave me sympathetic looks. Maybe they felt sorry for me because I'd lost my girl. Or maybe they'd heard I spent the night in jail.

Whatever.

Outside, the sun was blinding. I had to get my blood circulating, but given how I felt, a run was out of the question. Curro had locked my red bike to the rack out back, and I was in no condition to walk all the way to Pepe's. I got on the bike, only to again hear the sound of sirens. I was not about to go down Whitehead, so I crossed Duval and turned up Simonton. Was the air crisp, or was I shaking from the alcohol still in my system? Hopefully coffee would solve both. At Caroline Street I turned right and double-timed it toward Pepe's, now late to meet Nardi.

5

THE CHATTER WAS LIVELY IN THE SMALL RESTAURANT, FILLED WITH speculation about the robbery. There had been many attempts over the years, none of them successful. Until now. It was big news, but there was still no report, at least publicly, on the extent of the theft. Donny said the thieves had cleaned them out but hadn't offered any specifics.

Out of what? And how many whats?

Frank Nardi was perched on the edge of his seat.

"About freaking time, Buck."

"What happened at Treasure Salvors was crazy, huh?"

"Yeah, that's why I'm in a hurry," he said. "We've been scrambled to go on patrol."

"Why, did buccaneers make the heist?"

"Don't joke. What better way to make a getaway on a remote island after a theft of that magnitude? They have road blocks every ten miles up the Keys and haven't found shit, so either the goods are still on-island, or the bad guys left by boat."

"With what, exactly?"

Nardi said he didn't know the magnitude of the theft, but agreed that what was on display and in the gift shop was likely worth millions. Which made it the biggest crime in the long and notorious history of Cayo Hueso.

"Anyway, that's not what I wanted to tell you about," he said.

The waiter came and I ordered fried eggs and their famous refried potatoes along with a tall mug of coffee. Frank only had time for a refill of orange juice.

"What's up?" I asked.

"A piece of non-sensitive intel you might find interesting." He smiled and hunkered down on his crossed arms atop the table. I leaned in closer. "We've received some transcriptions of radio chatter from boats out of Cuba involved in a salvage operation."

"There's a lot of old Spanish galleons sunk in Cuban waters," I said. "No surprise there. Fidel plundered quite a few, though, so nobody's sure what's left—"

"I'm not talking Cuban waters or a sunken galleon. I'm talking Manny Gutierrez's ocean racer you sank on the Cuban territorial line. Interesting thing is, it doesn't seem to be a government salvage team but a private one, not that there's much sanctioned private enterprise in Cuba."

Frank said something about how things were changing rapidly in Cuba since both the Castro boys had died. The power vacuum and ensuing struggle had grown in intensity. All of this was interesting, but my mind had anchored on the news that Gutierrez's boat was being sought for salvage. The memory of my waterproof pouch sinking with the boat was etched in my mind as the moment my bankruptcy became irreversible.

At least until last week's revelation in Geneva, when Ben and I recovered the originals from my parent's Swiss bank account. I'd tried to find that wreck three times over the past months so I could retrieve my pouch. Given the hasty departure we'd been forced to make the day my maps and key were lost, I never thought to record the GPS coordinates.

"The boat sank in international waters," Nardi continued, "so there isn't anything we can do about it, but I thought you'd be interested."

"He was a spy, Frank. Isn't Homeland Security worried about what else might have been on board?"

"Not based on what they recovered from Gutierrez's home and art gallery. He was just an observer and distributor of funds to small cells around Florida. He left all his records intact. His operation was more defensive in nature, in case we launched an assault on Cuba. They had a series of counter-attacks planned." He paused. "But, yeah, you'd think the intel-types would have already salvaged that boat. And maybe they did. They wouldn't have told anybody."

If our government had salvaged the wreck, then they would already have my copies of treasure maps—which would be fine, since they could care less about that kind of stuff. But if a well-funded private group got hold of them, my now having the originals wouldn't matter. I didn't have the resources to compete.

"Buck, are you listening to me?" Nardi said.

"Sorry, I was just remembering that day. Maybe Gutierrez had some cash or art on board someone found out about. Maybe that's what they're after."

"More likely Gutierrez is after it himself. After his hero's welcome in Havana, and with Fidel and Raul now dead, he's been building a powerbase within State Security alongside Director Sanchez that could have him well positioned in whatever government emerges. Maybe there's something on the boat that will help him do that."

The waiter delivered my food, but my appetite had vanished. So had my hangover. My mind was now moving at high-speed as I imagined Gutierrez having my maps and pouch. Our showdown on the water left me with a thin scar on my forehead that now throbbed. It would not be a warm reunion if we ever met again.

Nardi got a call on his cell phone and had to scamper as the Mohawk was readying to patrol for the museum thieves. Before he left, he handed me a gift I could have used a month ago: the coordinates for the wreck written on a piece of his Coast Guard stationary. He said that based on the chatter it didn't seem the Cubans had the exact location, but they were getting close.

I mounted my bike, left Pepe's, and turned from Caroline down William Street. I'd planned to ride back by the Atocha Museum, but Nardi's news changed the plan. At least the Cubans didn't have the exact GPS location of the wreck. The Cuban Navy vessel never got within a half-mile of us. And if it was Gutierrez, he'd have a hard time finding his former boat.

I blew through the intersection at Southard, where a horn and the squeal of brakes caused me to jump the curb on my bike. The driver waved a fist from his Jeep window. I stood on the sidewalk, surprised at how deeply in thought I'd been lost.

A century-old two-story Conch house with a widow's walk stood before me, tired and abandoned, and somehow having not been updated during the past decades of modernization. I felt a momentary kinship with the worn-out structure. It had good bones and with enough attention—and money—could one day be a masterpiece.

With greater attention to my surroundings I pedaled across town to Blue Heaven in the heart of Bahama Village. I thought I'd find Conch Man behind the bar readying for the lunch rush but was surprised to see him at one of the tables with a couple of serious- faced men. In resort wear, they almost looked the part, but their flowered shirts were pressed, their hair was closely cropped, and black shoes and socks peeked out from below their creased khaki slacks. Trouble?

Lenny spotted me and said something to the men, who turned to glance at me as Lenny strutted over. Tall, muscular, black as night with a million-watt smile and stellar sense of humor, Lenny naturally drew people in.

"Police or accountants?" I said.

He laughed. "Political consultants. Willy's determined to get me on the ballot for the City Council in a couple months. Figured these boys out of Tallahassee could teach me a few tricks of the trade." He paused. "Like they gonna tell me how to connect with my own people."

Lenny's uncle, Pastor Willy Peebles, was well known for turning the island's troubled youths' lives around. Lenny was one of his top projects, and his subsequent reputation as an outspoken man of the people earned at the pulpit of the bar at Blue Heaven had won him the name Conch Man. But he was more Chris Rock than Barack Obama, so these consultants had their work cut out for them.

"I came by hoping you could help me out. I'm going out to salvage our favorite wreck."

"Hell you talking about? Another one of them sunken treasure ships?"

"Not exactly. Gutierrez's speedboat. Seems some Cubans are searching for it and I'd like to get there first, which means I need to get out there ASAP, like today or tomorrow."

"Again? Boy, you never give up. We already tried to find that thing—"

I held up Nardi's note with the GPS coordinates.

"Got the numbers right here, Lenny."

He glanced back at the men, who openly stared at us. "I'm booked with these boys for the next four days, morning and afternoon, in between breakfast, lunch, and dinner. You in a hurry, I can't help."

Damn.

One of the results of my having checked out from the mainstream world was that I'd left most of my old friends behind. The conscious decision to maintain a low profile here limited the number of friends I had made. Bottom line was I only had a short list of people I could count on, and Lenny was at the top of the list.

"Sorry, Buck, my handlers await." Conch Man smiled broadly, pumped his eyebrows, and returned to the mirthless consultants.

I pitied these men if they thought they could turn Conch Man into a cookie cutter politician. His political viability was in his deep connection to Key West's history, people, and the issues facing them, not because he'd be the slickest of Tallahassee-groomed candidates. The thought of him engaged in a political campaign made me smile. Any debates with opposing candidates would make for fine entertainment.

But Lenny's candidacy wasn't going to help me with my immediate problem.

6

I EXCHANGED THE BIKE AT THE LA CONCHA FOR MY '72 LAND ROVER BEFORE heading to the airport. Why would Cubans be diving on that speedboat? I couldn't believe American authorities wouldn't worry that Gutierrez might have left some sensitive information on board. And I couldn't take the chance that our government might have already salvaged the boat, either.

What if it was Gutierrez himself? What if he was after all the old maps, letters, charts, historic accounts, and summaries of missing treasures scattered around the Caribbean, South America, European, and Far Eastern waters that had been the culmination of my work at e-Antiquity? He hadn't fled with much when he left Key West, so he must have recognized their value.

The copies were almost as good as the originals. If someone with access to sufficient funds attained them, they'd be in a far better position to pursue those treasures than bankrupt Buck Reilly. I could sell the originals to cover my expenses for awhile, but the archaeological value represented more to me than I'd yet been able to put in clear thoughts, much less words. Maybe I wanted to prove that when the Wall Street Journal proclaimed me "King Charles" it wasn't a flash in the pan, and that I wasn't driven only by getting rich.

I found Ray Floyd poring over the flight records of a Beech Baron that had been confiscated by the DEA and sold to a local businessman. He'd gotten an incredible deal, but the plane had never run right, leaving Ray challenged and perplexed by its issues.

"Hey," he said. "I thought you'd have been down at Treasure Salvors looking for a way to get involved."

"I've got my own problems right now, old buddy."

"Old buddy?" Ray's loose smile faded. "What do you need?" he said.

I feigned a look of hurt. "Gee, Ray."

I walked to the machine in the back of the hangar, bought two soft drinks, and gave one to him.

"Okay, now I'm really worried," he said.

"I just need you to take a flight with me and stay inside Betty while I take a quick dive. No big deal. Should only take a half-day, max—"

"Provided it can wait a week, sure, but I can't take a half-day any time soon. This damn Baron's driving me crazy, and I've got—"

"Tomorrow, Ray. It can't wait any longer." He studied the serious look on my face. "Nothing illegal, don't worry . . . not even quasi-illegal," I said.

"Do I need my passport?"

"We can't get too far and back in half a day, can we?"

"If anyone else asked me that question, I'd say no, but with you I've learned—"

"I finally got the coordinates to Gutierrez's wreck from Nardi, okay? We can leave at dawn, that way you can get back as early as possible. What do you say?"

He rubbed his palms on the front of his Margaritaville flowered shirt, then down across the sides of his cargo shorts.

"Fine, I'll do it, but the quicker the better. I promised Bobby Spottswell I'd have this thing working before next weekend, and I still can't figure out what's wrong with it."

"It's never run right because it's jinxed. Drug planes always are," I said. "Spottswell's pissing money away on that thing."

"A fool and his money are my best friends," Ray said.

I spent the rest of the afternoon renting scuba gear, stowing it inside Betty, checking tomorrow's weather, and planning the flight and dive. Based on my charts and the coordinates Nardi had given me, the depth in that area was about a hundred and twenty feet. It was outside the main flow of the Gulf Stream and there hadn't been any hurricanes since the boat had sunk, so with any luck it hadn't been swept too far off the mark.

If all went according to plan, I should be able to get in and out fast.

7

B ACK AT THE LA CONCHA, I WALKED UP TO THE FRONT DESK.
   "Hi, Bruce."

"Buck Reilly. You were a hoot last night, friend. How's your head this morning?"

"Never better. Can you get my mail?"

As the only month-to-month resident, aside from management, what little mail I received was held at the front desk. I missed the monthly stipend from my brother, and kind of missed Ben, too. Apparently my not being a blood relative gave him an excuse to write me off once and for all because I hadn't heard from him since Switzerland.

Bruce returned with a couple pieces of junk mail.

"You have a phone message, too." He handed me a folded piece of paper. One of the downsides of living in a hotel is that the staff knows much of your business. I unfolded the paper. *FBI agent T. Edward Booth. Call ASAP.* A number followed.

Bruce smiled. "Said it was urgent."

Perfect.

I headed for the front elevator, which led to the rooms that faced Duval Street. I hadn't heard from Booth since he twisted my arm into agreeing to help with the odd job every now and then in return for keeping the heat off the on-again-off-again investigation into the charges of insider trading at e-Antiquity. I imagined Detective Johnson of the KWPD followed instructions and called Booth to report my arrest for public drunkenness, but had he mentioned my being found at the front step of the Atocha Museum shortly after it was robbed?

I glanced out the window of my sixth-floor corner suite. Duval seemed quiet. There was a light breeze rustling what foliage there was in this part of town, and I wondered whether I should make a run to the wreck site now instead of in the morning. Nah, it was pointless to go alone, and Ray had been adamant about needing to work on Spottswell's Baron today.

As little as I wanted to return Booth's call, curiosity got the better of me. I dialed the number from the room phone, wondering as I often did whether the hotel operator was listening in. I'd deep-sixed my cell phone and all other non-navigational electronic devices when I came to Key West as part of my technological detox, which had been a liberating sensation. I no longer jumped at the buzz on my hip, nor did my fingers twitch to text-related jingles. If you wanted me now, you could call me at the hotel and leave a message. It had taken awhile to get used to, but damn if it wasn't a better quality of life.

"What took you so long to return my call?" Booth said.

"How'd you know it was me?"

"Because you're the only one who has this number, Reilly. I set it up specifically to run you from."

My nerve endings were not happy with this news. I could feel them twitching.

"Why don't I feel honored?"

"So you and brother Ben took a little trip recently, huh? Buying chocolate and fancy watches in Geneva, maybe?"

Before I could deliver a comeback he sailed on.

"No, it wasn't a shopping trip, was it, Reilly? Unless you consider removing the contents of your parents' account at Swiss Bank shopping. Tell me, was it worth it? Is your bankruptcy going to be a distant memory? Are you planning to move from the hotel into one of those fancy Key West mansions?"

"How the hell do you—are you monitoring my private activities, because that's got to be a violation of my personal rights, or some laws, or—"

"Interpol requires Swiss banks to keep them informed on accounts associated with suspected criminals or victims. You happen to be both. So, I'll ask you again, should I alert the IRS and let them know you have some new income to declare?"

"No such luck, Booth. Nothing but old letters and memorabilia." Damn. To what extent did Interpol actually monitor these things?

"Aw, that's too bad, kid. But take this as a warning that you're still under the microscope, not only here, but abroad, so if you're lying to me, we'll find out sooner or later. If you all of a sudden have a lot of cash, or buy some fancy shit, we'll descend on you like a hailstorm of pain. You and your brother."

"You've got nothing better to do than keep me on a tight leash?"

"Choke chain, hotshot, and don't forget it. But that's not why I called, or I should say, why I'm calling you into duty."

I rolled my eyes. Here we go . . .

"I assume the coconut telegraph down there has pounded all day over the Atocha Museum being cleaned out?" he said.

"Yeah, it's all over—"

"But you probably don't know that the Sea Lion's missing too, along with your friend Clarence Lewis, its captain."

Truck?

A switch clicked in my brain. It was him I'd seen last night, with another guy, carrying a crate. *No!* Truck had punched me? Damn. Truck had punched me. He was part of the heist?!

"You still there, Reilly?"

"You called to report a missing tourist boat, Booth? Have you been demoted?"

"I'm told the security cameras on the waterfront next to the museum show that the Sea Lion tied up in the middle of the night, just before the theft, and left just after. There's video of Lewis schlepping boxes onto the boat, along with a number of other characters."

I swallowed hard. Video? What was the breadth of those cameras? Could they have captured me, too?

"That's got to be a mistake, Truck wouldn't—"

"We're tracking multiple vessels in all directions now, but it takes time, and we can't reach them all fast enough, which is why I'm calling you.

Nothing dangerous, no front-line work, just a sightseeing charter for you to go fly around toward the Bahamas and look at boats. You call me on this number every few hours and let me know where you've gone, what you've seen, and right away if you spot the Sea Lion. Can you handle that, Reilly?"

Double crap. A Cuban salvage team's zeroing-in on my waterproof pouch, and Booth wants me to waste hours, maybe days, flying around looking for . . . I still couldn't believe Truck would be involved with the robbery. The lump on the back of my head was still tender, though, and I did recall a vague image of his fist cocked.

I needed an out.

"As a matter of fact, no, Booth, I can't help you. As you've already mentioned, I'm broke. I barely have enough money for rent, and I certainly can't afford gas money to be out joy riding for you."

"I've got a credit card coming your way, Reilly, so you're covered. Expenses only, mind you. Now get your ass out there and start looking. Call me before the day's out."

He hung up on me.

I slammed the phone down.

"Shit! Fuck! Damn!"

8

How well did I really know Truck Lewis? Could he possibly be involved with the Atocha theft? He was a friend and certainly no Boy Scout, but would he do something that crazy?

I couldn't come up with any way to derail Booth's demands, especially in light of his knowledge of Ben's and my trip to Switzerland. The last thing I wanted was for him to demand to see the "letters and memorabilia" I took from my parent's account. It could all be confiscated as well as lead to charges of fraudulent conveyance of assets, the same charge that landed my former partner in a federal penitentiary.

Booth hadn't mentioned anything about Detective Johnson of the Key West Police Department. Had Johnson seen the security video? Did it show Truck and his associate coming over to talk to me? Would that bite me in the ass?

Right now the only thing that mattered was that I was Booth's bitch on call, and my maps on the speedboat were in jeopardy of being recovered by the Cubans. Best I could do was get out searching ASAP, find the Sea Lion, and figure out what the hell had happened. But the news about Truck, and my recollection of seeing him—no, of his knocking me out—just didn't make sense. I had to do some digging first.

The Sea Lion was part of a full service water-sports company called Footloose Fantaseas, owned and run by Lou Fontaine. I rode my bike to his office on Greene Street, just a couple blocks from his fleet, at Key West

Harbor. I'd never met Lou but I'd heard he cut corners on maintenance and that Footloose had the least dependable fleet on the island.

Bookings were done at the dock and in various hawker-booths around town, so the office was in a small space that had been an antique shop. I walked in and was greeted by a burly woman wearing a Hog's Breath t-shirt and what looked like a permanent scowl.

"Mr. Fontaine available?" I said.

"Who wants to know?"

"Buck Reilly. I'm looking into the missing Sea Lion."

"You look too rumpled to be a cop, unless they're wearing flip flops and letting their hair grow these days. You some kind of reporter?"

"Just a friend of Truck Lewis—I'm trying to find out what happened to him."

"Oh, geez. Listen, sonny, I'm not sure you want to be asking about Truck right now, given the situation."

While she talked I was watching two men in the back of the room. When I mentioned Truck's name, one winced and the other shook his head and looked back at his computer screen.

"But that's exactly why—"

One of the doors in the back swung open and a short, plump, bald man burst in.

"Goddamn that fucking insurance—" He stopped suddenly when he saw me, the cigar clenched in his teeth lowered an inch. "Who the hell are you?"

"This here's Buck Reilly," the woman said. "Friend of Truck's looking into his disappearance."

"Buck, friend of Truck, huh? The sunuvabitch who stole my schooner? Not only that, but brings cops and reporters down on Footloose Fantaseas with all kinds of crazy allegations, like maybe Lou Fontaine had something to do with the Atocha robbery? Sunuvabitchin' Truck Lewis." He had a New York accent and kept waving his cigar around when he wanted to emphasize a point, more or less with every sentence. "After all these years of my keeping him on after a zillion guests complain he's rude and scary when they have a little too much booze, after all his showing up late and sometimes not at all, the sunuvabitch goes and steals my hundred-year old schooner and disappears? *That* Truck Lewis?"

Footloose employees stared at me while Lou scanned me head to toe with the cigar clamped at the corner of his mouth.

"Donny Pogue, the manager of Treasure Salvors, asked me to help in any way I can." Slight exaggeration, but he *had* mentioned a reward.

"You?" Lou said. "The hell can you do that the cops can't?"

Even if I could say so, nobody would believe I was sniffing around on behalf of an FBI Special Agent, and I hadn't yet considered how I'd explain my interest in the matter, having only been inserted into it thirty minutes ago.

"I run Last Resort Charters and Salvage from my flying boat, search and rescue is one of the things I do."

"You here looking for work?"

"I've already been asked to search for your boat, Lou, I just came around to get your thoughts on what happened."

His face took on that getting-something-for-nothing-so-why-not look. He put a lighter to the cigar, expelled a puff of green smoke, and nodded.

"Come back to my office."

I wanted to ask for an oxygen mask—there were ashtrays on each of the three desks, and Ms. Hog's Breath lit a long black cigarillo herself. Lou's office was like a flat spot on Mt. Trashmore, with papers, old brochures, invoices, photos, and printed materials spread in no discernable order all over the cramped room. He sat in an old wooden chair, leaned back, and put his hush-puppied feet on the desk. There was nowhere for me to sit, so I crossed my arms.

"Does the boat have a transponder of any kind on it?" I said.

"It did. They found it in the water behind the museum, along with the radio. Ruined. Sonuvabitch."

"When did you realize the Sea Lion was missing?"

"Not till this morning. They came back from last night's sunset cruise, docked, the passengers left, the rest of the crew told me they washed her down, and left Truck behind talking on his cell phone. Must have been calling his partners, the crooks who robbed the museum."

I considered this. "Did the rest of the crew—how many others were on board last night?"

"Two others."

"Did they report anything strange to the police about any of the passengers? Or the way Truck was acting?"

"Nah, just the usual booze-cruisers, makeout artists, dreamers. And Truck was his usual charming self. Only one complaint, from a dyke who said he insulted her by calling her butch."

"So other than the boat disappearing and the video from the dock behind the museum, there's no evidence Truck stole the boat?"

"My boat's gone, he was caught on camera, and now I'm left to fight out the value with the insurance company for an irreplaceable hundred-year old ship, the oldest in Key West, not to mention my fleet's now reduced by twenty-five percent. I really don't give a shit about the details. Either the cops get it back or I'm screwed."

"How long has Truck worked for you?"

"Eight years. Aside from scaring the shit out of some of my customers, he really wasn't a bad captain. Never sank any boats, at least. Who knows what happened? I just hope they find my schooner. Intact."

Something occurred to me. "Where does Truck live?"

Lou made a face. "With his brother. Goes by Bruiser. He's an animal."

I knew Bruiser oh-too-well, and Lou was right.

"They rent a duplex on Patterson."

I thanked him and left.

Outside Footloose Fantaseas, the cigar stench clung to my skin like a layer of mold. I hadn't learned much from Lou Fontaine, certainly nothing that totally convinced me Truck had turned into a thief, even though I'd seen him toting crates at the scene of the crime. I had what was left of the afternoon to dig, but speed was important, and even though I couldn't beat the Cubans to the sunken speedboat, at least I had the exact coordinates. But seeing how it was Truck who hit me, and Treasure Salvors who got robbed, and the two were possibly connected, going after my maps would have to wait. Especially if I was on that security video too.

That possibility gnawed at me. Experts would enhance, review, and re-review the security video, so I wasn't in the clear yet. I could just imagine how Booth would react if he spotted me on the tape. I'd be his bitch for life—if I didn't wind up in jail as an accessory.

I had to find the Sea Lion.

9

THE RIDE TO PATTERSON AVENUE TOOK ME PAST GARRISON BIGHT MARINA and the city charter boat docks. It was a gorgeous day, and I realized it had been a hell of a long time since I'd been able to pursue what had once been a passion: billfish on light line. Images of pitching live bait to sailfish and blue marlin tail dancing were fond memories from my days of international travel, wealth, and high-net-worth friends.

I hadn't seen Bruiser Lewis since our boxing match a few months back. I crossed over Truman, coasted along Patterson, and though I didn't have the exact address it wasn't hard to figure out which place belonged to the Lewis brothers: a Key West police cruiser was parked in front of a house with Bruiser standing on the porch, arms crossed.

I pulled up onto the sidewalk and got off my bike. The cop climbed out of the car.

"Can I help you?" the policemen said.

"Reilly, that you?" Bruiser yelled.

I leaned my bike against a scrubby fichus, nodded at the policemen, and walked up under his stare to the porch.

"The hell's going on?" I said. "Where's Truck?"

Bruiser looked past me, scowled, then nodded toward the door. I followed him inside. Boxing trophies, glass tables, leather and metal chairs, and wood floors with Rothkoesque-patterned throw rugs created an altogether different environment than I had expected.

"Some serious shit going on, man," Bruiser said. "They saying Truck robbed Treasure Salvors and took off on the Sea Lion. You believe that shit? Fucking crazy, man."

"I tend to agree with you." I pretty much meant it, despite the evidence and the knot on my head. Truck *might* be involved in the heist, but he was no criminal mastermind.

"Did he ever say—"

"Don't even go there, Buck. He may be stupid but he ain't fucking insane. And ain't no way he'd of done something like that without me knowing." He shook his head. "Nah, man, something fucked up's happened. He must of been kidnapped or something, that's the only thing I can think of."

"Have the police—"

"Motherfuckers wanted to tear this place up. Good thing I was here. They ain't found shit, 'cause they ain't shit to find."

"Can you think of—"

"No, man—like I said, he must of been boat-jacked, or hijacked, or fuckin shanghaied if what they saying's true."

Bruiser's eyes were more intense than I recalled from the time we squared off in the ring. Boxing was his business, and as a pro he could measure the effort required and regulate its distribution to meet the need of the moment. He was that good. But seeing him here, in a situation he couldn't control, with his older brother missing and accused of a major crime, his response was anger, aggression, and something I never thought I'd see in Bruiser: fear.

I wanted to ask more questions, but he hadn't let me finish one yet.

"Look, Buck, I know you help people with your airplane," he said. "I'll pay your ass to get out and look for him."

That made three people who wanted me to go out and search for Truck in the same day. Not that I would ever share Booth's demand with Bruiser. If I did, he'd see me forevermore as one of *them* and he'd never trust me again. I might have seen Truck at the scene of the crime but I would come to my own conclusions, and if I learned anything more, well, I'd tiptoe through that minefield when I reached it.

"You don't have to pay me anything, Bruiser. I'm going up first thing in the morning to look for Truck anyway."

He stared at me and plopped a sirloin-sized paw on my shoulder.

"You all right, man. Keep me posted." He scribbled his cell phone number on a piece of paper. "Take this, too. Truck's emergency frequency he uses if he's got problems. Or if he's trying to get me and the cell don't work, we use this."

"You let me know if you hear anything, okay?" I put the scrap of paper in my breast pocket. "I'll do the same."

When I left, the policeman still on the curb watched me climb onto my bike. I felt his eyes burn holes in my back as I pedaled up Patterson. I was surprised he didn't ask for my ID. Could Booth have told the police I was helping him? I suddenly felt dirty, as if I'd lied to Bruiser by omission. If word got out I was helping the FBI, I'd be finished on this island, and another chapter of my life would end abruptly.

I couldn't let that happen.

10

"**C**ONCH BAIL BONDS."

"Curro, it's me, Buck."

I was at a phone booth next to Strunk Lumber. A convoy of forklifts were unloading a tractor-trailer that had just arrived loaded to the hilt with wood of various dimensions. I hoped it didn't mean a late season hurricane was headed this way, because here in the Keys you start to worry when you see sheets of plywood.

"What's up, cuzzie? You get some sleep?"

"Got a favor to ask you."

"Another one already? What now?"

"I'm heading out to hunt for the Sea Lion and wanted to see what you knew about Truck Lewis."

"Shit, cuz, he's no altar boy, but I wouldn't peg him for something like this."

"Despite the video I tend to agree with you, but what else can you tell me?"

"Little bit of B&E, couple minor assault cases, maybe a DUI or two, you know, typical for a local boy."

"Has he done any time?"

"Nah, nothing beyond a couple nights in the local jail. Never been convicted of anything. Guess maybe that'll change, huh?" A rhetorical question, but Curro's next one wasn't. "And what video you talking about?"

Crap. "Donny from Treasure Salvors mentioned it. The security video from the museum."

"Shows your boy?"

"Apparently so," I said.

"Hmm. That's his ass."

"Does this seem like something he'd be a part of?" I said. "Maybe just muscle and transportation for a cut?"

"Truck? Not really, cuz, but I see shit that surprises me every day. Fact is nothing makes me shake my head anymore. So sure, he could have got tired looking at all the crackers coming down and making money off all the old houses, and with everything costing so much here, he might of snapped, said fuck it, and went after his piece. Who knows, but hey, you find him, make sure he has my number, will you?"

While he talked I was trying to think of how I could ask the real question behind my call. With Curro, though, there was only one way, because he smelled bullshit better than anyone I knew, which considering his clientele was a necessity.

"One other thing," I said.

Silence.

"That security video from Treasure Salvors is the main evidence against Truck."

"Yeah, so?"

"I'm sure KWPD has it, and, well, your cousin . . . the one I, um, met this morning?"

"Sweetwater works in the jail, not the evidence locker."

"I just want to see it myself, Curro. You have any other cousins who might be able to sneak me a peek of that video?"

"Damn, boy, you got some big ones."

I swallowed, not knowing what to say. "Well, it's been—"

"I'll look into it," he said.

"Thanks, Curro. I'll owe you, big time."

"No promises, but yeah, you damn sure would."

THE COAST GUARD BASE BUSTLED AS THE MOHAWK'S CREW PREPARED TO embark on their hunt for the Sea Lion. The 230' cutter had all the state-of-the-art detection and tracking hardware, a crew of one hundred, helipads for up to three helicopters, three rubber-hulled inflatable boats (RIBS), and a long record of success in these waters for everything from refugee interdiction to intercepting drug smugglers to catching Cuban spies. Frank Nardi was the Officer of the Deck, which made him responsible for the safe and proper operation of the ship while at sea. Big job for a laid-back guy with a nice outside jump shot.

The security guard at the main gate wouldn't let me through but called aboard the Mohawk and told Nardi that I was here. Several other boats were tied up at the piers where the water depth allowed submerged nuclear-powered submarines to enter undetected by the outside world. For decades a missile base on Tank Island, just across a narrow canal, had been considered the first line of defense against the Soviet fleet in Cuba. When the USSR ceased to exist and their patronage of Fidel Castro evaporated, the Tank Island missile base was quietly cleared out. Someday the old missile silos would likely be reconfigured into condominiums.

Nardi hustled over, dressed in his dark blue Operational Dress Uniform.

"We're getting ready to sail, Buck. What's up?"

"I heard about the Sea Lion."

"Yeah, so?"

"Truck Lewis is an acquaintance. I've met with his boss at Footloose Fantaseas and his brother, Bruiser. I've got mixed feelings on whether he's really involved."

"That's not the intel I have, sorry."

"Have you seen the video footage of them loading crates onto the Sea Lion? Are you sure it's him?"

"I just follow orders, Buck. It's not my job to critique evidence. What are you doing here?"

"I'm heading out in the morning to search too and thought we could share information. You know, while we're out and about."

"Between the Mohawk's capabilities, satellite tracking, Fat Albert, and our air support, you really think you're going to find something we won't?"

"Not if we're looking in the same place," I said. Booth's directions had been clear, but Nardi was right. It'd be a waste of time to cover the same water they were. "I'm thinking of heading toward the Bahamas."

He looked both ways down the dock. The security guard was on the phone, laughing with someone on the other end. Nardi lowered his voice.

"Then stay to the north, otherwise it *will* be a waste of time because we're headed to the southeast."

"Based on what?"

"Common sense, mostly. Either that boat headed up the Keys or high-tailed it to the Bahamas, because they're the closest islands to get lost in."

"Besides Cuba, you mean."

"We talked about that, but if Truck's involved, his having been arrested and kicked out of Cuba is well-documented. Nobody believes he'd go back there. Problem is, that old wood boat doesn't have much of a thermal signature for infrared detection so she's not easy to track. And they dumped their radio and cell phones in the water so there's no GPS signal to follow. We don't know whether that was smart planning or dumb luck, but either way we need a visual sighting to find them."

A loud whistle sounded along the pier.

"That's my cue, Buck. Let me know if you find anything."

"And you'll do the same?" I said.

"Sure, just keep your television on and watch the news." He winked and took off at a jog toward the sparkling white cutter.

As I made my way home, another fact ate at me. Why hadn't anyone said anything about me being passed out at the scene? Or on the video? I had a bad feeling, but couldn't identify why.

FROM MY SIXTH-FLOOR CORNER WINDOW OVERLOOKING DUVAL STREET, I watched the sun setting on another day in *Cayo Hueso*. Even though Fantasy Fest was still a week away, the streets were filled with body-painted tourists who'd likely be gone before the real party started. With the influx of newsies, law enforcement officers, and party-hearty tourists, you could feel the build-up like barometric pressure before a storm.

Not that I was in a party mood. It was the first time Booth had called me into action, and I didn't like it one bit. I had friends on both sides of the issue and I hated lying to them about what I was doing.

There was no message from Curro, and since I was leaving early in the morning I figured I wouldn't get to see the security video. I confirmed that I'd meet Ray early at the airport but had yet to let him know our plans had changed. He responded with silence when I suggested he bring his passport, just in case.

The worst part, though, would be if we found the Sea Lion and I had to call Booth to report the location. How would I explain that to Ray? Or Bruiser? I hadn't told anybody about seeing Truck last night, nor would I until I was certain of his role. So when I told Ray we were going to look for the Sea Lion instead of dive on the sunken speedboat, I'd have to convince him we were not only trying to help a friend but also going for a reward. Everyone would expect me to go after the Sea Lion as a salvage project, but to perfect a salvage claim you either had to rescue a foundered vessel, be asked by the captain for help, or have possession of the vessel. And if we found it, and I mysteriously had a direct line to the FBI, that would lead to questions I wouldn't want to answer.

I poured four fingers of Pyrat rum over ice.

One crisis at a time, Buck, just take it one crisis at a time.

11

THE SOUND OF POUNDING WOKE ME. WAS IT FROM THE TOP UPSTAIRS?
Bang, bang, bang.

It was at my door.

I rolled over. My clock read 5:13 a.m. What the hell?

Bang, bang, bang.

"Coming! For crap's sake . . ."

I jumped up in nothing but my boxers and yanked the door open without looking through the peephole.

"What!"

"You gonna to make me stand out here, Reilly?"

Special Agent T. Edward Booth pushed past me and flipped on a light switch. I blinked.

"Put some clothes on," he said. "You seem a little too excited to see me."

"You woke me—what the hell?"

I went into my bedroom and pulled on shorts and a t-shirt. 5:13 in the morning!

He held up a CD/DVD jewel case. "This was leaning against your front door, sleeping beauty. I trust you're not bootlegging music or movies now too."

I yanked the case out of his hand. There was a sticky note attached with a message: "Here's the video you wanted. Damn right you owe me. Curro."

Good grief!

The Atocha Museum's security video, taken or copied from the KWPD evidence locker and hand delivered by Booth, no less.

"How come you're not out in the Bahamas like I told you?"

"It's still dark outside!"

I placed the jewel case in a drawer and rubbed the sleep from my eyes.

"You didn't go out searching yesterday, either. Did you think I was joking, or that I wouldn't check up on you?" Booth wore his trademark khakis, blue blazer, and penny loafers. His hair was cut short and his eyes were red. Probably drove all night down the Keys, or flew on a boondoggle government jet from Miami.

"I was asking around, trying to learn something before I—"

"There you go, playing junior detective again. Did I tell you to do that? Did I *not* tell you to keep a low profile?"

He squinted and leaned into me, causing me to step back.

"You have a learning disability, Reilly? On top of being an inside trader, fraud, and potential murder sus—"

"Spare me the bullshit, Booth. I'm going out at six-thirty. I needed a spotter and couldn't get Ray Floyd's help until this morning, so just back off." I turned on my coffee machine.

"The Coast Guard and Marine Patrol haven't found anything, and time's slipping by. I need you out in places I can't go, *tout de suite*," he said.

I gathered my gear while Booth updated me on how his promotion to Special Agent in Charge of the Southern Region was getting him a lot more exposure in Washington, and how he needed more high profile cases to keep his ascension going. Fortunately, the investigator extraordinaire didn't realize he'd just handed me hot evidence I hoped didn't feature my drunken self as the comic relief.

"Am I supposed to give a shit about this, Booth?"

He stared at me, eyes lowered to slits.

"Don't think I'm not aware of you being found drunk and passed out at the steps of the Atocha Museum, hotshot. If you weren't pissed out of your mind last night you'd still be behind bars. So what's good for me keeps the heat off you. Remember that."

I swallowed. Okay, he's not as stupid as I thought.

If Booth could get promoted out of Florida, maybe that would get him out of my life. In which case he was right, helping him would help me.

"Why'd you come down here, since you already have me doing your dirty work?"

"One, because you're not my only asset, hotshot. Two, to give you these." He pulled a cell phone out of his breast pocket, plopped it on the counter, then took a credit card out of his pants pocket along with a wad of cash.

"And three, to keep my eye on you."

I hadn't had a cell phone or credit card since I'd filed for bankruptcy three years ago. I couldn't help but smile. There were also six hundred-dollar bills.

"It's not Christmas, Tiny Tim. This is for communicating with me, expenses and gas. I'll also be able to track your GPS signal from the phone and receipts for fuel while you're outside the country. Remember that if you get any stupid ideas."

I drank my coffee.

"I need to shower and get moving. Do you have anything of value you can share with me, other than your personal advancement plan?" I said.

"The museum contained no fingerprints of interest, with the exception of your boy, Truck Lewis. He's obviously not the brightest bulb of that operation."

"What about the note?"

Booth paused but did an admirable job of maintaining a poker face.

"What note?"

"The one that said: 'This was never yours.'"

A slow smile bent the corner of his lip for a brief second. "Impressive, but inaccurate. The translations off."

"Translation?"

His smile returned. "The note was in Spanish. It said: '*Esto nunca se intento para ti*,' which our linguists translated to mean: 'This wasn't meant to be yours.'"

"What's the difference? 'Was never', or 'wasn't meant to be', so what?"

"I'm not saying there's a material difference, just that your read was off." Booth took a long swallow of coffee. "Our people don't have a line on that yet. Could mean—"

"Former investors, pissed off competitors, disgruntled partners," I said.

Booth put the coffee down. "All right, Sparky, you get a cookie. My number's the only one stored on that cell phone, and any other number you call will be tracked, so just remember, it's for government business, not calling your cute little blonde downstairs."

Booth's intel was off too. He didn't know Karen was gone.

"I'll be staying at the Holiday Inn," he said. "Call me at the end of each day. I may have you out for up to a week, but we'll play it by ear. Now, get to work."

"After I shower."

I didn't like that he was here in Key West, or that he'd come by the La Concha. I meant to tell him to keep my involvement confidential, but it wouldn't make sense for him to tell anyone anyway, not that Booth's actions ever made sense.

After he left, I put the DVD in the machine. Another sticky note inside said: "Fast forward to 2:52."

As the machine sped ahead I could tell that the lighting wasn't very good, and at 2:37, ghost-like figures raced across the screen. I slowed it down and watched as several men appeared all at once, then twenty minutes later started coming out, two-by-two, each group carrying boxes. I hit pause and tried to study their faces, but the picture was too grainy.

At 2:52 there was motion in the foreground, and a leg rolled into view but only for a moment. Then, a couple seconds later, a puddle appeared on the sidewalk. If you weren't looking for it, you might not see it. I rewound the video and watched the sequence three more times. My stomach dropped at the sight of a Tommy Bahama flip-flop, clearly visible, clearly my foot. I could also see the front wheel of my bike, with the reflector on the front wheel turning in circles as the bike lay in a heap on the sidewalk.

Crap!

A few seconds later, Truck and another man emerged from the foggy background and walked forward, their faces illuminated by the streetlights. I saw my hand wave briefly in front of them but not my head or face. The other man seemed to whisper to Truck, who a moment later drew his fist back and plunged it forward, off the screen. He then stepped back and the other man came forward and swung a club once before Truck grabbed his arm.

Thank God. At least they didn't want to kill me.

Both of them faded back into the gloom.

If it weren't for me showing up and calling him over, it would have been impossible to identify Truck from the video. Unfortunately, there were enough flashes of me, my bike, and my puke puddle to confirm my presence there, along with my discussion with the thieves. It was circumstantial, but it was enough to accuse me of being an accomplice, a lookout, or the mastermind, for that matter. And with everyone else missing, I could be the one to take the fall. Assuming you overlooked the fact that I was dead drunk at the time in question.

Beautiful.

I had to run to meet Ray. Getting out of town now seemed like a really good idea. The hunt for Truck, the Sea Lion, and the Atocha treasure now had new importance. Not only were my treasure maps in the waterproof pouch at risk, so were my freedom and the few friends I had here in Key West. Time was my enemy, and the government unfortunately had come up with no other suspects in the twenty-four hours since the robbery.

The mission for Booth, an inconvenient distraction from my salvage plans, was now critical to save my own skin.

Flyin' for the Sea Lion

A BUCK REILLY ADVENTURE

12

THE AIRPORT WAS QUIET, ONLY A FEW EMPLOYEES AND SECURITY TYPES around. I carried my flight bag and a small backpack through the private aviation hangar and out onto the tarmac. Ray was down the row of planes next to Betty. The gas truck was parked in the taxiway behind her, but Chet, the driver, was inside the truck talking to Ray through the open window.

"There you are," Ray said. "I thought we were leaving a half-hour ago. I need to be back by three or four at the latest. Spottswell wants to have the Baron ready to get out of town before Fantasy Fest starts next week."

I stowed my duffel in Betty's nose. "Hey, Chet, you fill her up yet?"

Ray and Chet exchanged a glance.

"Ah, well, Buck, we've got a little problem. Stephanie says you're too far in arrears to get more fuel, at least until you can pay down your balance some."

Stephanie Baldwin was the FBO manager and had control of the fuel concession for the private aviation side of the airport. She'd been pretty good to me, and the truth was I'd strung her out and was woefully behind on my expenses.

Ray climbed aboard Betty, probably to avoid embarrassment.

Being broke was a humbling experience.

"What exactly *is* my balance, Chet?"

He held the clipboard close to his face. "It's $2,287.51. Exactly."

He tried to smile, but grace is futile when someone owes you money and you have no confidence in their ability to pay you back.

I reached into my breast pocket and removed Booth's credit card.

"Go ahead and pay it off, and charge this morning's fuel too."

When I handed him the card his smile was just beautiful. Then he studied the card for a moment.

"Ah, what's South Region SAC?"

Crap. It had been so long since I had a credit card, I hadn't even thought to look at the name.

"That's the client I'm doing some work for. They said I could cover my expenses. *All* my expenses."

He turned the card over and looked at the signature block.

"It ain't stolen, right? I don't want to get fired. Ain't nothing else I'm good at."

"It's fine, Chet, I wouldn't do that to you."

He nodded and hopped out of the truck. "Stephanie'll be tickled, that's for sure. Boy-oh-boy, can't wait to tell her!"

Ray, who'd listened to all this from the open cockpit window, stuck his head out the hatch.

"All the scuba gear's secure, Buck. You brought a spear gun?"

"Maybe we'll get lucky and find a fat grouper on the wreck."

Once inside, we settled into the cockpit and donned the headsets. I finished the pre-flight checklist and fired-up the twin Lycoming engines. They started smooth, ran smoke-free, and hummed sweetly. Four months ago the port engine would hardly run, and with what little money I had left, Ray had rebuilt them both, along with the props. Now she was good as new. Ray watched my expression and must have read my mind.

"Damn I do good work, don't I? This old Widgeon didn't run this good out of the factory." He was beaming. "I'm like a surgeon, I tell you. These hands," he held them up, "these hands were touched by—"

"They weren't touched by grease remover from the look of them," I said. "Don't get that all over my interior. And yeah, you do great work."

Since the taxiway was so long, I locked the free-castoring tail wheel, kept the downwind engine at idle, and taxied until we turned toward the west at the end of the runway. After the run-up I added power, released the brakes, and we began to roll. A half-minute later we accelerated into a gentle climb that took us out over Smather's Beach.

"I figure it'll take about thirty minutes to reach the wreck site," Ray said.

But he looked at me like he didn't believe that's where we were going. Did he know me *that* well?

"Change of plans, Ray. We have to postpone the salvage operation, briefly I hope."

Ray waited. In his red Hawaiian shirt he looked more like a tourist than a crack aviation mechanic, but that was his signature style. Cover boy for Margaritaville.com. Plus-size edition.

"Did you hear the Sea Lion's missing?" I said.

"Truck's boat?"

Omitting my cameo, I explained that the security cameras at the Atocha Museum caught Truck and the Sea Lion on tape, and he was now subject to an all-out manhunt by the Coast Guard, FBI, Marine Patrol, and Lou Fontaine. Ray was astonished but didn't whine, and given that Truck was a friend, he understood the need to go look for him. I didn't tell him about my encounter with Truck last night, either.

"So where're we headed?" His voice had risen an octave. A fastidious pilot and navigator, Ray didn't like to make changes on the fly.

"The Coast Guard's headed to the southern Bahamian islands, which is where we were directed to look."

"Directed by who?"

Way to go, moron. "I meant that's the direction we're headed. But if that doesn't pan out—"

"I have obligations, Buck. A schedule to keep—clients. Spottswell—"

I handed him the cell phone Booth had given me. "Call and tell him you're running behind. It's Truck Lewis, Ray. He's either committed multiple felonies and may do serious time, or he was kidnapped, may even be dead."

Ray took the phone. "Since when do you carry a cell phone?"

"My client gave it to me to keep in touch."

"South Region SAC? What kind of company's that, and why do they want you to look for the Sea Lion?"

Ray had obviously heard every detail of my discussion with Chet.

"Don't worry about it, okay? Just pull out the charts and plot our course for the Bahamas. The Abacos, Nassau, and Freeport."

"Spottswell will not be happy." He grinned. "But that doesn't mean we can't hit the casinos on Nassau."

"Hopefully we'll find Truck fast so we can get out to Gutierrez's speedboat."

I had no interest in wasting time or money in casinos, whether in the Bahamas, Vegas, or Monte Carlo.

We searched the western Bahamian waters for the rest of the day. We saw watercraft of all kind but no hundred-year old schooner full of pirates, treasures, or friends named Truck. To placate Ray, we landed on Nassau at dusk, where at Odyssey Aviation we refueled and tied Betty down for the night. While he showered, I checked in with Booth to tell him where we'd searched and to confirm that the credit card he gave me would cover our room and dining expenses. He told me I had a $150 *per diem*. A quick call with Donny Pogue at Treasure Salvors revealed only that his insurance company had threatened to cancel their policy and they were riding him hard for answers. The Coast Guard had found nothing and was shifting their search even further south in case the Sea Lion was headed toward Puerto Rico.

Was that based on the note having been written in Spanish? Or did they have new evidence?

Smartass Booth said he'd been tracking me on the cell phone's GPS, so he was glad my report matched what he already knew. While I showered, Ray inquired about casinos, and it was watching him throw quarters down the throat of a one armed bandit at the Crystal Palace that made me realize why my mood was so rotten. I hated being at Booth's beck and call, and his tracking my every move called for retaliation.

"Hi, sweetie."

I looked up and saw a gorgeous, caramel-skinned woman smiling, not at me, but at Ray. A loopy grin came over his face.

"Having any luck?" she said.

Ray glanced at me, flared his eyebrows, and turned back to the vision in front of him. She had to be 5'10," all legs, an orange mini skirt, and a white sequined top that had barely enough material to cover her breasts.

"Not really," Ray said.

"Come find me if you want that luck to change." She winked at him, looked me up and down, and sashayed away. Those legs . . .

"Damn, Buck, she was flirting. With me!" Ray ran a hand through his hair and got it off his forehead. "Did I blow it? Should I go after her—"

"She's a hooker, Ray."

He snapped back toward me, his smile now a sneer.

"Why, because she flirted with me and not you? That makes her a hooker?"

"Looks that way to me, but maybe I'm wrong."

I wasn't.

I booked us a suite next door at the Wyndham on Cable Beach. Once Ray lost the rest of the hundred dollars he'd set himself as a limit for the night, we went to the hotel's restaurant, Moso, and got a table facing the water. We feasted on seared Ahi tuna and whole Laine snapper. Between dinner and the room, we used up a week's worth of Booth's per diem.

"I'm liking this client of yours, " Ray said. "Even if South Region SAC sounds like some kind of government agency."

"Just don't drink too many mojitos, we have a long day ahead of us to—"

Past the beach, something caught my eye.

It was a large sailboat. A schooner.

On my feet, I tried to make out its features in the dark. Too much distance, not enough light.

"What're you doing?" Ray said.

"Be right back."

I ran out the side door and down onto the powdery white sand and to the water's edge. A firework shot up from the boat's bow, and when it burst with a small pop, it illuminated several smiling faces on board.

Party boat.

Probably a sunset cruiser back from its circuit. Similar to the Sea Lion, but many of that genre were. Tourist cruisers were often old sailing ships that had no other contemporary use than to evoke the romance of old-time seafaring days.

My heart settled back to its normal pace. As I climbed the steps up from the beach back to the restaurant, I saw a brute of man in black jeans and a t-shirt with the sleeves cut off, sporting a beautiful woman on each of his tattooed arms. I spotted the orange mini skirt and white sparkly midriff just as they passed Ray at the table.

Ray's eyes perked up as he looked over his three empty mojito glasses and smiled. The girl with the orange mini-skirt was looking at him, and I saw Ray's mouth move. I read his lips: "Hi, beautiful."

The brute stopped in his tracks, swung the girls to the side, and descended on Ray. I hurried in their direction. Great, Ray, flirt with an escort accompanying a guy who looks like he plays linebacker for the Miami Dolphins. I saw the man reach out and take Ray's hand as if introducing himself, but Ray's face immediately twisted into an expression of agony and he fell to his knees. The brute was squeezing his hand like a nutcracker.

"Excuse me," I said as I ran up. "Can I help you?"

The man looked over his shoulder. Reflective blue sunglasses covered his eyes, but the sneer on his mouth was unmistakable.

"Hi, sport," he said. "Friend of yours?" He nodded toward Ray, still on his knees.

"You mind letting him go?" I said.

"He called me 'beautiful,' the man said. "Least, I assume he was talking to me, 'cause if he was talking to one of my lady friends, I'd have to kick his ass."

Everybody heard him, because nobody else was talking in the restaurant. The girls that had been with him had vanished. Waiters scurried behind the scenes and nodded in our direction. None of this was lost on the brute who finally released Ray's hand and turned his attention to me.

"You boys spoiled my night." He spread his arms wide. "The bitches left—so I didn't get any dinner, I don't get any pussy. Now what the fuck we going to do about that?"

Ray slid lower under the table, clutching his right hand and watching me. The man was around my height at 6'3" but outweighed me significantly.

He looked stone sober and ready to eat nails. Not a combination I wanted to challenge, or attention I could afford to attract. I couldn't clear my name, find Truck, or placate Booth, much less get to Gutierrez's sunken ship, if I was in jail or the hospital.

"We're on our way out, friend," I said. "Sorry for the confusion. I'll tell our waiter to put your dinner on my card."

He stared at me as I pulled Ray up by his left hand and we skirted our way around him. I avoided eye contact but he was grinning as we maneuvered past. Some guys live for confrontation, some love the fight, and some just love making other men buckle. He might have had all those going, but I didn't care, I just wanted to get the hell out of here. He was too big, and we had more important things to do.

My heart rate finally settled when we locked the door on our room. If Booth had watched the GPS that closely, he'd probably do the same with the credit card. I could imagine him cussing up a storm when informed of our night's tab. I fell asleep in the palace suite with a smile on my face.

13

AT DAWN WE WERE BACK AT THE AIRPORT AND ON OUR WAY TO BOARD BETTY when Ray blew a wolf whistle behind me. He'd stopped next to a glistening private jet strapped down next to Betty. I had been too absorbed in planning the day to notice it.

"You walked right past this baby," he said. "Gulfstream G-IV. My dream plane."

The clean white fuselage had a pink glow in the early dawn light. e-Antiquity had once had a G-IV at our disposal through Net Jets, and I could picture it, from the cockpit to the gold-plated head, burled wood, and calfskin seats. Probably belonged to some high roller still bellied up to the craps table.

"Let's go, Ray. Night time's for dreaming and daytime's for scheming."

"What a beauty." His voice was a near whisper.

I loaded my gear while Ray spoke with the attendant, who came to ask if we needed fuel, drinks, or breakfast to go. I climbed into the left seat and just as I finished my pre-flight, Ray squeezed in past me.

"The gas jockey says it belongs to some guy who looks like a rap star," he said. "Can't believe I spent all those years at Embry Riddle when all I needed was a boom box, a shaved head, and a bunch of tattoos."

"Maybe his rapper name is Sado Masochist," I said.

"Why do you say that?"

I nodded toward the plane. A bold "SM" was emblazoned on its tail. "Forget the G-IV, Ray. Time to look for Truck."

A few minutes later we were over the Abacos, and we took turns at Betty's helm throughout the day. We monitored radio traffic, checked the news, and once when Ray napped, I checked Booth's cell phone and saw he'd called me a dozen times. There were messages, but I didn't know the pass code. I did, however, read his text message:

"NO MORE CASINOS OR FANCY DINNERS OR THE CARD WILL BE CANCELLED WITH YOU STRANDED ON SOME GOD FORSAKEN ROCK IN THE OCEAN. CALL ME BACK NOW!!"

Booth's text was the high point of my day, but when darkness approached and Ray suggested we try our luck in Paradise Island, I broke the news that my client wasn't too happy with our expenditures last night. So we landed at San Andros airport on Andros Island, where we again replenished Betty's fuel tanks. This time we ate fish sandwiches and drank a few Kaliks at the airport bar before we camped out inside Betty's cramped fuselage.

"Spottswell's not going to be happy with me, thank you very much," Ray said.

"Poor Bobby Spottswell, stuck in Key West for Fantasy Fest. I feel so bad for him."

We burst into laughter.

THERE'D BEEN NO NEWS ABOUT THE SEA LION, AND A FEW CALLS TO KEY West, including Lenny, Curro, and Donny Pogue, revealed no breaks in the case back home, either. I'd made a fortune at e-Antiquity listening to my gut instincts and following my intuition. Whether it came down to whom to trust, which direction to go, which lead to follow, or where to dig a hole, the success of those decisions had made our company a household name. I'd stopped listening to my inner voice when my world imploded and I lost everything overnight. That voice screamed at me now, and it said we were wasting our time in the Bahamas.

I fell asleep to that thought and awoke to an epiphany. While Ray still slept I slipped inside the FBO and ran some quick calculations, checked weather, and filed a flight plan for a new destination. Ray ambled in and pointed toward the small restaurant. His eyes were barely open and his hair looked like an asterisk.

I joined him at the counter. "Sleep well?" I said.

"Coffee," Ray said. "Egg sandwich."

The waiter looked at me and I held up two fingers.

"You see my favorite plane out there?" Ray said.

I thought for a moment. "The Sado Masochist? Sure you weren't dreaming?"

"Nope, she's out there tied down at the end of the line."

That struck me as odd. Private jets were common on Nassau, but Andros? It might be the biggest Bahamian island, but there's not much action aside from bonefishing. I craned to check out the window, and sure enough, I spotted the hulk of the G-IV behind an old Mooney.

The microwave beeped and the waiter dropped two steaming sandwiches in front of us, which we proceeded to wolf down. I asked Ray to buy a few bottles of water and munchies from the vending machine down the hall while I paid the bill. I knew he wouldn't appreciate my new plan, so I was going to wait until we were airborne to mention it.

Ray walked back in with his arms full—*what the hell?*

A huge man followed him. Not just any huge man, but the brute from the restaurant on Nassau. Shaved head, blue-mirrored sunglasses, tight black t-shirt stretched taut by what had to be steroid-nourished muscles adorned with exotic tattoos. As they approached, the man pushed past Ray and up to me.

"Buck Reilly, right?" He didn't extend his hand—for which I was grateful, considering how he'd brought Ray to his knees last time.

"Who are you and what are you doing here?" I said.

"Call me Gunner." He pushed his sunglasses up on his head. "That's your piece-a-shit Widgeon out there, right? We both came outta Key West, and we're both after the same target."

Target? "You're the G-IV?"

He bared small, square teeth in a smile or a sneer, I wasn't sure which.

"Sweet, ain't she? Outfitted with the best tracking and communications gear money can buy. I can monitor the Coast Guard—hell, I can hear the Key West police order doughnuts."

"So that night at the restaurant was . . . what?"

"A test. I wanted to see what you boys were made of." He smiled. "You did all right. But this one?" He nodded toward Ray. "Poontang blindness, which makes me wary of him for a partner."

Partner?

"That G-IV's too big to fly single-handed. You have a co-pilot?" I asked.

"You looking for a job? Sorry, I got a pilot *and* a co-pilot."

"Listen . . . Gunner, was it? Sure, we're out of Key West, but I don't know what target you're talking about, unless you're here for bonefish like we are."

He stared at me, eyes cold.

"Find any bonefish on Nassau at the casino? Or while you were flying a search pattern around the Abacos yesterday, with me tracking you five miles high like a fucking AWAACS?"

Ray's eyes were round as sand dollars.

"Go start the plane, Ray," I said.

As Ray hurried from the restaurant he dropped one of the water bottles but didn't stop to pick it up.

"We're both after the Sea Lion and the treasure on board," Gunner said. "Difference is, I'm not butt buddies with one of the thieves."

"I don't—"

"Don't waste my time, Reilly. I came to make you a deal. You lead me to the Sea Lion, I retrieve the treasure, and everyone's happy."

"Why would that make everyone happy?"

"'Cause the opposite of happy is *un*happy. Trust me when I tell you that unhappy would really suck."

Wheels spun in my head. This was just like the days when other, more ruthless men were after the same archeological finds as e-Antiquity. I searched my memory. Could Gunner have been—

"You still with me, Reilly?"

"Just trying to remember if we'd met before, when I ran—"

"e-Antiquity? Sorry, friend. When you were off making a fortune, then pissing it away, I was at the sharp end of a stick in garden spots like Yemen, Mogadishu, Kuwait, Afghanistan."

There were a lot of years between the conflicts he was alluding to, yet he didn't have the bearing of a man who'd spent that much time in . . .

"Military?"

The square teeth reappeared.

"Too many rules that cramped my style," he said.

Mercenary? Could he be another of Booth's private operatives? Didn't he say I wasn't his only asset? I swallowed, hard. The sound of Betty's twin engines starting up caused a hum in the restaurant.

"I don't know what you're talking about. We're on our way back to Key West this morning."

"Giving up so soon?" He stared at me, expressionless. "Two days on the trail and that's it? No wonder you went broke. And not much of a friend to Clarence Lewis—if he's innocent, that is. Me? I don't give a shit. When I find that old sailboat they won't know what hit 'em." He smiled. "I'm a take action and ask questions later kind of guy."

"What are you, some kind of bounty hunter?"

The smell of rank coffee washed over me when he laughed.

"You watch too much TV. Technically I've been hired by an interested party to find some stolen goods, but with millions of dollars of treasure on that boat, I may forget who I'm working for."

I slid my change off the counter. "Good luck with all that, Hummer."

I walked past him and felt his hand grab my shoulder, stopping me in my tracks.

"It's Gunner, and don't you forget it."

I jerked my shoulder out of his grasp. My body felt numb as I approached Betty. Would Gunner be able to find the flight plan I'd just filed? Did he really have the gear to track us, no matter where we went? Who was the 'interested party' that hired him? Would he kill Truck if he found the Sea Lion first? Had Ray pissed his pants?

It was going to be an interesting day.

14

GUNNER WOULD FOLLOW US IF HE BELIEVED WE COULD LEAD HIM TO THE Sea Lion, so I initiated what evasive actions I could.

Good thing Ray missed most of Gunner's comments or I'd have a mutiny on my hands. I explained he was hired by someone to search for stolen goods, whether it was the Atocha treasure or the Sea Lion, but said he seemed more interested in making some fast cash. I was impressed—and worried—at the way he'd manipulated us last night at the restaurant, and glad I kept things under control. I might not have that luxury if he showed up again.

"How's he afford that G-IV?"

Good question. Planes like that cost $15,000 to $20,000 per day, easy. Could Gunner own it? Or did his client provide it? Had to be the latter, but whom? Booth couldn't provide that kind of support, could he? Hell, all I got was a credit card and cell phone. That reminded me . . .

"You bring your cell phone?" I asked.

Ray reached down into his flight bag and pulled it out. "Yep. Never use it much but never leave home without it, either."

"Good. Save this number, will you?" I handed him the phone, and once he stored the one number I slid open my side hatch window and dropped Booth's phone into the sea a mile and a half below us.

"Hey, what'd you do that for? What about your client?"

"I don't like being so accessible."

"But that was a nice phone." Ray's expression made it clear he thought I was nuts. He'd be certain of it before long.

I guided our flight path down the Keys. Ray happily recited the names of the islands he recognized and guessed at a few others. I felt bad since he thought we were headed home, but hopefully Gunner would too. As the chain angled west and we didn't, Ray's face drooped.

"What's up, Buck?"

"Something occurred to me this morning, which is why I was in Flight Services before breakfast. Donny Pogue told me the thieves left a note that said: 'This was never meant to be yours.'"

"So?"

"It was in Spanish."

"*So?*"

I hadn't worked it all out yet, but when Booth told me the note was in Spanish, some pieces started to come together in my head.

"You watched the news much lately, Ray?"

"I moved to Key West to avoid the news. It's too depressing."

"Read any papers? New York Times? Washington Post, USA Today?"

"Solares Hill Gazette."

"There's a civil war brewing in South America, maybe even a border dispute between Peru and Bolivia."

"Peru and Bolivia? Who cares?"

"Seems some nationalistic Peruvian rebels have made a claim for reparations against all the nations who stole their raw materials—"

"No, Buck—"

"Including the Spanish, who back in the 1500's and 1600's raped the Peruvian silver and gold mines to fund their imperialism throughout Europe and the western hemisphere."

"Buck, we can't—"

"The Spaniards carried tons of riches away in galleons, several of which fell to pirates, and several others were lost at sea in storms and hurricanes. Like la *Señora de Nuestra de Atocha* and the *Santa Margarita*, both of which sank in September 1620 and were salvaged by Treasure Salvors."

Ray looked at the compass, which showed a heading toward the southwest.

"Please tell me we're not going to Peru."

"No, Ray, I wouldn't do that to you."

"Bolivia?"

"Nope."

"Thank God, 'cause—"

"We're going to Panama," I said. "The canal to be exact, which if I'm right would be how the rebels would get the Sea Lion to the Pacific and Peru. Now, in the 1600's, when the Atocha sailed, there *was* no canal, so the Spaniards had to dismantle the ships and carry them and their cargo in portage over the land that's now Panama. Then they'd reconstruct the ships and sail out of Porto Bello. Lucky for the rebels, it's a lot easier now."

Ray took his headset off and rubbed his eyes, then ran his hands up through his long, dark hair.

"Yeah, lucky for them."

"By my calculations this morning, if the Sea Lion is making about six knots, the four and a half days she's been gone will have her just about to the Canal Zone. So we need to hustle our asses down there because I'd much rather meet up with them in the Caribbean than in South America." I paused but didn't look at Ray. "When e-Antiquity ran into its . . . problems, I, ah, may have left a few big clients hanging in Panama. Some other South American countries too."

"*Which* other South American countries?

"Pretty much all of 'em." My best Cheshire cat smile did nothing to soften Ray's expression. "We just need to get safely past Cuba, and with one stop for gas we'll be at the Canal early this afternoon."

He looked back out the windshield.

"Yeah, because they *really* love you in Cuba. Right?"

I didn't answer him. It was a rhetorical question.

15

IT TOOK TWO HOURS TO REACH COZUMEL, MEXICO, WHERE WE STOPPED FOR fuel. We'd radioed ahead and the truck met us on the tarmac, which saved us from having to clear customs.

Ray's sour mood darkened when he called his answering machine and learned that Bobby Spottswell had showed up at the airport in Key West yesterday to check on his Baron, only to find it in so many pieces inside the hangar. Bobby wasn't the kind of guy who cared about Truck Lewis or the Atocha museum's loss.

I thought of times past here in Cozumel, diving on the reefs, Palancar in particular. From the tarmac I saw tourists come and go, their lives on hold while they took a precious few days off to relax, enjoy the talcum-white beaches, maybe scratch the surface of this Mexican island that had been a fertility destination—utilizing everything from prayers and ceremonies to bloody sacrifices to help women get pregnant—long before it was called Mexico.

Several small ruins reclaimed from the forest that had consumed them for millennia now served as a backdrop to the airport, helping create the mood sought by the Mexican Tourist Board. In reality, they'd razed the largest concentration of former Mayan civilization on the island to build the runway I was now standing upon. The Mexican government deserved some credit, though, for letting e-Antiquity, and a team of archeologists from the University of Mexico, exhume a vast collection of subterranean ruins. e-Antiquity's ability to assemble the best and brightest international team led to what remains one of the finest collections of its kind, now housed at the university's main campus in Mexico City. We were allowed to keep and sell twenty percent of the find, which caused yet another surge in our stock, a couple of years before it hit the wall and went the way of the Mayan people into extinction.

There'd been a nice story on e-Antiquity at the Mexico City exhibition, but my guess was it had been removed. Where I was once greeted as a renowned guest of the nation, I now sought to pass through quickly, undetected and unrecognized.

Reminiscing about that gave me an idea. I grabbed Ray's phone and dialed one of the only numbers I still had memorized from my former life.

"Harry Greenbaum, here."

"Hi, Harry, it's Buck."

"I say, young man, good to hear from you. Not in trouble again, I trust?"

"No, Harry, everything's fine."

"And the Atocha theft, tell me you're not up to your neck in that?"

As e-Antiquity's largest venture capital investor, Harry had lost a fortune when the company filed Chapter 7, but first he'd cashed out far more than his principal investment, so I didn't feel too bad for him.

"Only my ankles, Harry. A friend captained the boat the thieves absconded on. I'm out searching for them now."

"Of course. When I heard about the incident I assumed you'd get in the middle of it, one way or another. I'm just glad to hear you're not on that old schooner yourself."

When I told Harry why I'd called, he promised to do some checking. I didn't have much information other than Gunner's nickname and the conflicts he claimed to have participated in. That and the "SM" on the tail of the G-IV.

"If any of the sixty-two companies you own pieces of can provide any information, Harry, I could sure put it to good use."

"Sixty-four now, Buck. At least this bloody down market's provided some plum acquisition opportunities. Yes, I'll inquire in the proper places and perhaps a few improper ones too," he paused. "So you finally rejoined the modern world and purchased a cell phone?"

"Nope, it belongs to a friend, but that's where you can reach me. And thanks, Harry. I'd say I owe you one, but that'd be redundant."

"So it would, young man. Cheers."

I always felt better when Harry was involved. With my parents gone, he was the closest thing I had to a senior family member, and even though we'd been estranged for a couple of years after e-Antiquity cratered, he'd been kind enough to forgive if not forget the troubles we caused him. He was a perfect British gentlemen tempered with Yiddish sensibilities, which in combination had helped build a fortune that allowed him to invest in businesses that captured his imagination and promised substantial profits. His vast array of companies offered a broad network of information sources he was savvy enough to manipulate to his benefit, and occasionally mine.

I hoped my intuition would lead us to Truck Lewis. Booth had already threatened to cancel the credit card, so I held my breath here. The FBO processed the card for the fuel and sundries just before we began our run-up and taxi toward the runway.

"I still can't believe you threw that phone out the window," Ray said. "At least you held on to the credit card."

Crap. Even without the GPS tracking device in the phone, Booth would be able to track our course with the credit card. And he'd go ape-shit when he saw we were in Cozumel.

I looked around the tarmac one more time and was relieved not to see Gunner's G-IV. Maybe the trip down the Keys had lost him after all.

We climbed to 8,000 feet and flew for an hour before I added ten degrees of flaps and began to descend. Ray looked out the window and glanced at the chart.

"We're still a couple hours outside Panama," Ray said. "Why are you reducing altitude now?

"There's been a head wind much of the way, might have slowed the Sea Lion's progress."

"Assuming they came this way," Ray said.

"Let's start searching from here on in."

We leveled off at 1,000 feet, low enough to spot boats of the Sea Lion's size clearly but still high enough to see a significant distance. We flew a straight course on autopilot so we could both study the waters with binoculars. Two hours of that produced nothing but 35 container ships sighted and mounting fatigue for Ray and me. Now within thirty minutes of Colón, I went through the motions of landing prep.

I caught a whiff of something and saw that Ray had perspired through his shirt.

"What's bothering you?" I asked.

"I've never been to Panama." He wiped his brow. "I used to have this video game called *General Drug Lord* and the bad guy looked just like General Noriega. He was a bitch to track down. Took me a year to reach level twenty and finally nail him."

I edged forward on my seat. "Do me a favor and hand me the small leather phone book out of my flight bag."

Ray dug into the bag and produced the worn leather booklet, secured shut with a leather strap.

"Open it up and find the page marked with Panama on the top," I said.

He paged through the book. I had a flashback of better times, when the book in Ray's hand was my private listing of contacts, friends, and not so friendlies I'd met hunting for treasure around the world.

"Argentina . . . Costa Rica . . . Ecuador . . ."

"Should be in the middle," I said.

"Nicaragua?" He hesitated on that page. "Did you really know Daniel Ortega? Nicaragua's president?"

"Between his presidencies. Should be the next page, Ray, and please, ignore the notes. Just look for Enrique Adolfo Jiminez."

He flipped the page. "Got it. Who's he?"

"It's not a he. It's the name of the airport in Colón. The airport code is MPEJ. There should be a listing for Jaime Escobar with a phone number on that page."

"Yep, here it is."

I asked Ray to call Jaime, hoping he was still alive, had the same number, and wouldn't hang up on me. Ray put it on speakerphone. After a long delay, the number started to ring and Ray threw the phone to me like it was a hot potato.

I sucked in a deep breath.

Someone answered in Spanish.

"Jaime, is that you?"

"Sí, who's this?"

"Charles Reilly, old friend. How the hell are you?"

"*Charles?*" Ray shook his head.

"Oh, my. I hope you're not in Colón. Señor Acosta would be very inter-ested to see you," Jaime said.

"No, Jaime, I'm not in Colón, but I might be soon." I felt down to where I kept my new waterproof pouch in the slot below my seat. "I'm on my way there."

"You have some *grande cojones*, Charlie, let me tell you—"

"I need to see Señor Acosta, can you arrange it?"

Silence.

"You there, Jaime?" I checked the window on the cell phone. We were still connected.

"I can reach him, but what will I tell him? You know about killing the messenger, King Charles?"

"I go by Buck now. You can tell him I'm bringing his map back."

"Ay yi yi!" Jaime said. "Just like that?"

"Actually, not just like that," I said. "There's a catch."

Jaime laughed. "With you, there's always a catch."

16

NOT FIFTEEN MINUTES AFTER I HUNG UP, RAY'S CELL PHONE RANG. HE HELD it up so I could see the caller ID: "South Region SAC."

"How'd they get my number?" Ray said.

"Turn the phone off."

Booth knew Ray was with me, and he must have received notification of the credit card being used in Cozumel. A trace on Ray's phone would show that we'd continued south to Latin America, so he'd be apoplectic by now—or Gunner was high above us reporting our every move. I didn't want to answer the call with Ray here, but I might have no choice—if he froze the credit card we'd never get home. For now I'd stall, wait until I had something to report.

Ray clenched his palms together and interlocked his fingers. He looked like he was about to pray.

"Why won't you tell me who South Region SAC is, or why this Acosta's pissed at you?"

"I told you—"

"Spare me the client bullshit, okay? Why would a new client pay off two grand of your gas bills unrelated to whatever you're doing? Or hire you to look for Truck—"

"It's irrelevant, Ray."

He squirmed sideways to look at me squarely.

"Irrelevant? Really? How do I know we're not going to be grabbed at customs—"

"We're not going through customs, Ray. MPEJ doesn't even have a border station. In fact, there's no FBO, either."

His mouth hung open so wide I could count the fillings in his molars.

"We're not going to be here long enough to—"

"What, go to jail?" Ray said. "That doesn't take long—"

"We're not going to jail." At least, I hoped not. "Raul Acosta's the governor for the Panama Canal Zone. He and I used to do business together when I was studying the overland travel routes from the Pacific. Remember I told you how the Spanish would dismantle the galleons? I paid him handsomely to allow me to study those routes by air, then on the ground."

I took a deep breath and debated what I'd say next, but I owed Ray an explanation. I reached down below my seat for the waterproof pouch, rifled through my notebook, and pulled out a map.

"He lent me this map, which dates back to around 1600. It documents the overland route traveled by a Spanish armada."

"Big whoop. What good's that?"

"Only half the fleet made it across. The rest were ambushed and a hundred men were killed. Another hundred died from disease. Those who escaped reported that they buried their cargo to be recovered later."

"Damn. What happened?"

I handed him the piece of old brittle paper in the sealed plastic sleeve.

"This is what they drew to document their journey." He held the map like it was a newborn infant. "It's the original, Ray. A one and only four-hundred-year-old map."

"Holy crap."

The map could hardly have been more fragile. The hand-drawn route was on yellowed parchment that was stained, torn, and crumpled. Thanks to the plastic sheath it was in the exact same condition as when Acosta lent it to me four years ago. He was supposed to get half of anything I found, or I'd return the map after thirty days. So I was a little late.

"We were never able to decipher the notes, and our expedition found nothing but unmarked graves and rusted armor over old bones. But there was no doubt something of incredible value was buried along that path, and it pains me to come to Panama for any reason other than to take up the search where I left off."

Ray scratched the stubble of beard on his chin.

"What about South Region SAC?"

Colón appeared on the horizon, the waters that led to it littered with a vast array of ships loaded with colorful containers, all funneling toward the canal.

"Let's just remember we're here to find Truck, okay?"

I lined us up due south, aimed at runway 18, and held my breath. There would be no announced approach, vectoring, or guidance from the small tower. A chill passed through me.

My plan rested on Raul Acosta's being honest with me. And why should he? I hadn't been with him.

The jungle seemed to press in even closer since the last time I was here. Our wheels touched down and Betty bounced along the rugged runway. All we could see were transport planes, aside from a handful of small propeller planes and a green, military-looking helicopter. I taxied Betty to the end of the runway and pulled off onto the tarmac near an old fuel truck.

"Want me to power her down?" Ray said.

"Not just yet." I unbuckled and climbed into the cabin. "Wait here," I said.

Ray's expression told me he agreed with this idea but he damned well wasn't happy about it. He and I had never argued before, but he wasn't giving up on wanting to know who South Region SAC was. I couldn't blame him, but I couldn't tell him the truth, either.

Once I was on the tarmac I stretched my arms and legs. Ten minutes passed. I saw people watching us from the hangars in the distance, but nobody made contact.

A black sedan approached at high speed. My sphincter tightened as the car adjusted its course directly toward me. The driver came into view first, but all I could see were dark sunglasses. He wasn't smiling. The car screeched to an abrupt stop and the back door swung open.

Jaime Escobar jumped out and stared at me with his hands on his hips.

"Can't believe it's you." He shook his head. "You one crazy sum'bitch."

There was no doubt about that.

17

"THE SIZE OF YOUR BALLS HAVE NOT SHRUNKEN, EH, KING CHARLES?"

"Call me Buck. Wish I could say the same about my financial statement."

Jaime laughed, then shook his head. "Yes, Señor Acosta told me you had gone broke. Hard to believe—but in this world, in this time, many have."

"Where's Acosta?"

"Waiting for you. What about your friend?"

"He'll stay here and fuel the plane." And keep an eye on it.

Jaime removed a cell phone from a clip on his belt, made a call, and turned to look at one of the hangars. He spoke in Spanish, then waved to the fuel truck.

"Credit card okay?"

He nodded quickly.

I stuck my head inside the plane and told Ray the gas truck would be here soon and to have them fill it up with the credit card I tossed him—I was going into to town to see Governor Acosta. He took the card without a word.

The ride to Colón took us around acres of containers stacked five high that covered a mass of land equivalent to the city itself. Business was good, but then, monopolies tend to be fruitful. If you wanted to get cargo from the Atlantic to the Pacific, you could either go through the canal or around Tierra del Fuego. I was only a kid when President Carter signed the canal back over to the Panamanians, which I now saw as a commercial and strategic blunder that weakened our nation in ways he never dreamed about, but then, he didn't ask my opinion.

Colón was pressed onto the muddy banks of the Caribbean Sea, just north of the funnel-shaped start of the Canal Zone. Ships as tall as skyscrapers floated in line in Limon Bay awaiting Panamanian pilots to usher them through a series of locks, all for a hefty fee. From here the canal looked like a broad river, the locks being several miles south. I remembered visiting Raul Acosta at his office near the locks, in the heart of the canal operations center. Jaime's driver had turned into town rather than continuing on toward the canal itself.

"Where are we going?"

"Señor Acosta does not want you to come to his office. He'll meet us here in Colón."

A jolt of anxiety pressed me into the back of my seat. When I hadn't returned the map previously, Acosta had been quite graphic as to what he would do to me if he ever saw me again. I slipped the map from my shirt pocket and kept an eye on Jaime and the driver up front. I needed an insurance policy.

The driver wound through the Byzantine town until he came to a small restaurant perched atop the seawall that overlooked the bay. We entered the building and were ushered upstairs into a small room where Raul Acosta stood next to an open balcony door. The breeze blew his gray hair back.

A huge grin revealed brown crooked teeth below his nicotine-stained moustache. His eyes didn't smile.

"King Charles, you finally returned. Here I thought you had stolen my map. Some of my partners wished to come find you—"

"I go by Buck now."

A quick lift of his eyebrows was the only recognition of my changed name. I suspected Raul was used to dealing with people who had many names.

"But, no, I told them, Charles is an honest man. He'll come back. There's no need for violence."

This last part caused Jaime to smile. Jaime, the man who introduced me to the governor originally. Jaime, the curator of the Porto Bello Museum of Fine Art and Antiquities. Like many men with similar titles at private and state-owned museums around the world, Jaime was intent on improving his collection, but even more intent on lining his pockets.

"And you have my map with you, King Buck?"

"Just Buck." I glanced at the bodyguards, who looked like they were anxious to administer tooth extractions without Novocain. "I need a favor first—"

"More favors. It's always favors with you, isn't it?"

The smile began to fade. Even Jaime's veneer of affability disappeared. Raul paused for a moment, then stepped out onto the small balcony.

"Perhaps we should discuss this favor out here where we can observe the sea."

The two bodyguards took a half step forward and urged me on to follow their master. Outside, the view was amazing. The restaurant was set directly above the water, and the balcony was cantilevered out from the cliff, suspended high above the rocks and surf below. It took my breath away, but not just because of the beauty. The bodyguards, who now filled the doorway, were smiling.

My teeth were clenched tight. I waited for Raul to speak.

"Now, Buck, this favor you need?"

I cleared my throat, took a deep breath, and turned my back to the bodyguards.

"I'm looking for a missing boat out of Key West."

Raul looked at me as if questioning my sanity. But he was listening.

"I believe it was hijacked by Peruvian rebels."

"Peruvian rebels? Stole a boat in Key West, Florida?" He paused, shook his head. "And you think they plan to pass through the canal?"

"It's the only way home."

Raul scratched his chin, shook his head again, and went back to scratching his chin.

"These the same rebels who argued for the return of raw materials stolen hundreds of years ago?"

"That's my guess," I said. "Ironic, isn't it? I'm here to return the map drawn by Spaniards who crossed Panama with Peruvian silver and gold— while searching for a ship hijacked by Peruvians seeking to return through the Panama Canal."

My gut told me that while the Atocha theft was big news in Florida, and good Internet fodder in the States, word had not traveled into Latin America yet, especially since the extent of what was taken still hadn't been made public. My gut had better be right, or what I'd just done was like telling the cagiest fox in the forest the chickens are loose and on the way past his den.

"And you have my map with you?" Raul said.

"I do."

He said something in Spanish. One of the bodyguards withdrew a cell phone, punched a couple of buttons, and handed it to Raul. Once again wishing I'd learned the language, all I could tell was that Raul spat out an order and after a few seconds asked a question. He lowered the phone and looked back at me.

"The name of the boat and type?"

"Sea Lion. She's a hundred-year-old schooner."

The corner of his lip curled. He hesitated, maybe embarrassed to pass this on. But he did—the one thing I made out was the name of the boat. A moment of silence passed and I chanced a glance at the bodyguards. They remained in the doorway, and I swear not one of them blinked. Jaime was almost completely hidden behind them, but I could see his shoes and figured he had his ear pressed close to hear what was happening.

Another burst of Spanish followed, then Raul slapped the phone shut.

He stared at me. And stared.

"Any luck?" I said.

"Give me my map."

"I've got it. Just—"

"I'm losing my patience, Charles." He looked past me to the body-guards. "I want my map!"

I felt them move closer. "Okay, okay. It's close by—"

Raul flung his wrist and one of the bodyguards had me around the waist and off my feet. I swung an elbow back and caught him on the nose. The sensation of crushing bone reverberated through my arm. The grip around my waist loosened, but the other bodyguard stepped in, and the three of us crashed into Raul Acosta. He tried to step aside, but the balcony was too small. He yelled at them in Spanish, and I pressed harder into Raul to block them from tossing me over the side.

"Hold on!" I shouted. "Hold *fucking* on, Raul, I've got the damn map!"

Pinched against the railing, he glanced from the wall of flesh that pressed against him, to the rock and liquid grave that awaited us all below. His concern had me worried. What was this little balcony's weight capacity?

A torrent of Spanish from Raul, and the guard released his grip. Another fusillade of shouting and obvious threats sent them scurrying back inside the restaurant. The two of us stood there sucking wind as if we'd just sprinted a mile.

"It's in the car, Raul . . . it's in . . . the fucking car." He shoved me back inside the restaurant. "Under the floor mat . . . backseat floor mat."

He yelled at the guards and waved them off toward the door. They literally ran, looking like Keystone Cops. Jaime, Raul, and I stared at each other until they came running back after only a minute, one holding the map aloft in its sealed plastic sleeve, waving it as if he'd just found a winning lottery ticket.

"Give me that damn thing, you fool. It's *four hundred years old!*"

Raul took the sleeve from the man and placed it on a table, then gently withdrew the map. I remembered how I felt when I saw it in Geneva just a few weeks ago. God, it was hard to relinquish it now.

Raul glanced up with what can only be described as sheer lust in his eyes.

"The Sea Lion?" I said.

He offered a small smile. It spoke so many things. Intrigue, hesitation, wonder, and what I feared most, double-cross.

"The Sea Lion." He looked back at the map and laughed. "Captain Clarence Lewis requested passage an hour ago."

Truck? Damn.

"So they're through?"

Another laugh set me back a step.

"What, you think the Panama Canal is like one of your pizza restaurants? Call up and get delivery in thirty minutes? The volume of traffic requires a half-day's wait for most ships, especially pleasure craft, which is how they declared themselves. I'll alert the Panamanian Navy to intercept them—"

"No!"

My shout made him flinch. The bodyguards rushed to his side like the trained pit bulls they were.

"No navy, Raul. At least not yet. I need to, ah, try to handle this myself. A friend's on board as a hostage, and if the navy closes in, he might get hurt. Let me try first."

"You? Alone? Against the so-called Peruvian rebels?"

It was my turn to smile. "But first, I need one more favor."

18

JAIME DID NOT ACCOMPANY ME BACK TO THE AIRPORT, WHICH WAS FINE WITH me. I'd had enough reunion time for one day. The driver didn't speak English, so our ride was without small talk. As we drove through town, around the landscape of multi-colored freight containers, I watched the scenery pass and pondered the effort that had gone into searching for the treasure purportedly buried pursuant to the map I'd returned to Raul Acosta.

I tensed up when the driver drove past the entrance to MPEJ. Raul may have seemed grateful, but men like him rarely let somebody take advantage of them without recompense, so I expected retribution somewhere down the road. I just hoped it wasn't this road to the airport, right now.

My concern was alleviated when the driver took another entrance, also marked with MPEJ and a sign that said *Aviación Privada*. We rounded a corner that led through the overgrowth around the airport, passed between two hangars, then turned onto a road parallel to the taxiway. Betty was visible in the distance but so was another, larger plane next to her.

I immediately recognized the bold "SM" on the tail of Gunner's G-IV. My driver closed the distance and deposited me at Betty without fanfare, threats, or wounds, but he didn't drive away. Nobody else was in sight.

Betty's hatch was open.

"Ray?"

"Inside." His voice was *more* than an octave higher.

I peeked through the hatch and saw him seated in the left seat with Gunner behind him in one of the jump seats.

"Wow, what a coincidence to find you guys here in Colón," Gunner said. "Great town, isn't it?"

Had he tracked us here himself? Or was he Booth's other asset, tracking the signal from Ray's cell phone? If that were the case, it meant Booth had double-crossed me. Was he mad at me for going radio silent? None of those scenarios made me feel any better.

"What the hell are you doing inside my plane?"

"Ray invited me in out of the heat, but good point. Why are we sitting in this junker when we could be enjoying the air-conditioned luxury of my G-IV?"

"When did he get here, Ray?"

"About a half-hour ago."

I saw no bruises, but Ray was no fighter. He was a manatee of a human being who got along with everyone and hated confrontation, not counting video games where he was a virtual Rambo. Right now he stared at me like he wished we'd never met.

"So, Booth told you where we were?" I said.

Gunner had his reflective blue sunglasses on, and just like when we last met, his face was impassive. No recognition, no confusion.

"Bold move coming to Panama, men," he said. "What led you here? Or was it bonefish again?"

"Billfish, actually. Perfect time of year for sailfish and blue marlin," I said.

"So you're going to shoot them with that spear gun you have in the locker?"

He'd searched the plane. My breath caught. Had he found the waterproof pouch under the seat?

"Actually, we were just about to head out, Gunner. Feel free to follow us in that rocket ship of yours. By the way, what does the 'SM' on the tail stand for?"

"Sick Motherfucker," he said. "Appropriate, don't you think?"

"Who am I to argue?"

"So who did you meet with in Colón and where's out next stop, fellas?"

"I always wanted to see the Panama Canal—"

Gunner grabbed Ray by the throat. Ray's eyes bulged and a sound like air being let slowly out of a balloon escaped from his mouth. He grabbed hold of Gunner's broad, colorfully tattooed forearm but couldn't budge it. I darted forward—

"Stay back or I crush his windpipe like a beer can. Who's in the limo that dropped you off? Tell me what you learned."

"I called ahead for the car. It took me to Port Operations, where I found out the Sea Lion's already passed through the canal."

"And they gave you the information, just like that?"

"Amazing what a couple hundred bucks will do, asshole. Now let him go!"

"When did the schooner pass through?"

"This morning, about eight hours ago. They're sailing toward Peru and we're going to head them off. There, that's all I know, now let him go, Goddamnit!"

Gunner released his grip and Ray grabbed his neck, rubbing it and clearing his throat, over and over.

"That's more like it, partner," Gunner said.

"We're not partners," I said. "Now get out of my plane."

"You gonna make me?"

Straight ahead was going nowhere, so it was time to zig and zag.

"Ray invited you on board my plane, now why don't you show me yours?"

He smiled and shimmied toward the hatch. I followed, grabbing my dive knife out of the open duffel by the locker. Though I was tempted to stab him in the back, the thought of jail in Panama encouraged me to shove the knife in the waist of my pants and cover the handle with my shirt instead.

Gunner jumped out and landed like a cat. A big cat.

"Airplane envy, huh?" He laughed. "Sure, come take a look inside a plane built in this century, Reilly."

Gunner was empty-handed, so I assumed he hadn't found my stash of maps. I poked my head back inside Betty.

"Start the engines, Ray, this will only take a minute."

I spoke loud enough for Gunner to hear me and nodded at him when I turned around. We walked toward the G-IV, which I hated to admit was a beauty. The pilot watched us from the side window and the door popped open and dropped slowly to the tarmac as we approached. I studied Gunner from behind. He was agile on his feet and had a gait that matched his cocky attitude. He'd be a serious challenge hand-to-hand, especially because a battle with him would likely include feet, fingernails, teeth, and head butts, for starters. I'd have to rely on smarts against this one, but he might match or surpass me there, too.

He bounded up the six steps into the plane, paused, then flashed his square teeth at me.

"Check this out."

Inside was a combination of plush comfort, light-colored woods, soft tan leather, and an impressive display of electronic equipment. It smelled good, and the air had a nice chill. Gunner turned to face the wall of electronics, many of which I recognized.

"All the latest tracking gear," he said. "Satellite, GPS, sonar buoy drops with tracking capabilities, heat seeking, thermal imagery, radar—you name it, this baby has it."

Betty wasn't exactly stock, but the best she had on board was a hand-held Garmin GPS and radar for weather.

"Pretty cushy for a guy like you, Gunner. I thought there'd be some real hardware."

"Count on that, partner."

He popped a clip on the wall, and a built-in locker slid open. Inside were two automatic weapons. One looked like an M-16, the other was smaller, an HK MP-5 fitted with a silencer. There were a couple of handguns, but my eyes bulged when I spotted two green tubes I recognized as anti-tank missiles.

"See what I'm telling you, Reilly? You can't escape the fact that I'm going to be up your ass like one of them Key West masseuses you're probably used to. And if you don't cooperate and I find the damn boat first, I'll sink the bitch and everyone on board, mark its location, and come back with dive gear to recover the treasure. Not to mention blow you and that antique jalopy out of the sky for target practice, know what I mean?"

"You've made your point. I told you what I learned here, and we're headed out to search the Pacific waters toward Peru. This plane can't go as slow as my Widgeon's fastest cruising speed, so following each other won't work. Let's keep in radio contact."

His ugly sneer made my skin crawl.

"Now you're thinking, boy." He pounded on the cockpit door. "Start this bitch up!"

"See you at the next stop," I said.

I took my time down the steps and gave him a nod before I stepped off. The door lifted as soon as I was off the steps, which is what I'd hoped would happen. Betty's engines sounded strong and the hatch was open. I took a deep breath.

I was about to make Gunner one very unhappy mercenary.

I pulled the dive knife out of my waistband, ducked under the G-IV's wing, and stabbed the port tire with all my strength. A loud pop and ensuing hiss of air made me jump but didn't slow me down from repeating the same maneuver on the other tire. Alarm bells had to be sounding inside the G-IV's flight deck, so I sprinted around Betty's tail and dove inside the cabin.

"Go, Ray! Go! Go! Go!"

I saw the door start to open on the G-IV as Betty jumped forward.

Could Gunner pop open his gun locker, grab one of the automatics or one of the anti-tank missiles, and blast us as we accelerated down the runway? Not enough time, was there?

"Woo-hoo!" Ray's shout and wild eyes made it clear he'd seen my sabotage.

"Pedal to the metal, bro!"

I held my breath as Betty hurtled down the runway and lifted off without so much as a single 9mm round or errant missile lighting over our wings.

"See you, *partner*," I yelled.

19

After Betty was off the pot-holed runway and airborne, Ray and I switched seats. Once settled, I depressed the left pedal and commenced a gradual bank to port.

"Thanks a ton for leaving me alone in that hell-hole," Ray said. "Those gas jockeys gave me the creeps, and when Gunner showed up I thought I was dead meat." He rubbed his neck.

"We couldn't leave Betty alone, and we needed fuel."

"Still, I'm feeling like the red-headed stepchild here."

I didn't respond. Ray's agitation was getting worse, and I needed his cooperation. I spared him the details of Gunner's armaments and tracking equipment, and my reunion with Raul Acosta. Ray had a spastic colon, and too much stress and fear could sometimes result in his soiling his shorts. My sense of smell and Betty's upholstery weren't up to that, just now.

"Were you serious about going to Peru, because Spottswell—"

"Peru was bullshit, but we're not going back to Key West yet either."

"Why—"

"The Sea Lion's out here in the Bay of Limon awaiting entry into the Canal Zone. Governor Acosta will stall, but there's not time to get Nardi and the cavalry down here. We're going to have to try and stop them ourselves."

Ray smiled. "Ha! Wait until Gunner figures that out. And all that business back there at the airport, with the limo, and the creepy-looking—will you listen to me ramble on here?"

"I'd rather not, Ray. I'm actually trying to come up with a plan."

"Why can't the Panamanian Coast Guard, or whatever they have here, just intercept the boat and send Truck home with the goods?"

"That'd be the logical thing to do if we were back in U.S. waters, but not in this part of the world." I paused. I had a sudden urge to come clean. "And there's one other thing, Ray. Remember the night of Karen's going away party?"

"You mean the night you were so hammered you vanished without saying goodbye?"

"Right, and when I vanished, as you put it, I rode my bike home. Down Whitehead Street."

I hesitated and he stared at me, waiting for more, then his eyebrows popped up.

"What are you saying?"

"I was drunk as a skunk and could hardly walk, much less ride the bike. In fact, I crashed into the curb and slammed down hard on the sidewalk, where I barfed out all those nasty shooters and good Barbados rum. But when I stood up, I saw two guys carrying a crate through the darkness."

"No shit!"

"Yes, shit. One of them was Truck Lewis. I called out to him, and he and another guy came over. I don't remember anything besides Truck clocking me. I tried to get up but the other one hit me with a club or something. Next thing I knew, I'm waking up in the KWPD drunk tank."

"No shit!"

"The police grilled me but I didn't remember the incident until later when Curro drove me by the museum."

Ray closed his eyes for a long moment. Finally he opened them and heaved melodramatic sigh.

"So you're telling me Truck's guilty after all? We're sticking our necks out—I've pissed off Bobby Spottswell—and Truck's *guilty?*"

"All the evidence says that's the case, but—"

"Hell, Buck, you're an eyewitness!"

"Nobody disputes he was there, the video proves that, but I still think there's a chance he was forced to go along. And if Gunner or the

Panamanians or Peruvians get to him first, they may kill him and nobody will ever know either way."

"So this is about finding the truth and not a reward?"

"One other detail. My drunken arrival during the robbery shows up on the security video too. When the police figure that out, who do you think will take the fall for all this if the Sea Lion gets away?"

Ray was quiet. He shook his head, probably wondering if his being with me would make him an accomplice.

"Finding Truck and the Sea Lion may be the only way I can clear my name. If we can get a reward, we'll do that too, don't worry."

Ray shook his head and stared out the window. I dug into my breast pocket.

"Punch these coordinates into the GPS. Raul has the Sea Lion circling a small area just outside the container ships."

He stared at me a long second, then pulled the hand-held GPS off the Velcro that attached it to the instrument panel. Ray Floyd was a helluva mechanic, a surprisingly astute social philosopher, and an all-around nice guy. I'd never seen him hurt a mosquito, much less get into a fight. But he also spent every waking minute away from the airport wired into every kind of military shoot-em-up video game on the market, so he had a mean streak in there somewhere.

"All those years of training on the joystick in front of your game station, Ray—now's your chance to try it in the real world. Just think of these guys as terrorists and let's kick some ass."

He pressed his lips together and I could see the corners of his mouth twitch. Yep, here came the smile. The GPS plotted a course, and to our mutual delight, the Sea Lion's position was less than five miles away.

"Do me a favor," I said. "While I keep my eye out for them, go through the checklist for a water landing."

When I explained my loose idea of a plan, Ray got very quiet. After several moments of paralysis he took the clipboard and ran his finger down the checklist for our landing in the Bay of Limon. I kept the altitude low so the Sea Lion wouldn't spot us and so we could land quickly once we find them. Truck would certainly recognize Betty, and if he *was* involved he'd smell a trap. We'd find out soon enough.

As we flew around the bay getting into position, I was amazed at the number of huge cargo ships awaiting passage. Colorful containers dotted ship decks, some stacked five high. Products from all over the world destined for Pacific ports and consumers.

I spotted a sailing ship in the distance, the size of a toy compared with the freighters. The twin masts and yellow hull left no doubt that it was the Sea Lion. I banked to port and added flaps. While Ray called out the checklist we made a bouncy landing in the washing-machine chop and came to a quick stop. Our GPS location was exactly where Raul told me to be. I reached for Ray's cell phone.

"Hello, Buck, you in position?" Jaime said.

"Just landed. Go ahead and ask Raul to issue instructions."

We disconnected and I stumbled into the back. I imagined Gunner parked on the tarmac, enraged as his radar showed us just a couple miles off shore. I only hoped we could make this happen faster than whatever he came up with.

"The depth finder shows fifty feet here," Ray said. "Drop anchor?"

"There's plenty of line."

While he fumbled with the bow hatch and anchor line, I donned my wetsuit. When I felt the pull of the anchor jerk us into position, I took a deep breath.

"What if your Panamanian buddy doesn't do what he promised?"

"He will." I bit my lip. He'd better.

I used my binoculars to scan the waters to the northeast and finally spotted the Sea Lion. It was on a reach perpendicular to our position. Come on, Raul. I watched for five minutes—nothing. Another five minutes, and still no change in course. The seas sloshed in all directions, and Ray was looking a little wonky and muttering to himself. I hated doing this to him and I really appreciated how game he'd been. He could have whined or refused to come, but he sucked it up. Ray didn't know Truck as well as I did, and he certainly didn't have an FBI agent manipulating him, so he was doing all this for me, pissed or not.

The Sea Lion tacked in our direction.

"Okay, she's coming our way," I said. "Raul's people must have made the call to the Sea Lion."

Ray clung to the bulkhead, trying to watch the horizon out the window. I tossed him a life vest, which he needed no coaxing to put on. I swung the buoyancy compensator and scuba tank over my shoulder, buckled up, sat in the hatch, pulled on my flippers, cleaned my mask, took a deep breath from the regulator, then fell forward into the water. When I looked up, Ray stood in the hatch and handed me the tools I hoped not to need. I then turned face down to float on the surface.

I did what I could to calm my breathing, but as I floated in the seventy-five- degree water, staring into the murky blackness of the Bay of Limon, I had too much time to think. The meeting with Raul Acosta had been a painful reminder of my success, and his calling me King Charles cut like a knife. At least he hadn't asked about Heather, my ex-wife, who'd helped charm the Spanish map away from him in the first place.

I looked up and Ray nodded at me. I glanced down the bay and saw the Sea Lion closing fast. I sucked a deep breath of dry, compressed air, and the shiver turned to a wash of adrenalin.

Places, everyone, the show's about to start . . .

20

THE SEA LION HAD DROPPED HER SAILS AND COASTED TO A STOP NEXT TO Betty but didn't drop anchor. I kept an ear out of the water so I could hear what was being said. Problem was, much of it was in Spanish. I cocked my head and saw three men at the rail, one at the helm, none of them Truck. They were dark-skinned Latinos but more Indio than black.

I bit down hard on my mouthpiece.

"How long was he under water?" someone said from the sailboat.

"About seventy minutes, but at that depth it was too much," Ray said. "He's got nitrogen poisoning, the bends. There's a decompression chamber in Colón, near the harbor, if you can take him."

"Why not fly your plane?" It sounded like he said *"jor plan."*

"He's the pilot. I'm just along for the ride."

Next glance saw the men on the Sea Lion in heated debate. I hoped Raul's people had poured it on thick, as charity from this bunch was unlikely. Their spirited argument ended abruptly.

"We will take him, but what about you and the plane?"

"I can't leave it, I radioed for a pilot to come help me. They were trying to find someone who knew how to fly one of these."

Ray was doing great.

I saw the men drop a rope ladder over the side of the Sea Lion. My breathing began to escalate along with my heartbeat. Still no sign of Truck. Did that mean he was dead?

Damnit.

One of the men climbed unsteadily down the ladder. The waves and chop rocking me around made the Sea Lion move unpredictably.

"Here, take this line and we can try to pull ourselves closer together!" Ray said.

I felt the plane and ship close in on me, and suddenly feared getting crushed.

"Is he conscious?" one of the men asked.

"He was. Can you reach him? Almost . . . you're really close."

I saw a hand reach out to me. Another man was just behind him, clutching the ladder in one hand and my rescuer in the other. A short pang of fear caused me to hesitate. Then I felt the hand grab me by the hair, the man yanked hard, and the pain pushed me to action.

I reached up and grabbed him by the belt. His eyes barely had time to grow wide. When I spun my body and pulled him, he fell heavily into the sea. His partner swung for a moment on the ladder, then caromed into the water too. A bright flash turned the water's surface bright orange, and the smell of phosphorescence and a shrill scream told me Ray scored with the flare gun.

The men in the water started to react after their partner on the boat, his chest ablaze, shrieked in agony. One began to swim toward me, then stopped when I raised the spear gun up from below the surface. But it was the fourth man on deck, the one unharmed by the flare, who pulled a rifle up to his shoulder. With no time to chicken out, I lifted the spear gun, centered it on his chest, froze for an instant, lowered the gun, then pulled the trigger and nailed him in the thigh with the untethered four-foot spear. He dropped the rifle overboard, which crashed into one of his associate's heads.

With my spear spent, the man who'd made a move toward me before now came at me hard and knocked my mask askew. I felt awkward and vulnerable, burdened by the scuba gear. Ray couldn't shoot these guys with the flare gun without hitting me.

Something came over my shoulder and jabbed at the man who was twisting my head. It was the boat hook—Ray jabbed the man in the chest with it!

I took the opportunity to submerge, get my wits about me, and resurface next to the Sea Lion. I came up behind the man who was struggling in the water, trying to reach the ladder. With my dive knife now in hand, I grabbed hold of the ladder and pulled him into my chest with the knife over his throat. He instantly stopped struggling.

"Hey!" I shouted. "I'll cut his freaking throat!"

The other man in the water let go of the boat hook that he was trying to pull away from Ray. He treaded water and stared at me. I kicked off my flippers, brushed the mask off my head, pulled the release strap on the buoyancy compensator and dropped the tank, then pushed the other man away and high-tailed it up the rope ladder onto the Sea Lion.

On deck, the charred Peruvian lay still but groaning, and another one clutched the spear that had passed through his leg, with blood squirting out and pooling below him. I could hear Ray yell at the others, threatening to shoot another flare, but knew that wouldn't last. There was another rifle leaned up against the bulkhead, which I grabbed and trained on the men in the water. Ray and I exchanged a glance, and I think we felt the same way, anything but victorious, just sick at the carnage we'd imposed.

But the Sea Lion was ours.

I waved the others on board, and after Ray checked Betty's anchor, he jumped into the water with a shriek and climbed aboard to help me secure the men and tend the wounded. I handed Ray the rifle and left to search the ship. A sudden concern stopped me in my tracks. What if there was nothing here? How would I explain our attack? I could add piracy to my résumé and Panama to the list of countries where I was under investigation.

The hatch that led below was locked from the outside. I flipped up the hook, pulled open the door, and stepped down the ladder. The only sounds were the lap of the waves and the creak of the hull throughout the main cabin. Four crates were piled on the floor. My memory was too fuzzy to tell if these were the same ones I'd seen the night of the robbery.

I was looking around the cabin for a tool to pry open a crate when a sound from behind the closed door to the bow caught my attention.

It was a grunt.

I moved forward cautiously, then stood at the door. It too was locked from the outside. I heard a rustle inside and a steady scratching sound. What I found when I opened the door made me laugh.

Truck Lewis, tied and taped to a bunk. It must have taken all four men to corral him—the guy had the physique of a linebacker. His mouth was covered with duct tape, which I removed first.

"What in the hell you doing here?" he said. "We back in Key West?"

"Not yet, old buddy." I smiled. "Before I do anything, though, I want to know what your role is in all this and why you punched me when I saw you the other night."

Truck rolled his eyes. "I was trying to save your life, fool. You showed up drunk and asking questions and them motherfuckers wanted to kill your ass."

I felt the back of my head where the lump had been.

"Gee, I guess I should thank you, then."

"All right, wise ass, just get me the fuck outta here."

I made quick work of his bonds and he stood unsteadily, holding himself against the cabin door.

"You bring the Marines?" he said.

"More like the Air Force. Let's go."

I clambered around the four trunks in the cabin and started up the ladder.

"You already unload some of this treasure?" Truck said.

I paused on the steps. "What do you mean?"

"There were eight of these damn things. About broke my back hauling 'em down here."

Aside from the cabin where Truck had been tied up, it was wide open below deck. There were no other crates.

Truck stretched and shook his arms to get his circulation going while I searched.

"Only these four crates now," I said. "What happened to the rest?"

"We stopped several hours into the trip."

"Stopped? You mean you went ashore somewhere?"

"Man, we were still at sea. They had me captain the ship until a big speedboat showed up out of the dark. Then they locked me in the cabin, but I heard talk and the sound of the crates moving around." He paused. "Get this, I heard one of the Peruvians mention a name I recognized, then heard the voice to go with it."

"What are you talking about? When?"

"When we met up with that other boat." He grinned. "I'm pretty sure our old homeboy Manny Gutierrez was there. He must have off-loaded some crates."

I realized I was holding my breath and exhaled.

"Gutierrez—"

A loud crash on the deck above us made me jump.

"The hell was that?" Truck said.

I was already halfway up the ladder.

21

THE MAN WITH THE SPEAR THROUGH HIS LEG HAD COLLAPSED. BLOOD WAS everywhere. The one Ray had shot with the flare was still upright but hanging on the rail and groaning. Ray held the gun on all four men. The two I'd wrestled in the water were in their late twenties, had ochre-colored skin and the pointed features of Native Indian descent.

Ray's expression bespoke concern and confusion. All in all, the scene was a mess.

"Damn, you fucked these guys up good," Truck said.

"Got a first-aid kit on board?"

"Man, this is a tourist boat. People getting drunk and falling over all the time."

Truck went below and returned with a white box adorned with a red cross. I took the gun from Ray, who wobbled over to the mast and slumped against it.

Truck applied a tourniquet to the impaled man, then cut off the pant leg above where the spear passed through his quadriceps. One of the Indian-looking men and Ray helped hold the wounded man while Truck pulled the spear the rest of the way through. Fortunately the shaft was smooth and there was nothing tied onto the end, but the man writhed and moaned anyway—it had to hurt like hell. Truck cleaned the wound with hydrogen peroxide, applied Neosporin to the neat holes on both sides, and wrapped the leg with gauze.

Next came the burn victim, who tried to take a swing at Truck when he peeled off the man's shirt to check his wounds. Truck dodged the blow, then clasped a hand around the man's throat.

"Try that again, Poncho, I throw your ass to the sharks." He looked from one to the next of his former captors. "You boys have seriously fucked with the wrong dude. I'll clean your asses up, but you mess with me once more?"

By the looks on the guys' faces, these kids—none of them looked like they'd made it out of their twenties yet—they got the message.

"Where the hell are we, anyway?" Truck said once he'd completed his ministrations.

"You were about five miles from passing through the Panama Canal," I said.

"You shitting me? Damn, boy, the Sea Lion made it here like a champ. Always dreamed of sailing her down through the Spice Islands to find me a nice little Trini. Um- hmm." He shook his head and smiled like a proud parent.

"You should have seen the scene in Key West," I said. "Television crews from all over, police, state troopers, FBI. Unbelievable." I chuckled. "And your boss was real concerned about your well being."

"Lou Fontaine? Yeah, I bet he was. Probably figured I ran off with the loot and his boat to boot."

"Yep," I said. "And so do the KWPD and the FBI."

Truck looked over at Betty rolling in the light seas, then back at me. "Now what?"

"There was a crazed mercenary in a private jet following us to get to you," I said, "but we left him disabled in Panama. We can't trust the Peruvian government and I can't fit all those crates on board Betty."

"What're you saying?"

"Can you get the Sea Lion back to Key West on your own, or do you want Ray to stick with you?"

"Piece of cake." His gaze passed quickly over the four captives. "These boys'll be fine down below."

I turned to the one who wasn't wounded and nodded my head at him. "Peruvian?"

He shrugged and turned away. The one who'd been shot with the spear opened his eyes and looked up at me.

"Si, Peruvian."

He continued passionately in Spanish, nodding at Truck, then pointed below deck. All I could make out were the words *oro* and *plata*, which I knew meant gold and silver.

Maybe these men were connected to the Peruvian rebels in the news and had sought to repatriate the treasure taken by the conquistadors from Potosí back in the 1500's and 1600's. Whatever their intent, I didn't care. I was just glad to have found Truck safe and relatively innocent.

But Manny Gutierrez? Could Truck have been mistaken? How could a Cuban colonel in the Secret Police be involved with Peruvian thieves or rebels?

I suggested we call the Coast Guard and ask them to meet Truck en route back to Florida, but he reminded us the pirates had tossed the radio overboard back in Key West. I sent Ray to get the spare radio we'd brought, along with his cell phone.

"Keep my name out of it," I told Truck while Ray was gone. "You take the credit, okay?"

We set the wounded captives up below as comfortably as possible, bound their hands and feet, then more thoroughly tied the others to the same bunk where Truck had been. Once the cabin door was secured, we all turned to the crates.

"This should be interesting," Ray said.

They were simple wood boxes, nailed shut. I pulled the dive knife from the scabbard on my calf. The sound of nails ripping from wood shrieked again and again until Truck was able to fit his fingers under the crate's top and pull it loose.

The light from the cabin windows illuminated deep gold and dull silver bars. Emeralds and rubies sparkled, wrapped in gold chains. Ornately decorated boxes were partially buried amidst the loose cob coins, pieces of four and eight, and gold doubloons.

Staring at the four-hundred-year-old booty, I couldn't help but think of how it had gotten here. Mined by slave labor; fashioned by hand; carried by horseback, carts, the backs of slaves; transferred from ship to shore; hauled overland again in portage; reloaded in galleons; sailed to Havana only to set sail again a day before a hurricane ultimately took hundreds of lives. The two sister ships, *Atocha* and *Margarita*, both sank into the quicksands between shoals in the Marquesas and weren't discovered again until 370 years later by a California chicken farmer who lost several family members of his own over a fifteen-year search, followed by a court battle with the State of Florida and the Spanish government. After a couple of decades at the museum, the treasure was spirited away again by these Peruvian nationals who sought to repatriate assets stolen from their ancestors by foreign imperialists.

Now Truck, Ray, and I had written ourselves into the history of the cursed treasure of the *Señora de Nuestra de Atocha*. I only hoped we wouldn't meet the same fate as those who had possessed it before us.

"Can't we just sail to a nice little Banana Republic and live like kings?"

Surprisingly, it was Ray who asked the question.

"That's what I'm talkin' about," Truck said.

I started to ask what we'd do with Betty but stopped and swallowed hard. Exactly. Why not run away and live extravagantly in some remote paradise? These crates contained millions in irreplaceable objects.

Visions of my good old days pulled at me like a black hole. But those days were the result of a legitimate business, albeit built on an unsustainable model. Life on the lam would bring entirely new problems. I thought of my partner, Jack Dodson, still in jail. I thought of the accusations by various authorities after my parent's deaths. Finally I thought of Special Agent Edward T. Booth.

I'd had enough law on my back the past few years. I picked up the lid and placed it back over the crate, then hammered the nails back in place with the butt of the dive knife. Truck and Ray watched in silence. I handed Truck the knife when I was done.

"Party pooper," Ray said.

I thought of Betty and the dive trip Ray and I had planned to recover my waterproof pouch. We still had the dive gear, and it was on the way home. I dialed Frank Nardi's cell phone number aboard the Mohawk and handed Truck the phone.

He hemmed and hawed, then broke the news. I couldn't hear Nardi's side of the conversation but could tell he was amazed that Truck had escaped, captured his captors, and was just this side of the Panama Canal. Truck didn't mention Gutierrez. They agreed to sail toward one another, and for Nardi to send choppers toward the Sea Lion once they were within range. I felt I'd done everything I could to ensure Truck safe passage home.

"It's not the only treasure in the sea," I said. "Let's get out of here before the Panamanians get curious."

Ray headed straight for the ladder.

Reluctant Goodbye

22

W E CIRCLED THE SEA LION ONCE. HER SAILS WERE FULL AND SHE WAS pointed north. Truck waved from the helm. In his other hand was the spare radio we'd given him.

I suddenly wondered whether he'd really sail toward the Coast Guard or return to Key West at all. Wouldn't that be a kick in the ass if he didn't?

Ray programmed the GPS, checked weather, adjusted the transponder, and estimated our fuel capacity. Once set, we cruised with minimal conversation until we landed back at Cozumel for fuel. I knew he was still brooding about my holding out on him, but at least we were on the way home.

What if Booth had cancelled the card? We'd been incommunicado for twenty-four hours, and he had to know about our stop in Cozumel. I needed to check in and give him the news. There'd be enough daylight left to make a quick dive on the sunken ocean racer if we kept an aggressive pace.

I spotted Ray's cell phone clipped to his flight bag. I glanced out the window and saw him pointing out features of my 1946 Grumman Widgeon to the fuel jockey. Once I energized the phone, three service bars appeared, so I dialed the number Ray had saved for me. Plus, if Gunner was one of Booth's guys, I wanted to make sure he called him off—

"Where the hell have you been?"

Damn! I'd been hoping just to leave a quick message.

"You called earlier, how'd you get this number?" I asked.

"I'm with the FBI, Reilly, what do you think? Why the hell did you leave the Bahamas and go to Cozumel, Mexico—"

"Relax. I found the Sea Lion at the mouth of the Panama Canal." I heard a sharp intake of breath.

"Was Lewis on board? The treasure? What about—"

"Present and accounted for. Truck was tied up below deck. Four Peruvians had him hostage."

"I'll be a son of a bitch."

"No argument here."

"What about the treasure, Reilly? You didn't call to say goodbye, did you?"

The thought of toying with him was hard to suppress, but the concern that popped into my head earlier about Truck's vanishing hadn't entirely gone away. Nor had my brief fantasy about disappearing, for good.

"Truck called the Coast Guard. The Mohawk and Sea Lion will meet somewhere along the way. There were four crates of treasure and four slightly damaged Peruvians on board, along with Captain Lewis, anxious to get home."

"How the hell did you manage that? Last I saw you had nothing but dive gear and that cherub of a mechanic. Four armed Peruvians?"

"I have some connections in Colón from my e-Antiquity days—"

"Smugglers and mercenaries, no doubt."

Did he know about Gunner?

"I haven't heard jack from the Coast Guard," he said. "They would have called me. Or I'd have heard an alert—"

"This only happened an hour ago. Maybe they're waiting until they reach the Sea Lion."

"You're not bullshitting me, are you, Reilly?"

"I never bullshit the FBI, Special Agent Booth."

A chuckle surprised me. "Nice work, kid. I knew you'd be useful—"

"The Sea Lion was headed north to Key West, and so am I." I swallowed. I didn't want Booth to get too comfortable with this relationship. "And you can call off your other asset, too. My job is done."

"What other—"

I pressed the end button. *More than done.*

"Who were you talking to?"

Ray's voice made me jump. He was looking in my side vent window, slid open to offset the heat. When would I learn?

"Nobody, just checking messages at the La Concha."

"Oh yeah? So Karen's replacement is named Special Agent Booth? Sure sounded like you said, 'I never bullshit the FBI.' I've risked my ass, and for what? An attaboy back in Key West?"

I unclipped my seat belt. "I'm going in to use the head. We need to get airborne, ASAP."

"How about the truth, Buck!"

I bit my lip. Ray was one of my best friends—hell, one of my only friends.

"Promise I'll come clean when we get back to Key West, okay?"

Ray shook his head. "Sure, Buck. Later. In Key West. If it's not too dark, or too late, so then maybe tomorrow, or maybe never."

Damn.

BEFORE WE TOOK OFF I CHECKED IN WITH HARRY GREENBAUM, WHO'D garnered some interesting information on our friend Gunner. His actual name was Richard Rostenkowski, and he'd been thrown off the Chicago police force for excessive violence only to disappear for a decade. A recent scandal that involved a Blackwater security team in Afghanistan resulted in criminal charges, again, for excessive force and the murder of civilians, which caused the expulsion of a man known only as Gunner, whose fingerprints matched those of Officer Rostenkowski. Blackwater wouldn't reveal any information, but word was that Gunner was now self-employed and pursuing work that could yield him significant sums of cash.

He said he was hired to find "lost goods," but hired by whom? Booth wasn't paying any big rewards, so it had to be someone else.

Just the kind of guy I didn't need to have a grudge against me.

I decided to put all that behind me. The Sea Lion was found, I'd made the report to Booth, and Truck had contacted the Coast Guard. As for Ray, he wasn't talking to me. He either ignored my attempts at conversation or was sincerely asleep.

With about a thousand miles of water to cover, I had plenty of time to think about the imminent dive on the ocean racer. It had been months, but I was certain the integrity of my waterproof pouch would hold up. Gutierrez must have salivated at the contents. At least a dozen maps, letters, articles about missing galleons, descriptions of hidden caves, missing cities, buried valuables. Even though they were just copies, their value could hardly be more obvious.

I reached down and felt the new waterproof pouch below my seat, in the new shelf I'd built after Gutierrez trashed the last one. Now, I had the original maps and information stashed there, fresh from the numbered account in Switzerland. I might be crazy to keep them there again, but I wanted them with me at all times. Gutierrez was back in Cuba climbing the ranks of the Secret Police, and nobody else knew I'd kept the pouch there, except Ray.

Now if I could just recover the copies from the sunken ocean racer, I'd have the only ones in existence. Someday, if I had the money, I'd be equipped to find some of the world's greatest missing treasures. I could even go academic and pursue the treasures for posterity using public grants. The Great Recession may have ended, but I was still in the no-man's land between recovering materialist and socially responsible activist.

Big territory, and new to me.

And what about Gutierrez? Could he be the one Nardi said was searching for the boat? Could Truck be right about his involvement with the theft of the Atocha treasure? He'd lived in Key West for years and certainly knew the museum well. But the two matters were totally unconnected. What were the odds of his being tied to them both? Remote, but I had learned the hard way that with Gutierrez, you never knew.

I was dying to use Ray's phone to call Nardi and see how close they were to Truck, but the last thing I wanted was to arouse Ray's curiosity. The time flew by as my thoughts ricocheted between the treasure on the Sea Lion, whether I'd see Truck again, what to tell Ray, the maps under my seat, the sunken ocean racer, and what Karen was doing in New York. A ping in my headset brought me back to the present. Cuba was ahead, the western tip visible on the horizon.

My palms broke into a sweat. I wanted to steer clear of their airspace, so I banked to the north. Lightning may not strike twice in the same place, but it would sure strike me if I got too close to Cuba while Gutierrez was still around. I sat up straight in my seat.

Only about fifteen miles to the coordinates Nardi had given me.

23

RAY FINALLY SPOKE TO ME.

"Where are we?" he said.

"Halfway through my landing checklist."

He rubbed his eyes, took a deep breath, and studied the instrument panel. It was nearly 5:00 p.m., maybe an hour of daylight left given the time of year. If the GPS coordinates were accurate, it should be enough, but I could tell by Ray's long glance at his watch that he wasn't sure we'd make it.

"Plenty of time," I said.

Before he could comment I pushed the yoke forward and began our descent. We'd passed a number of boats and ships as we skirted Cuban waters, some of them still visible in the distance, but the landing site was clear of any impediments. The GPS alarm sounded as we passed over the target during our approach. My heart bounded in my chest and a smile pulled at my lips—but only for a moment. The remains of Gutierrez's partner might still be on board the sunken boat.

As we touched down, a spray of salt water shot up the sides of the fuselage and catapulted off the props in every direction. Calm seas welcomed us and made for a smooth turn and taxi on the step back over the dive site. The depth gauge showed approximately a hundred and ten feet of water, and sonar depicted a smooth bottom.

"Can't we come back another day for this, Buck?" Ray said. "It's been a hell of a week."

"I know you're pissed, Ray, and I'm sorry, but we're here. Let's get this over with."

Ray shook his head and stared at the window. The GPS sounded again. I pulled back on the throttles and we came off the step and settled into the deep blue water. Anticipation tingled in my fingers. I unstrapped my harness and stepped out of the flight deck. Ray slid over and took control of the helm.

I peeled off my shirt as I opened the aft locker. With the gear laid out, air turned on, GPS location programmed into the rented dive computer, I flipped open the hatch. Water splashed around, but Ray did a nice job keeping us pointed away from the swells. Had it been a little earlier, the conditions would have been perfect. Clear day, no wind, no rain, and optimal visibility. I figured there should still be enough sunshine to get me through the dive.

Once I had on the BC, tank, and fins, I held the mask in my hand, checked my watch, and adjusted the bezel.

"I should be back in twenty minutes, max." I had to shout over the sound of the engines. "If it takes longer, I'll need to hang for ten to decompress, but I won't have much more air than that."

Ray stared straight ahead. I could tell he was determined not to look at me.

"How will I know if you need help?"

"I'll be fine," I said.

"Okay, how will I let you know if *I* need help?"

I had to remind myself that Ray's world is all about precision, accuracy, planning, and predictability. This whole week had taken him off his axis. That and my not being straight up with him. I reached into the aft locker and pulled out my anchor line.

"This has a hundred feet of line attached to it. If anything goes wrong just throw the anchor in over the dive site and I'll come right up."

He nodded. It wasn't exactly high-tech, but I didn't expect the precaution to accomplish anything other than to ease his anxiety a little.

"Okay, now?" I said.

He was silent.

Good luck to you, too.

I dropped into the chilly autumn water. As soon as Betty passed me, I spun over and began to descend into the blue depths, with no bottom in sight.

24

THERE WAS MINIMAL CURRENT AS I PROGRESSED STEADILY TOWARD THE bottom, alternately equalizing pressure in my ears and watching the depth gauge. At forty feet below the surface, details on the ocean floor began to materialize. Patches of sea grass, small coral heads—and there in a sandy ravine was Gutierrez's black ocean racer. The boat rested flat on its hull like a sleeping nurse shark. My old green kayak was still stuck through the cockpit, and memories of the chase were still fresh. After several attempts, here I was, taking back what Gutierrez and his partner had stolen. The thought added confidence to my kick.

The boat gently rocked on the bottom. I arrived at its stern. The hull was covered with green algae, and coral had started to grow on the exposed metal. Parrot fish, sergeant majors, purple tangs, a fat angel fish, along with dozens of wrasses and other smaller fish swam in and out of the grills on the engine cowling and around the double stainless steel props partially buried in the sand. I checked the starboard side but couldn't see in the side window, which had remained intact. It too was coated with sea life. I took a deep breath, which lifted my body up a few feet and allowed me to hover over the kayak to see where it had crashed through the windshield. I couldn't see inside—damn, I'd forgotten a flashlight.

Brilliant move, moron.

That could be a problem, given that the windows were covered with algae. Air bubbles from my regulator whisked past my ears and provided the only sound as I circled around to the driver's side door, ajar and swaying slowly in the current. Crap. What if the pouch had been washed out?

I checked my depth gauge: 108 feet, which only gave me another three minutes to avoid any decompression stops. I'd already used over a third of my air. Time to get inside. I took hold of the door, pulled hard, and swung it open—

A green flash exploded in front of my eyes, and I kicked away from the boat. A massive moray eel craned its fat head out and stared me down. It was dark inside the cabin, and the limited light at this depth caused him to glow an iridescent green.

Crap, crap, *crap!* Not only had I forgotten the flashlight, I'd left the spear gun on the Sea Lion. With two minutes of bottom time left I swam hard around the back of the boat to the starboard side door. A crust of coral and muck coated the handle and filled the seam separating the door from the hull, but I took hold of it and pulled. It opened a little. I positioned my fins flat against the hull and used the leverage to tug as hard as I could, and the door pulled free.

The moray lunged at me, but I kicked back hard, separating myself from the ship.

I ascended ten feet and stared down. I again swam over to the port side but stayed far enough away so the eel wouldn't feel threatened. With both doors open, I could now see inside. The human remains were gone, no doubt consumed over time by my fat friend. The moray was coiled and staring at me like a giant rattlesnake.

I scanned the inside as best I could but saw no sign of the yellow plastic waterproof pouch. As I started to swim back around to the other side, I was astonished to see Betty's Danforth anchor come hurtling toward the sea floor, then jerk to a stop ten feet above the sunken boat.

Are you kidding me, Ray?

What the heck could possibly be wrong?

Son of a bitch!

A quick glance at my watch confirmed that I had a minute of bottom time left. Ray was going to have to wait. I peered in the passenger side door and spotted the pouch wedged on the top of the boat's dash, pressed against the windshield. It appeared green—of course. The sun's rays lose intensity at this depth, and yellow fades to dark.

Bingo!

Now, how to get it without losing an arm to the moray?

I looked around for an answer, noted the eel's position, and had an idea. What worked once, just might again. I sucked in a deep breath that lifted me up above the boat, where I exhaled and kicked hard. With my arms locked straight I shoved the end of the kayak hard and fast inside the cabin. I felt it move under my pressure. I backed up and repeated the effort, pushing as hard as I could. The kayak had gone another two feet through the windshield.

I chanced a quick look at the anchor that dangled above me and saw that Ray was now lifting and dropping it up and down to emphasize his distress message.

"I'm working as fast as I can, Goddamnit!" I shouted. All I heard was a groan and more bubbles blasting past my ears.

I peeked through the broken windshield into the cabin and saw the moray pinned under the kayak, still alive and squirming like crazy.

God, he's pissed.

He'll rip my head off if he can. I took a deep suck of air, plunged my arm inside and grabbed an edge of the waterproof pouch and tugged . . . *Damn!*

It was stuck!

I pulled again, harder this time, and felt the muck, sea anemone, coral roots, and eel crap slowly give way just as the fat moray sensed my presence and whipped around to inhale my arm. I felt his teeth graze my forearm as I withdrew it from the cabin, and a long track of four slices filled with blood on my arm. I kicked hard, sucked air like a sprinter, and scissor-kicked wildly toward the surface.

Was the damn eel coming after me? I didn't see him but couldn't be sure.

SCUBA 101 kicked in and I slowed down a little to prevent my lungs from exploding and took quick shallow breaths, now worried about Ray's alarm.

As the light above grew in brilliance I could hear the distant sound of boat engines. Was that the problem? A boat coming?

I checked my watch and knew I should hang on the anchor line for a few moments to ease the nitrogen from my bloodstream, but considering Ray's urgency, there wasn't time. I'd have to count on there being a built-in grace period in the recreational dive tables.

I broke through the surface by the anchor line. Ray shrieked at my sudden appearance and fell backwards inside the cabin.

"Where the hell have you been? Didn't you see the anchor?"

"I'm here, Ray what's the emergency?"

"The Cubans are coming, damnit! The fucking *Cubans*!"

The sound of the boat grew louder as I scrambled up into the fuselage. I got stuck in the small hatch as Ray lunged for the left seat. I dumped the SCUBA gear into the water, then kicked off the fins. There goes the security deposit.

"Cut the anchor line, we've got to get airborne, pronto!" he yelled.

Betty's engines roared to life and I was again grateful I'd had Ray overhaul them. I tossed the waterproof pouch on top of the instrument panel and Ray didn't give it so much as a glance. We bounced along the water's surface, which threw me from side to side as I struggled toward the co-pilot's seat.

"Oh, shit!" Ray said.

He flipped the speaker switch on the dash, and what I heard next surprised me a hell of a lot more then the moray had.

"Stop right there, sea plane! I command you, stop now!" the voice crackled over the radio.

Ray looked at me with wild eyes. "They sound really pissed!"

"You're violating Cuban waters and breaking international law!"

I felt the thin scar on my forehead from the last time I was on this very spot. When blood dripped into my lap, I looked at my gashes and realized how razor-sharp the moray's teeth had been.

Just then Betty broke free from the ocean's grasp and we lurched into the air. Ray banked to port and I spotted a large speedboat slicing through the water toward us.

The voice was Cuban but the English was excellent. Was I imagining it, or was the voice familiar?

Could it really be Manny Gutierrez?

25

NOW AIRBORNE, RAY BREATHED A SIGH OF RELIEF.

"Circle around, I want to see who's in that boat," I said.

"Are you crazy? We're outta here!"

The radio had gone silent, and the speedboat had stopped in the water near the wreck.

"Come on, Ray! It's not a military boat, it's just a speedboat. What can they do? We're in international waters. Circle around."

"I'm in the pilot's seat, and—"

"Now, Ray!" He was on my last nerve.

Ray hesitated, then banked hard to starboard.

"Damnit, Buck, I just want to get back to Key West. And we need to get out of here. We—"

"One pass, that's all, and get lower, I want to see their faces."

Ray circled and reduced altitude. As we got closer I could see four men standing on the deck looking up at us. The radio again crackled to life, now in the intimacy of my headset.

"You've got *cojones*, coming back to this place, but I knew you wouldn't be able to resist," the voice on the radio said.

I saw one of the men holding the boat's microphone as he looked up at us.

"Resist what?" Ray said.

"Get closer. Is that—?"

"That's close enough, damnit!" Ray said and banked to the north.

The man lowered the microphone and I caught a clear glimpse of his face. The air caught in my lungs. It was Manny Gutierrez, and I could swear he was smiling.

But why?

That's when I saw the guy on the bow of their boat lift a long tube and point it at us.

No . . . *No!*

"Turn, Ray, *turn!* Get out of here, *now!*"

I reached up and shoved the throttle handles down. Betty jumped forward.

"What the hell are you doing?" Ray said.

A flame and trail of smoke launched from the bow of the boat and was headed our way.

"ROCKET!" I screamed.

"*What*?!"

"Evasive action, quick! Turn!"

I saw the streak of fire headed right for us. Ray swerved hard to port and a fraction of a second later we were rocked by an explosion that sent Betty sideways with yaw into a slide.

"I can't . . . control her!"

Ray worked the yoke, pulled it back hard, and the engines screamed in a steady howl with both tachometers red-lined. I pulled back on the throttles, but we continued to veer uncontrollably.

"What's that smell?" he said.

Uh-oh.

I looked back into the fuselage. Fire was burning a hole through the roof near the tail.

"*Fire!*"

I jumped from my seat and fumbled with the fire extinguisher strapped behind the pilot's seat. I nearly fell into the flames before I shot the extinguisher into them. The fire died down but it was burning outside, too.

The hole grew bigger back toward the tail.

"Betty's on fire!" I yelled. "I can't get it out!"

"I can barely control her!"

"We've got to get her into the water or she'll burn to a crisp!"

"She'll sink if we set her down now," Ray said.

He suddenly banked again and I realized he'd been gaining altitude.

"What the hell are you doing?" I yelled. "We either ditch or we'll explode!"

Ray fought with the controls as I struggled back into the right seat. Sparks shot out from under the instrument panel.

"Ray, what're you doing? We have to land!"

"I can't swim, remember!"

He was eerily calm, eyes focused and his teeth pressed together. His resolve helped calm me down. We could only have seconds, minutes at best, before the flames reached the wings and Betty's fuel tanks ignited.

"What's the plan?" As I asked the question, I saw the answer out the window.

"Ray? No, Ray, we can't . . . Ray?"

He gave me a sidelong glance. "Better get your harness back on."

I buckled in, then looked back over my shoulder as the fuselage slowly burned forward. The hole in the roof kept getting bigger and the flight deck filled with smoke. Would the fuselage collapse before the tanks ignited? My eyes and throat burned. Ray dropped the nose and pointed us toward land. It was still in the distance, but I could see a beach jutting into the sea. Just then, the yoke fell forward.

The radio crackled again. "I'll find you, Reilly. If you live!"

Ray groaned. "The ailerons have burned through!"

The altimeter needle dropped like a rock. Our angle of attack was pointed down toward the shore just off the point of land.

Ray pressed his feet up and down on the pedals to no avail.

"The rudder's gone," he said.

"We're going down—brace yourself!"

I hand-cranked the flaps to keep the nose up, but with the tail controls fried it was like trying to sprint with one leg. Ray glanced over, calm as I'd ever seen him, and in the face of death he gave me a crazed smile.

"Always wanted to see Cuba," he said.

Betty dove toward the water, and through what could only be the grace of God, the nose lifted just before we hit. I tried to hold on, but the force of the impact wrenched us both forward and Ray smashed his head hard on the instrument panel. He slumped over, unconscious.

Betty bounced and skimmed, and with no ability to control our direction I cut the engines and dumped the fuel. The curve of the sixty-plus year old aquatic hull guided the powerless flying boat across the water like a skipping stone until we lurched forward with a loud metallic shriek. We ground to a sudden halt on the shallow bottom, a hundred yards off the western tip of Cuba. Water sloshed around my feet, which meant the hull had been breached.

As I reached up to cut the magnetos, the speaker crackled.

"Welcome back, Reilly."

I flipped the switches and killed the electrical system—to prevent additional fire and to silence the speaker.

"Fuck you, Gutierrez."

26

RAY WAS UNCONSCIOUS AND BETTY WAS SMOLDERING. WE WERE BEACHED ON a sand flat adjacent to a channel, a hundred yards from land. A quick glance at the shore revealed no buildings, houses, or people. When I shook Ray, his head flopped to the side. He had a gash on his forehead but there wasn't much blood. His breathing was raspy. I had to get him lying flat to assess his injuries.

The cabin was smoky, the floor covered with water, and spotted embers glowed above my head. The handle wouldn't work so I kicked open the hatch. I grabbed my bailing bucket and doused the roof with seawater until there was no more smoke. Ray still hadn't moved. I unclipped his harness, checked his limbs for any obvious breaks, relieved to find none. I grabbed him under the armpits and pulled him back into the fuselage.

He said something unintelligible, windmilled his arms, and tried to free himself from my grasp.

"Ray, it's me, Buck. You okay?"

He dropped a hand over his eyes and slowly felt upward along the sheen of blood to the gash on his forehead.

"I'm bleeding . . . What happened? Did we crash?"

He lurched up to a sitting position and looked around.

"Holy crap! We did crash. Somebody shot us down! That boat . . ." he paused. "You had to circle and see who it was!"

He was right. If I'd have listened to him we'd be halfway to Key West by now.

I pulled my flight bag from under the seat, along with the backpack that had a change of clothes. I grabbed the waterproof pouch from under the pilot's seat along with the one from the wreck and stuffed them in the flight bag. Ray stared at the hole in the top of the plane. He stood up, weaving a little, put his head through the hole, then made a 360-degree turn.

"The tail's toast, rudder, ailerons, half the fuselage is charred. Oh, man . . . we're *so screwed!*"

"Based on the sparks that were coming from below the instrument panel the electrical system's shot to hell too," I said.

From outside I could see a foot-long tear on the bottom of the fuselage where Betty must have caught on a rock. I pointed it out.

"We're beyond screwed, we're . . . we're . . . I don't even speak Spanish! Do you speak—*I don't speak Spanish!*" he said.

"Me neither, Ray. Come on, grab everything you can find that identifies us, or the plane. We need to peel the numbers off the tail—"

"The tail's fried, Buck! There are no numbers! There's no freaking tail!"

We dug through the plane and grabbed anything that could be traced back to me.

Was this happening?

Was I scuttling Betty?

Was she beyond repair?

I didn't doubt Gutierrez's threat that he'd come looking for me, but hopefully he'd dive the wreck first to see if I found the pouch. Wouldn't stop him from radioing some of his cronies in the Secret Police to come search for us, though.

I jumped out onto the soft sand flat, where Betty was wedged into marl and turtle grass. The channel we'd bounced over was just behind her. My heart raced, my body was soaked with sweat and salt water, and I more or less collapsed on the sand.

Betty was charred, torn, bent, and broken. She was all I had in this world, aside from two pouches of ancient clues to potential treasures. My business was now gone, Last Resort Charter and Salvage, done, beyond done—crushed, ruined, destroyed along with Betty.

Everything was ruined.

Rage grew within me and without realizing it I was pounding my fist into the surf and sand.

"Aaaaggghhhh!"

I stuck my face into the shallow water. I should just suck in a lungful and—I was being pulled up from the water by my hair.

"What the hell are you doing, man? Pull it together!" Ray said.

When I sat up something caught my eye.

"Oh, shit . . ."

Ray spun around to see where I was looking. A half-dozen fishing smacks were coming around the point straight toward us. It only took a few minutes until they beached their boats on the flat next to Betty. The first man yelled to us—in Spanish, of course.

"*No hablo Espanol*," I said.

"*Americano?*" one of the men said. He was the youngest of the deeply tanned and weathered bunch. "We saw the smoke streak across the sky when you crashed. What happened?"

"Fucking Gutierrez—"

I grabbed Ray's arm. "Electrical fire," I said.

"In the plane's tail?" The young man looked at Betty again and pressed his lips together.

"Where are we, anyway?" I said.

"Puerto Esperanza. Western Cuba."

The men were fishermen, amazed at the appearance of the crashed plane and Americans wearing Hawaiian shirts. Or maybe they were just amazed we'd survived the crash.

"Can you men help push the plane into the channel and tow it to shore?" I said.

The young Cuban spoke to the other men, who conferred a few moments in rapid-fire Spanish. I assumed they were questioning the sanity of helping us, but then one jumped out of his boat and felt around Betty's hull, checking the depth of the sand, eyeing the tear in the hull. He spoke to the others, and two other men jumped out and did the same thing. They then began to dig sand away from the hull with their hands, digging, pushing, pulling, and yelling instructions to each other. We all worked together, and after fifteen minutes Betty was afloat in the channel, tied to two of the boats, and on her way to shore. Ray was in the young man's skiff, and I was inside Betty bailing water as we went.

Even though I was happy to get her off the flat, the more I surveyed her damage, the worse I felt.

Here in the deep water a painful thought stopped me mid-bail. I should just let Betty sink so Gutierrez couldn't find us. If she were unfixable, it would be the smart thing to do. The thought only rattled in my head for a few seconds, then I started bailing again.

I just couldn't pull the plug on Betty.

I'd never done the smart thing before, why start now?

27

THE TRIP TO SHORE TOOK FOREVER—AS WELL IT SHOULD HAVE, SINCE THIS was a funeral procession not a salvage effort. I could hardly bail fast enough with the water pouring in from the gash in Betty's hull. When we finally rounded the point, a small fishing village appeared on the shore. Fisherman watching us in the darkness jumped into the water as the boats neared land, they encircled Betty, then guided and pushed until she was ashore, listing heavily to her port side, the green float dug into the brown sand.

I jumped into the shallow water. Betty looked like a beached whale that had been shredded by sharks. What would the Cubans do now? I glanced from face to face and saw the glow of excitement. They talked amongst themselves, gesturing toward the plane and looking back toward their village.

Women emerged from dark dwellings and stood with their hands on their hips. Children came out ran toward their fathers and brothers, chattering like so many birds, all in a rush to see the carcass first hand. The excitement was palpable, their voices vibrated on my skin, oblivious to our loss.

They would assume us to be rich, and once word spread we were Americans, the assumption would solidify. All Americans are rich, even bankrupt Americans, when compared to Cubans. If the village had a telephone or radio, would the word be out on the wire of an American plane shot down by a hero of the revolution? Manny Gutierrez strikes another blow against marauding imperialists? If only I had a picture of him in the Mercedes he abandoned in Key West when he fled all those months ago.

With the last glints of sun reflecting off the unburned portions of her silver fuselage, Betty was surrounded by curious villagers engaged in animated conversations all raging at once. Arms waved, reenactments occurred, and amazement slowly turned to concern, particularly in the women's faces. I heard the word *Americano* several times, and politics aside, survival in Cuba meant keeping off the government's radar. Maybe that would keep a lid on our appearance, at least long enough to get the hell out of here.

Ray remained seated in the younger man's skiff and stared into the water. In shock from the knock to his head, or just despondent? I wanted to throw up but couldn't afford the luxury. I was studying the fishing boats, dories, and skiffs, assessing whether any were seaworthy enough to cross the straits back to Florida, when the younger Cuban who spoke English stepped forward.

"My name is Juan Espedes."

"Thanks for helping us ashore, Juan. I don't know what we're going to do about Betty—sorry, the plane."

"It does not look good, Señor. I think she *es muerte*."

"My friend here's an airplane mechanic." I turned to Ray. "You okay?"

I checked the gash on his forehead. It was swollen but didn't look too bad. Ray pushed my hand away, stood up, wavered, then squatted down to steady himself on the side of the fishing boat. He had his cell phone in his hand but water dripped out of it.

"I'm sorry, Ray," I said. "For not listening to you, for not telling you the whole story, for getting you into this mess, for—"

"Forget it, Buck."

"I owe you the truth—"

"I don't—"

"I was drafted—forced, really—to do something secretly—well, kind of undercover—for a government agency." I paused. "I can't tell you—shouldn't even be telling you this much."

Ray raised an eyebrow. "You mean like a spy?"

"More like a fucking errand boy."

"That's an awful lot to swallow." Ray held his palms up. "But it doesn't really matter anymore, does it? Considering our situation." He rubbed his eyes. "And I'm sorry about Betty. I tried to steer—"

"You were great. It's my fault, one hundred percent."

He glanced back at Betty. "What are we going to do?" He shook the phone and more water flew out. "This thing's shot."

I glanced at the dories lined up along the beach.

"None of these boats go out into the gulfstream, Señor." Juan must have read my mind.

"Are there any others we could charter in Puerto Esperanza?"

"To go to America?" He laughed, and then looked contrite. "No, sorry."

A younger woman came up, took Juan by the arm, and turned him away from us. She spoke in quiet Spanish, nodding once toward us. After their brief exchange, she spoke to the other women, all of whom turned to look at us again, then she hurried back toward the cluster of small houses.

"Maria is my wife," Juan said. "She has asked you inside for the dinner and to sleep. Nothing more can be done in darkness."

Ray stood and stared at me. I shouldered my flight bag, nodded at Ray, and steered him in behind Juan. No, nothing could be done for Betty in darkness. Nothing could be done for Betty in daylight.

The question was could anything be done for Ray and me?

28

JUAN AND MARIA'S HOME CONSISTED OF ONE BEDROOM THEY SHARED WITH their two young boys, a bathroom, and a kitchen with a small table and an ancient couch. By American standards it would be considered miniscule, but here on the western tip of Cuba, they were proud to have a free standing home to themselves. Only Juan spoke English, a result of his growing up in Havana and having a father who worked for *Granma*, the State-run news agency, where he was a liaison to the U.S. based news agencies with offices there. Maria and the boys were kind, gracious, and curious. Juan had a busy evening translating every word we said.

Exhausted from one of the longest days of our lives, Ray and I were dozing off in our black beans and rice. Once dinner was over, Juan pushed the table against the wall and provided us with blankets. I gave Ray the couch and he started snoring before I hit the floor. I awoke once, after a dream about Betty in flames and my being unable to get the fire extinguished or get the unconscious Ray out of his seat.

I went outside with Ray's cell phone, but it still wouldn't turn on. I walked down the shoreline until I came upon Betty, a black silhouette askew in the sand, alone and discarded like so much jetsam. The smell of low tide and rotted fish burned my nose and heightened the sense of death. I ran my hand down the cool skin of Betty's fuselage until I reached what was left of her tail.

"I'm sorry, old girl."

Black waves lapped against the shore. The water was warm as I waded around Betty and studied the gaping hole, the charred ailerons and rudder. With an antique airplane you're always worried something will go wrong, or that you won't be able to get parts as things wear out or break, but this I never imagined.

Shot down?

"You got us safely to shore, Betty."

When I said her name aloud it reminded me of her namesake, my mother, which caused another missed heartbeat. She too died in an accident in a foreign land.

I walked in a fog of grief back to Juan's. Once inside, I fell right back asleep on the floor and stayed there until a horn sounded a short series of blasts that awakened the entire household.

Juan appeared in the door of his room with Maria hanging on his shoulder. Looking at their faces it was obvious that the horn was not a normal occurrence. Their hospitality suddenly felt like a huge mistake. If it was the Cuban police searching for the American pilot, Juan and his family could be in serious trouble.

"Is there a back door?" I said.

Juan shook his head quickly.

"How about a window?"

Juan nodded and I jumped up.

"Let's go, Ray."

Maria, who had left Juan to peek out the corner of the window, said something to him, her hand over her heart.

"It's a truck, a farmer's truck from Pinar del Rio," Juan said. "*Mi madre!*"

"You know him?" I said.

"I'll be back," Juan said as the horn blared again.

Out the window I could see an old truck with an older man standing next to it. It looked like Juan was asking what the heck all the honking at dawn was about. The old man pointed to Betty.

Double crap.

Juan held his arms up and lifted his shoulders.

"What's he want?" Ray said.

Juan pointed up the road and slung his shoulders again.

"Is he looking for us?" Ray said.

I swung back to look at him. "How the hell would I know?"

Ray shrank under my glare

"I'm sorry, but we need to get out of here," I said. "We can't put Juan and his family in danger."

We balled up the blankets and tossed them on the couch, then grabbed the flight bag. I saw Maria standing in the door to the bedroom, both boys at her sides, her hands over their mouths.

Crap.

The window in the back of the house was open, with a curtain made of burlap that fluttered in the light breeze. I smiled at Maria and rolled out the window like Butch Cassidy. I landed feet first on the ground, then hesitated while I listened. Ray fell on top of me and we both collapsed into the dirt.

"Oof!"

"Sorry!"

We edged around the house to the road. It was a dead end to the right, three houses down. The only way to go was left, where the old man's truck was parked.

"What are we going to do?" Ray said.

I looked at the old man talking to Juan. No uniform, no antennae on his truck, no cell phone on his belt. No gun, either.

"Come on." I stepped out from under the tree onto the road.

"What're you doing?!" Ray said.

Juan and the old man were having a calm conversation, until Juan spotted me coming down the road.

"*Buenos dias,*" I said.

Juan stood with his mouth agape, but the old man had a small smile on his face.

"*Buenos dias.*"

Ray came up behind me just as the old man let loose a long statement, or question, in Spanish.

"*No hablo Espanol,*" I said.

"Ahh, Americano." A bigger smile.

"I speak English," Juan said.

"I understand *Ingles* too," the old man said.

Juan asked some questions as if we'd never met, which Ray and I answered like the strangers we weren't. Yes, it was our plane, we had an electrical fire, landed offshore and idled until we beached her last night. They both nodded and stared at me as if I were supposed to have more to say. I realized nobody else had emerged from their homes and imagined each of the fishermen's families huddled under windowsills staring out and wondering what was being said.

The old man cleared his throat. "Are you CIA?"

Good grief!

Ray contributed a little shriek. I laughed.

"Actually, I'm a charter pilot and Ray here's my friend and mechanic."

Now the man laughed.

"Mechanic? You fix this plane?"

Ray shrugged but didn't answer.

The old man rubbed his whiskers. "I saw you last night, a flame across the night sky. I know this type of plane, a water plane. It is why I came to find you."

"Señor Maceo is a *veguero*, a tobacco farmer near Pinar del Rio, one of the best known in Cuba," Juan said.

"You own a farm?" Ray said.

The young man sighed. "The government owns everything. He's the manager, now. His family did own the farm, before the revolution. He's a little famous. The tobacco for Trinidad cigars comes from his land. They were the Beard's favorite."

Great. Why is a tobacco farmer so interested in us? If he makes the cigars that were Castro's favorite, does that mean he's wired to the government?

The old man started toward Betty, walking slowly, studying her. Now, in daylight, the sight left me speechless. It sunk in with painful clarity that the girl I loved was totaled. There would be no way to fix her in Cuba, especially on the run from Gutierrez, who'd search relentlessly for us. I inhaled a quick breath. If this old guy found us, Gutierrez couldn't be far behind.

We had to get out of here. I again examined each of the fishing smacks in the distance.

Could any of them make it ninety miles to Key West?

The old man said things to Juan that he agreed with (head nods), a few he didn't (head shakes), then some more that he did. Ray and I exchanged we're-fools-for-not-learning-Spanish glances.

"Come," the old man said.

Ray and I followed dutifully.

Where? Ray mouthed the word.

I didn't know the answer but followed anyway.

What choice did we have?

29

"MY FARM IS NEAR HERE." THE FARMER NODDED TOWARD RAY. "THAT cut on your head needs attention."

Ray stopped in his tracks and looked at me. I nodded, and he shook his head. I took him by the elbow and steered him toward the truck. We had to get out of here, whether we knew what the old man's intentions were or not. There were no boats or options here that would help us, so putting some distance between Betty and us made sense.

"I'm sorry about your plane," he said. "She was very old. We are accustomed to using old vehicles here, but I fear your friend will not be able to fix it. She's a Grumman, no? But not the Goose, too small, eh?"

Wow.

"She's a Widgeon," I said.

He'd said he was familiar with "water planes," but how, if he was a farmer?

Now at the truck, I cinched the flight bag up on my shoulder. The old man spoke in Spanish to Juan, who smiled and nodded his head. He looked from Betty to us and extended his hand to me.

"Good luck, Americano."

I tried to swallow but my mouth was dry.

"Can you keep watch over my plane? I'll be back for her."

The old man and Ray exchanged a shake of their heads. Juan nodded, and we got into the Chevy truck, vintage 1955, and sat three across the bench seat. Juan waved once and turned back toward his home.

I caught a last glimpse of Betty before she disappeared behind sea grape and casuarina trees. We bounced up the rutted dirt road, my heart in my throat, our future uncertain.

"Where are we going?" Ray kept his voice calm, but I could see—no, I could *feel* that he was a nervous wreck inside.

Señor Maceo didn't answer. He might have grunted, I wasn't sure. He drove with a hand loose on the top of the steering wheel and his head cocked toward the open window. The old truck was in decent shape. The interior had been replaced with odd fabrics stitched with care. The manual transmission shifted smoothly and didn't grind, smoke, or shimmy. I thought back to the last time I was in Cuba, impressed with all the old cars still in use. Few were in as good as shape as this one, though.

We'd hopped into the truck with this guy because we didn't have any other options. But why had he come to Puerto Esperanza to look for us? He said he saw Betty in flames as she streaked toward the west and that he recognized it as a seaplane, a Grumman in fact, but why did that matter to him? He wanted to know if we were CIA but hadn't indicated whether that was a good or bad thing.

Gutierrez and the authorities would hunt for Betty, and it wouldn't be hard to find her. I didn't think the fishermen would talk about it, but with the plane sitting on their beach, it's not like they could pretend nothing had happened. The logical thing for them to do would be to report it, but would they say we left with Señor Maceo?

Or would they burn Betty to the ground to get rid of the evidence? That thought twisted my gut, along with my awareness that no harbor was safe until we found passage out of Cuba.

If what Truck said was accurate and Gutierrez was involved with the Atocha theft, how crazy was it that we collided with him on the dive site? Could he have known we were coming? And how could he be connected with the Peruvians? Hero of the Revolution or not, he was just a colonel in the Secret Police. I pondered this for a moment. What about his boss, Director Sanchez? Now *he* could have connections to Peru, being a big shot in Havana, and all. Could Sanchez be the connection to the Peruvians, if in fact they were connected at all?

Having followed a coastal road for fifteen minutes, Maceo turned south and drove inland. The landscape changed quickly, becoming agricultural. Farms and shacks were scattered across the countryside, all of which seemed threadbare and dilapidated. Only a few had electrical lines connected to the single wire that ran along the road. This was one of the poorest regions of Cuba. Agriculture didn't require electricity, only mules, fertilizer, sunlight, dirt, and a lot of sore backs.

We had to pull over twice for horse-drawn carts to pass, and both drivers waved to Señor Maceo. He stopped to pass the time of day with one of them.

"Do you like Cuban cigars?" he asked.

"Occasionally," I said.

"Rum, too," Ray said.

"These farms are where the tobacco for the best cigars is grown. Partagas, Cohiba, Cuesta del Rey, Trinidad. The fields are nearly ready to be cut."

Large ramshackle barns with rusted roofs dotted the landscape. No John Deere or Kubota tractors were in sight. The harvest here was done manually. The broad tobacco leaves swayed in the breeze, bright green and dense in the fields. It looked like a bumper crop. In the distance, rugged gray mountains, plateaus, and buttes jutted up dramatically from the green surface.

"Pretty, huh?" I said.

"Sure is," Ray said. "I wonder if they need any mechanics around here."

Señor Maceo laughed, showing his tobacco-stained teeth.

"We Cubans are resourceful mechanics. Chevrolet does not ship us parts for these vehicles."

We drove another twenty minutes. I felt as if we were being sucked into the country's interior, ever further from any chance of getting back to Key West.

Señor Maceo waved his arm out the side window. "My farm starts here and goes as far as you can see."

"*Your* farm?" Ray said.

The old man sighed and was quiet for a moment.

"I still think of it as my family's farm. A piece of paper or government declaration does not change our history here."

Was that a note of political discontent? God, I hoped so.

He slowed the vehicle and turned down a dirt driveway that was better maintained than any of the roads we'd taken from Puerto Esperanza. A small but handsome farmhouse sat atop a slight knoll at the head of the drive in an oasis surrounded by tobacco plants. Multiple outbuildings were behind the house, including two large barns, one of which was built on the edge of a hill. A jungle of tobacco plants surrounded everything.

We pulled to a stop beside the farmhouse, which was situated just high enough to enjoy a spectacular view of the countryside and out toward the coast. An old Russian Lada was parked there too.

Señor Maceo saw me looking at the porch.

"I was seated here in my chair last night when your plane streaked through the sky," he said. "Through my binoculars I could tell it was a Grumman."

A door slammed, a young woman emerged from the house, and suddenly the landscape's beauty was eclipsed.

She walked with purpose toward Señor Maceo's side of the truck. She wasn't smiling. The moment the motor was off she began a short series of questions, pointing to us as if we weren't there.

Señor Maceo responded patiently, without raising his voice. He glanced toward us out of the corner of his eye, nodded, then answered another of her questions. Her hands were on her hips one second, a second later one was pointing toward the house, then toward us again. A roll of her dark eyes made it clear she was less than pleased to make our acquaintance.

"Oh, jeez," Ray said.

The woman, who looked to be in her late twenties, stomped back up the steps of the farmhouse, spun and waited, hands bunched in fists. Her long dark hair had swung around her neck. Her gaze was fiery yet controlled.

"My granddaughter," Señor Maceo said. "She manages the farm."

Ray and I exchanged a glance. No wonder she was pissed, and who could blame her? Gramps brings home a couple of Americans shot down by a colonel in the Cuban Secret Police? That decision could land them in jail. I again questioned Maceo's motive.

Once Señor Maceo got out, Ray pulled back the lever so we could walk over to face the beautiful granddaughter who ran the most successful tobacco farm in Cuba. She literally blocked the top of the steps, so we hesitated. I tried a big smile, which only precipitated another roll of her eyes before she stomped through the door and slammed it.

"Please excuse Nina," Señor Maceo said. "She takes matters here at the farm very seriously, as she should. I always did . . ." His voice trailed off.

There we stood—marooned, on the run from the Secret Police or at least Gutierrez, my plane destroyed, and now the spark in a family dispute. What else could go wrong?

"We must eat," the old man said, "but not until I show you why I brought you here. Come."

He stepped around us and continued on the gravel drive around the back of the house, without even a glance to see if we were following.

Ray shook his head and scowled. "Now what? A prize cow?"

I hitched my flight bag up on my shoulder and followed after Ray. Señor Maceo paused where the drive split in two directions. Each path led toward a different barn. He waved us to follow him toward the bigger of the two, the one built into the hill.

I glanced back over my shoulder and saw Nina, the granddaughter, watching us out the rear window of the house. Our eyes met and her expression didn't change, nor did she turn away. I felt like a trespasser.

I picked up the pace and caught up with Ray as the old man struggled to slide the big barn door open. We both pitched in and the door slid wide to reveal some antique machinery inside, with a wall of tobacco hanging behind it. The smell of decades' worth of dried tobacco was pungent, a rich, deep aroma that produced a sensory rush in the warm morning.

Ray looked at me, then at the ceiling. I got it. He was figuring the old man must want him to fix one of the ancient tractors.

"This is the big barn, where we dry the plants. We have two levels and can handle many hectares at once." His smile was proud as he looked around the room. "Upstairs is where the finest tobacco is kept, as it is even warmer there. The fumes rise from below, further saturating the leaves as they dry with the evaporated essence of these plants here. Other farmers have built barns to copy this one, but the aged wood and the many, many years of plants drying here cannot be copied."

"Impressive," Ray said. I heard his stomach growl from behind him. "Now, about some breakfast—"

"But this is not what I brought you here to see." The old man paused. His expression was serious, almost reverent as he looked down toward the ground. He grasped his hands together for a moment and suddenly got down on one knee. Was he going to pray?

He took hold of a gap in the floor where a handle was hidden, and lifted a trap door open. Still on one knee, he glanced back toward us.

"I have a secret I have kept in the barn for over fifty years, known only to myself and Nina." He looked from my eyes to Ray's and back. "I thought maybe someday someone would come for it, but nobody ever has. For decades while the Beard was in power, I lived in fear of it being found. Now, things are beginning to change."

Ray tried to look past the old man and into the dark hole.

"I have also thought that maybe there would be a sign of some kind." The corners of his mouth turned slightly upward. "Last night, that happened."

"What?" Ray said. "What was the sign?"

"Your plane. When I saw this from the porch my heart began to beat like it hasn't for many years. Then, at first light, when I followed the coast until I found you in Puerto Esperanza and I saw the small Grumman there on the beach, that's when I knew."

"Knew what?" Ray held his palms up.

Señor Maceo lowered one leg into the darkness, turned, and lowered the other. He descended another step, then looked up at us.

"Come and see."

30

FOLLOWED HIM DOWN INTO THE HOLE. I COULD SMELL EARTH BELOW ME, mixed with the scent of tobacco.

"Wait for me!" Ray nearly stepped on my head.

I could hear Señor Maceo below, his feet now on the ground. It was a pitch-black void with only a narrow shaft of light from above, illuminating nothing. I was surprised at the depth of the room and had lost count of the number of rungs I'd taken. The steps were sturdy and wide, more like a ship's stair than a typical ladder.

"There's a light switch over here."

His voice sounded distant and there was a faint echo in the room, as if the sound bounced back off something close by. Instead of another ladder rung, I felt the ground. I moved aside and put a hand on Ray's back as he approached the end. Just as he stumbled off, caroming into me, a few light bulbs illuminated the cavernous basement.

I saw Ray's eyes widen and heard his sharp intake of breath before I spun on my heel to behold the most surprising sight I could imagine.

"I don't believe it!" Ray said.

I couldn't speak. This was—

"I've had this here since April 15, 1961. Early morning of that day, to be exact."

"Why does that date sound familiar?" Ray said.

"It was the day that galvanized Castro, and the event that led Cuba into the waiting embrace of the Soviet Union," Señor Maceo said. "You call it the Bay of Pigs invasion."

"And this—"

"She too streaked across the sky with smoke behind one of the engines and crash landed, not in the water by Puerto Esperanza, but here in the fields of my family's farm."

Ray, his eyes lit up like a child's at Christmas, reached up and put his hand on the plane's fuselage. It was peppered with holes, much of its port wing was missing, and the port engine cowling was blackened from smoke.

"A Grumman Goose! I can't freaking believe it. A Grumman Goose!"

The old man nodded his head. He too had a big smile, no doubt happy to share his half-century-old secret with someone who could appreciate it more than a farm worker might.

"Yours was smaller, no?"

"The Widgeon's the smallest of the Grumman fleet," I said. "The Goose is the next size up, then the Mallard, then the Albatross."

The old plane was painted black but covered with thick dust and dirt from being in Señor Maceo's improvised hanger for so many years. There were no numbers or markings of any kind, anywhere. I walked around her and checked the damage. The plane lay flat on its belly, her wheels still tucked in place. Several holes, rips, and tears were visible on the fusclage, but given that she had crash-landed, she really didn't look that bad. The tobacco plants must have provided a cushion. I rubbed my hand along the port hatch until I found the handle. I turned to Señor Maceo, who stood just off my left shoulder.

"May I?"

"Of course."

I pulled the handle and the hatch popped open. Ray came running around the tail as I lifted the hatch up.

"Starboard engine looks fine," he said.

I peered into the darkened cabin and saw rectangular wood boxes stacked on top of each other. The flight deck was dark because of the windows being sooted over. The ceiling inside the Goose was a few inches higher than Betty's, so I had more headroom. One of the boxes was cracked open, and I peeled back the lid.

Wow.

Inside the crate were several guns, but not just any guns. I pulled one out, and even though it was dusty, I could feel and smell the oiled metal.

"What's inside?" Ray said.

I turned and his eyes nearly popped from his head.

"Is that a Thompson submachine gun?"

"Yep, and if that's what's in these other crates, we could start a war down here."

There were smaller crates too, which I assumed contained ammunition. My eyes had adjusted to the darkness and I crept forward through the fuse-lage to the flight deck.

Oh crap!

I ran and dove out of the hatch and landed hard on the ground between Ray and Señor Maceo.

Ray jumped but the old man didn't budge.

"What's wrong, Buck? Looks like you saw a—"

"Ghost," I said. "The pilot and co-pilot's remains are still strapped in. Two piles of fabric and bones."

Señor Maceo said he hadn't wanted to remove anything from the plane in case the authorities found it. If he buried the dead crew he might be accused of helping them escape. If he removed the weapons, he could be accused of arming dissidents. Had anyone ever come searching for the plane, he'd have shown them where it crashed. But since it was in the way of his neat rows of tobacco plants, he'd used his tractors to drag it into this basement.

"But how did you get it down here?" Ray asked.

I had already spied the answer. There was a set of solid doors on the back wall. The barn was built into a hill on the front, so from there no one would expect a rear set of doors. The old man said he'd nailed boards on the outside of the doors to conceal them after a few years had passed for fear of an accidental discovery by one of the transient workers who might expose his hidden treasure.

"I'm sure these men were important battlefield commanders who were meant to lead the invasion," Señor Maceo said. "Their deaths led to the mission's failure. They could be CIA—that's why I asked if you were. I thought maybe after all these years you had come to look for your compatriots."

Maybe the old man hoped we were scouts for another invasion. Couldn't blame him if he wanted his farm back.

"I have never flown on a plane," he said. "I was just a boy when the Pan Am Clipper used to come here in the 1930's. Those seaplanes were much bigger."

"Those were Sikorsky's back then," I said. "The Pan Am Clipper was founded in Key West where Ray and I live."

"I wanted to become a pilot," he said. "But I was destined to be a farmer, like my father before me." Señor Maceo had a distant look on his face as if he were back in that time, wondering what his life might have been like had he pursued his dreams. "But when this beauty landed here, well, I imagined fixing it up and flying across Cuba. A silly notion, yes? For an old man like me?"

"We're all dreamers, one way or another, Señor Maceo," I said. "There's nothing crazy about that."

He beamed a crooked smile. "I knew if I could find you, that you would understand and appreciate this wish." He paused. "I don't know why I kept her hidden, but after so long, there was nothing else I could do. Nina always thought I was crazy—"

"You *are* crazy, Papi!"

Her voice from the darkness by the ladder surprised me. She stepped into the light, and my first, redundant thought was how beautiful she was. She stood next to her grandfather as she gave us looks to kill. My second thought was that I knew why she was so pissed off. Their secret was exposed—and to Yankees, no less!

31

"**C**AN YOU GET THIS BEAST OUT OF HERE?" NINA SAID.

Ray shrugged. "She's in pretty rough shape, but we need a way home, one way or another."

"So you take my beauty, then?"

Señor Maceo beamed as he spoke of the Goose. No surprise there. But for the first time since our arrival, Nina's eyes lit up. Not only that, she looked at us without hostility.

Ray said, "I think we—"

"Ray, can I talk to you for a second, over here?"

I led him into the shadows by the ladder.

"She's in seriously rough shape, Buck, but what a great project!" Ray's voice was loud, his excitement uncontainable.

"We don't have time for projects." I lowered my voice to a whisper. "If Manny Gutierrez finds Betty, he'll learn that this old farmer picked us up. We don't have much time, a day, maybe two max."

"I'll never be able to—"

"And I don't want to restore the Goose, I want to strip her of any parts we need to fix Betty."

"Buck . . ." Ray hesitated and looked down at the ground. "Betty's . . . Betty's done, old buddy. She's in far worse shape than this Goose."

He looked up in time to see the quick convulsion of emotion that shook me, once.

"But—" The words caught in my throat.

"Truth is, we should take what we can from Betty to fix the Goose. Their specifications aren't all that close, but depending on how their issues match up, I might be able to pull it off. Just depends on the condition of these engines."

I took a few deep breaths. I knew he was right. I'd come to the same conclusion last night. And if Betty truly was dead, then I didn't care how we got off this damned island.

Maybe there was another way.

"What about Truck?"

"Truck Lewis?" Ray said.

"He should be passing by Cuba on his way back to Key West, tomorrow, or the day after. Maybe he could swing in and pick us up?"

"Just like that? Detour into Cuban waters and pick us up lounging on the beach?"

"Damnit, Ray, we saved his ass in Panama. It's called *quid pro quo.*"

I looked back at our hosts, who stood with their arms crossed and staring at us. Past them was the Beast, so dubbed by Nina. How could we possibly get that thing fixed enough to fly it out of here? Ray stepped up next to me, his face illuminated by the shaft of light from above. Was it excitement I saw in his eyes? Or awe at the prospect of such a challenge? If anyone could make the Beast work, it would be Ray Floyd.

"When all's lost, a man has nothing but his heart," Ray said.

All was lost all right, and my heart was crushed. I took in a long breath.

"Okay, " I said. "Check out the Beast."

"Gotcha." He leapt forward.

We walked back to the farmer and his granddaughter.

"Do you mind if Ray looks the plane over to see if she can be fixed?"

"Does he know what he's doing?" Nina asked.

Once I explained that he was a mechanic accustomed to working on antique planes, they were both excited at the prospect. Señor Maceo saw it as the culmination of his years of waiting and our arrival as a sign of things to come. Nina was thrilled at the prospect of getting the damn thing gone. But if I could get hold of Truck, there might be an easier way off this island.

"Do you have a radio transceiver here at the farm?

"To call the United States?"

"Actually, to reach a boat," I said.

"We do have a radio," Nina said. "It's in the office."

"Could I use it while Ray goes over the plane?"

She hesitated, then nodded. "Come, I will take you."

"I'm staying here to help Ray." Señor Maceo's excitement had turned his voice singsong.

Nina started up the ladder and I followed after her. I glanced up and was impressed to see how quickly she moved. My eyes were drawn to her rear end—I stubbed my toe and nearly fell—Be careful here, Reilly.

I thought about the secret she and her grandfather had kept so long from the State. It would be a win-win if Ray were able to salvage the Beast and get it off their farm. Assuming we didn't get caught in the process.

Once outside, the bright sunlight made me squint. In the dark basement so long, I had forgotten it was late morning. We walked together up the gravel road toward the house. Nina wore faded blue jeans and a white button-down shirt that accentuated her dark tan, brown eyes, and sun-streaked auburn hair. The muscles in her arms were evident below her sleeves, and her narrow waist was belted in a thick cocoa leather strap.

"How long have you managed the farm?"

"Seven years now, since Papi's first heart attack. He ran the operation for nearly fifty years and remains very involved. He tells everyone I'm in charge, but many of our managers have worked for him all their lives. They will never accept me as the *jeffe*."

We continued in silence, the only sound the crunch of our shoes on gravel. The smells of the plantation were strong and fragrant, tobacco the only scent I could identify. The humidity had built with the sun's ascent and I was sweating.

"Where in America do you live?"

"Not far, really. Key West, Florida."

"Ah, yes, almost as close as Havana from here. Many from this region have left for Florida." She sighed. "Only God knows how many made it."

She led me in a back door of the farmhouse, which turned out to be tidy and spacious. Homes of this size would hold three families in Havana.

We walked through the kitchen, down a hall, and into a small room in the front. I was surprised to see a computer on the desk.

"Can you access the Internet?" I asked. Or email?

"Sorry, it's only for inventory and recording each detail of the weather. We monitor humidity, rainfall, and temperatures, everything that might have an impact on the plants. After five years of study we have been able to predict crop yield."

Impressive, but it wouldn't help us get out of here. Behind the desk was an old Zenith radio connected to an antenna outside. She turned it on, and loud tinny-sounding voices burst from the speaker.

"If you have a particular channel you want, you turn this dial. Otherwise, you're free to speak with the Ministry of Agriculture, who it's connected with now."

She smiled and although her teeth were very white, her top front ones were slightly crooked. I found that the tiny flaw made her more distinctive, hence more attractive.

"I'll leave you alone, but remember, the government monitors all radio frequencies. If you expose yourself, I'll have no choice but to turn you in. Be careful what you say, and don't mention where you are."

She closed the door as she stepped out. She was quite a woman, this tobacco farmer, and under different circumstances I'd have been more focused on her. Not with Gutierrez on the prowl, though.

The son of a bitch destroyed Betty.

The radio, of course, was in fine condition, well cared for, and worked like new. I thought back to when I saw Truck's brother. Bruiser had said he'd been trying to reach Truck on a certain frequency. What the hell was it? Then I remembered he didn't say it, he wrote it on a piece of paper, which I pulled out of my wallet.

I spun the dial clockwise until I was in that approximate location. A steady static hummed from the speaker. I edged closer and took the large microphone in my hand.

"Calling the Sea Lion, calling the Sea Lion. This is . . . this is . . . Betty the Widgeon, calling the Sea Lion."

I repeated the same hail a dozen or more times and micro-adjusted the dial in case I was off the frequency. I was about to give up and try again later when the static was suddenly broken by a voice in English.

"Come in Betty, this is the Sea Lion."

Got to love Truck Lewis.

"Howdy, Sea Lion. What's your twenty?"

"My *twenty*? Damn, Buck, you a cross-country trucker now?"

"I have a little problem, Sea Lion, need your help. And it's *Betty*, got it? How far out of home port are you now?"

"Not sure I have a home port no more, *Betty the Widgeon*."

Uh-oh. Ray had speculated on whether or not Truck would head to the rendezvous point with the Mohawk, given the treasure he had on board. My stomach sank. Is that what he meant by being unsure of his home port?

"You're not—"

"Cutting and running? All this good hooch on board? Shit, man, what you think? I've steered myself in circles at every damn island I pass. Could be living like a king down here, man."

The line turned to static, and I swallowed.

"But no, my mama'd track me down and kick my ass, that's for damn sure. Your buddy Nardi calls me every hour. We should meet up by dawn. We're about two days out of home port, Betty."

Truck had given me his most serious military voice with the last part. His most sarcastic one, too.

"So, what the hell's your problem anyway?" he said.

"Remember our favorite island, to the south of home port? Well, we had a little problem and a hard set down here, real hard, and now we have no way off. We're darn close to the end from where you'll be sailing by, could be available for a pick-me-up when you pass."

"Brother, I swore I'd never go back to that place after what happened last time. Those motherfuckers nearly made a stew out of me, man. You know what I'm talking about. Weren't for you, would of happened, too."

"Time to repay the favor, Sea Lion. Our old friend who moved back here has the hots to find me and wants a reunion in the worst way. In fact, it was his explosive summons that caused the unplanned stop here and inability to leave. So, time's of the essence, Sea Lion."

A long static followed on the line.

"Betty, I'm sorry to hear that, I truly am. But you gotta remember what I've got on board this old sailboat. And I can't exactly haul ass if'n they come after me, know what I'm saying? And like I said, I'm hooking up with your friend before long. So how about I have the orange stripes come bail your ass out?"

It was my turn to go silent. Damnit to hell.

As much as I wanted to be pissed at Truck for refusing to come, he was right. The Sea Lion was 100+ years old, sail only, and had the Atocha treasure on board. At least a lot of it.

"Matter of fact, Betty, after you bailed me out down south, I persuaded my . . . guests here on board to reminisce a little. They confirmed what I told you about your boy. The one who wants to get even with you for his boat."

"Oh, he got even already, trust me."

"Yeah, well, he took half the crates."

"Half? Is he the brains behind the deal?"

"They made it sound like he was working with or for some others from that rotten island. So, no, just middle management, but maybe making an end run."

Didn't surprise me. Gutierrez lived in Key West for years, probably loved going to the museum, and once he blew town could have dreamt of coming back to steal that treasure.

"Makes sense, Sea Lion." I swallowed hard. "Listen, don't mention us to anybody just yet. If what you suggested is true, and the orange stripes—or worse, the Washingtonians—start making a stink, the hunt on this side will only intensify and we might disappear for good."

"You might be right about that, Betty."

I checked my watch. "I'll try you again around this same time tomorrow. We have one other option we're working on that might do the trick. Drive that boat straight home, Captain, and don't upset your mama."

We signed off, and as good as it was to hear a friendly voice, it left a hollow feeling. No cavalry was coming for us. Not even an old pirate ship like the Sea Lion.

I imagined him sailing into the Key West Bight with a Coast Guard escort, TV crews lined up along the seawall, Donny and the Treasure Salvors gang smiling ear to ear, Marine Patrol boats in the harbor, state police, Key West cops, Monroe County sheriff—*uh oh* . . .

What about the FBI? Special Agent Booth would be waiting too, the only scowl amidst a sea of smiles. He'd push his way through and demand to know where I was. Then, when Donny discovered that half of the treasure was missing, along with Ray, and me, Booth would come to his naturally paranoid conclusion that we'd absconded with the missing gold, silver, and jewels. Would he believe Truck's story that Gutierrez had the goods? Or that Ray and I were stranded here? If Booth had seen that security video, he'd tie it all together in a nice, neat little conspiracy.

Damn.

32

RAY MUTTERED TO HIMSELF IN A SELF-INDUCED AVIATION MECHANIC'S FANTASY of doing the impossible in a ridiculously short amount of time. Even if he did, we'd have to risk our lives to see if it worked. We needed to buy some time.

I pulled Señor Maceo aside. "Can you take me back to Puerto Esperanza? I want to try and camouflage Betty—the Widgeon—so it can't be seen from the sky."

The old man turned toward the Beast.

"But Señor Ray, he needs my help with the Goose. I, ah, I don't think . . . Nina. Tell Nina I said to take you."

I left them in the dark hole and set out to find her. The farmhouse was empty, the truck and Lada were still in the drive, so I made my way toward the other barn. It was filled with old farming equipment, looked like a warehouse of agricultural antiques about to go on display at a museum. No Nina.

On the way back to the farmhouse I heard a rhythmic, fast-paced gravel crunch headed my way from around the next bend ahead. I dove into the thick plants along the path and held my breath as I tried to imagine what could make such a sound. After a few seconds, I found out. Nina ran by at close to a sprint. She wore shorts, tennis shoes, and a tank top. Her legs were every bit as muscular as her arms, and she moved in a swift, sure motion up the path before she disappeared over the rise. I remained hunched in the tobacco plants and thought about how good she looked and what fine shape she was in until I suddenly felt like a voyeur and stepped out of the bushes. A moment later she walked back down the path, wiping sweat from her brow, breathing hard but not panting.

She saw me but her expression didn't change. She kept coming and I tried not to stare at the sweat-soaked tank top that clung to her breasts.

The situation was complicated enough, I couldn't make it worse. Nina was off limits.

"Good run?"

She smiled and wiped her brow again.

"My idea of the *siesta*. I like to be in good condition before the harvest begins."

A flirty response came to mind, but I bit my lip.

"I need to go back to Puerto Esperanza, and I'm afraid your grandfather volunteered you to take me. Would you mind?"

She grumbled something in Spanish and turned toward the barn, ready to go chew her *abuelo* out, but she stopped. The gears in her mind turned quickly, and she gave me a nod.

"If it helps get rid of you faster," she said. "I'll change and we can go."

Back in the farmhouse she pointed me toward their refrigerator and instructed me to make some sandwiches from the meager contents while she changed. Ten minutes later, with a canteen of water, sandwiches, and some fruit in a canvas sack, we were headed back up the road toward the coast. Nina drove much faster than her grandfather and sped right past the neighbors who waved from a horse-drawn cart.

"Can you slide down in your seat, please? People will start talking when they see you with me."

"No need to get anyone jealous." Damn. The words just came out on their own.

"Very funny. You look a hundred percent gringo. If the police are searching for you, I'd rather not have them find you with me." She cast a quick glance at me. "And there's nobody to be jealous. I don't keep men around long enough to get jealous."

Focus, Reilly.

As we made our way to the coast, I asked about her family's history here in the Pinar del Rio.

"My relatives were successful and wealthy before the revolution," she said. "They were forced to continue their legacy as managers on their own plantation after. Papi sent my grandmother to Florida—"

"By herself?"

"He promised he would follow but never did. The farm was too important, she was safe, and he refused to leave me. They haven't spoken in over twenty years."

"What about your parents?"

"My father was to succeed Papi, but he died of cancer twenty-two years ago when I was a child."

Nina spoke in crisp, idiomatic English, used few hand gestures, and showed no emotion whatsoever—until I asked about her mother. She looked at me, unguarded. It was only for an instant, but the depth of pain made me feel that I was intruding just by seeing her face.

"She was raped and killed by soldiers. The men were shot for their crimes."

I didn't ask more questions. Given what Cuban families had suffered these past fifty years, especially those who'd been stripped of their possessions and marked as virtual traitors, their scars naturally ran deep. At least families like the Maceo's, with expertise in key areas like agriculture, were indispensible, even under the Communist regime.

"And what about you and your family, Buck Reilly?"

My pause caused her to glance over. I still hadn't developed a concise response to that question.

"My parents died in a car accident a few years ago."

"I'm sorry," she said. "No wife?"

"Not any more."

"Ah, sorry again."

"She left me when my company went out of business. We'd been very successful and she couldn't stand the thought of being broke. I do have a younger brother."

"Are you close?"

"Not really. He bought me the plane, though—the one that's now a ruin in Puerto Esperanza."

She too stopped asking questions.

"For the past couple years I've used my plane to run a charter and salvage business out of Key West. It's called Last Resort Charter and Salvage. Or at least it was."

Another sidelong glance. In her eyes I read the conclusion: no more plane, no more business, no more wife. And here I was stranded in Cuba. Then came the last straw, a sympathetic smile.

We drove the remaining ten minutes in silence. I recognized the sandy road that descended toward the small enclave of beach shacks and we both tensed.

"Better slow down. I'm not sure what we'll find here."

She downshifted and we lurched along toward the water.

When a fishermen walking up the road saw Señor Maceo's truck, he looked back over his shoulder and quickly held his hand up in front of his chest. Nina stopped the truck. The fisherman checked behind him again, then hurried over. He bent down, peered at me, and exchanged harsh whispers with Nina. I heard a quick intake of breath from her and she jammed the truck in reverse.

"Wait!" I said. "What's the matter?"

"The PNR are guarding your plane. It's too late, we must leave before we're seen." She released the clutch and we started back. "That means policia—"

"Wait, Nina! Just stop a minute and let me out."

"You can't go in there, what if they see you? You don't even speak the language, and—"

"I look a hundred percent gringo, I know." I pretended as if the concern in her eyes was for me, but she didn't want to get caught, and I didn't want to place her in danger. "Just let me out and drive up the road a half-mile. I'm not back in twenty minutes, go home and forget you ever saw me."

"Why are you doing this? You can't hide the plane any longer, they've found it! And the fisherman, he says a colonel from MININT is on the way. That's the Secret Police, in case you didn't know."

"Twenty minutes, that's all I ask."

"Fine, get out."

I eased out of the door and closed it quietly. We met eyes.

"You're a fool, Buck Reilly."

If only I had a dollar for every time someone told me that.

33

I MADE MY WAY THROUGH THE WOODS ALONG THE SHORE SLOWLY TO AVOID making noise. Once I was close enough to hear the water lapping at the beach, I spotted Betty through the brush. I squirmed closer until I saw a guard with a rifle standing on Betty's port side. He smoked a cigarette and kicked gravel into the water.

All the fishing boats were beached and none of the fishermen were in sight. I looked at Juan's shack. The curtains were drawn, and although I could see light inside, I couldn't see him, Maria, or their kids. Every shack was the same, buttoned down tight.

Damn. If Gutierrez were on his way, he'd do whatever was necessary to find us. Could he know that Ray and I intercepted the Sea Lion? Or did he just want my maps back? Or to get even? No other vehicle was visible, so the PNR must be alone.

I returned the way I'd come, then jogged up the road. My twenty minutes was nearly up and I doubted Nina would give me a grace period. I saw the truck ahead, on the side of the road, with the engine running. She must have been watching from the side mirror, because she waved to me without looking back. I jumped in and we started up the shore road.

"You must leave the farm now," she said. "Take your friend and go. I'll drive you to Bahia Honda, maybe you can hire a boat."

She was right, of course. If the PNR had found the plane, it wouldn't take long to figure out who picked us up. We raced along at what had to be close to the old truck's maximum speed.

"What did the fisherman say, exactly?"

"He said the PNR arrived an hour before, in a car with another man. He left once they found your plane and returned to Havana, or maybe to Viñales, I'm not sure which. They were very excited and told the fisherman that Colonel So-and-so of the Secret Police would be here tomorrow and that they had been looking for this plane."

Tomorrow?

"You never told us the Secret Police were looking for you!"

The rest of the ride was white-knuckled and chilly. She flew up the driveway, threw the truck in park, and ran into the farmhouse. Before I got to the top of the steps she stormed back out and said her grandfather and Ray weren't inside. We hustled over to the barn, shimmied down the hole and were astonished at what we found.

The barn doors were now open, and afternoon sunlight streamed in. A wall of tobacco plants stood five feet high beyond the door. Ray and Señor Maceo had strung cables and pulleys from the large truss that held the floor above and used a tractor to hoist the Beast up high enough to hand-crank the wheels down. The Goose now sat on two flat tires. Additional lights lit the old plane, which had been wiped clean. My earlier thought was confirmed—there were no markings or numbers of any kind, only bullet holes. Ray stuck his head out the hatch as we approached.

"Welcome back! This baby's in better shape than I thought!"

"We've got trouble, " I said.

Nina shouted in Spanish to her grandfather, who peered over Ray's shoulder.

"They found Betty. She's under guard, and some big shot colonel is supposed to be here tomorrow."

Ray's face sagged. He climbed out of the Beast, the equally droopy old man followed after him. Nina continued issuing orders and proclamations in Spanish, waving her arms around, pointing to me, then Ray, until Señor Maceo flung his hands toward her palms up and waved *his* arms while he talked just as intensely if less dramatically.

"The biggest issue is that one of the engines seems seized," Ray whispered.

"And what about that wing?" I pointed to the port wing, which was cut in half. The fuel tank on that wing was also torn open. Hard to believe the plane hadn't burned when it crashed.

"The port engine's the bad one, too. Overall, the electronics are rat-worn, but the hydraulic system seems okay, so the flaps, elevator, and rudder are working. The front windshield has some holes in it. I think the pilot and copilot were shot, which is probably why they crashed."

Nina was glowering at us. She had a torn look to her, and I felt responsible for the wedge between her and her grandfather. I knew she was right. Our putting them at risk was unacceptable.

"It doesn't matter, Ray. Now that they've found Betty we need to go—"

"No!" the old man said. He and Nina began another duel in Spanish I interrupted at the first pause for breath.

"She's right," I said. "We've already put you in too much danger. We—"

"But she can be fixed," he said. "Señor Ray says so."

"There's no realistic chance," I said.

"Think where Betty's damaged," Ray said.

I looked from him to the old man and back.

"Her starboard side, where the rocket hit," I said. "It fried the tail and burned up that side of the fuselage and part of the wing. Lucky we didn't explode."

"But her port wing and engine's fine, right?"

"Ray, don't even go there. Betty's done, remember? And if you're thinking of salvaging her to fix this beast—"

"With the proper weighting and balance on the throttles, I think it can work," he said. "The props are different sizes, but—"

"It can work!" The old man said. "This man is a mechanical genius! He must be part Cuban!"

Nina let loose a final barrage in Spanish and flew up the ladder two rungs at a time.

The three of us stood facing each other, under the crumpled port wing of the Beast.

"Nina aspires to run the Ministry of Agriculture," Señor Maceo said. "She has always worried the Beauty might ruin that for her, and now she is certain this will happen." He smiled. "Which is why we must get rid of it."

The two of them stared at each other with moon faces and goofy smiles. Ray reached into his shirt pocket and removed a piece of paper.

"Here's my list of what we need off Betty."

"I told you, Betty's under guard," I said. "More men are coming tomorrow, and I'm pretty damned sure Gutierrez will be with them."

The old man smacked his watery lips together, licked them, then smiled.

"That leaves tonight to get what we need from the *poquito* Grumman."

I looked at Ray. "Are you serious?"

"Yes, Buck, we're serious," he said. "Not to mention determined."

They stood staring at me, waiting. Immovable.

Fuck it.

"All right, show me the list."

A loud stereo hoot filled the underground chamber, and the two men jumped up and down and hugged each other like kids who just scored a goal in a soccer game.

Beauty or the Beast?

34

THE THREE-QUARTER MOON WAS PARTIALLY COVERED BY CLOUDS. I'D LEFT Ray in the truck near where Nina had waited for me hours earlier. Now nearly midnight, there was no activity of any kind unless you counted the mosquitoes that feasted on my exposed legs and arms. We'd synchronized our watches to give me time to get in position before Ray created the distraction I'd need to close the final distance. Negotiating the woods in daylight had been a lot easier—I was tripping my way through the darkness.

I heard a stick crack up ahead followed by a harsh: "Sssshhh!"

I crouched low and snuggled into a bush. As my eyes adjusted, I saw what looked like three figures, just inside the trees by the shore, not more than thirty feet ahead. I counted my blessings that I hadn't blundered into them. Were they watching Betty, or were they thieves?

A bead of sweat ran down my spine and made me shiver. I checked the time, worried Ray would drive into Puerto Esperanza before I was ready. One of the men sneezed.

"Goddamnit! The hell, Peruvians allergic to Cuba or something?" A laugh, then: "You boys'd never survive in Iraq."

I was surprised he spoke English, even more surprised that I recognized the voice.

"It's past midnight, anyway, so I doubt Reilly'll be coming back tonight. Let's get the hell out of here."

No doubt about it. Gunner.

The men stumbled from the woods out to the beach without any attempt to conceal their movements. A voice called in Spanish from where I estimated Betty to be, and one of the men who'd just left with Gunner called back.

Had Gunner teamed up with the Peruvians? How? And what about the slashed tires on the G-IV? Could the Peruvian bosses have been at the canal, waiting to rendezvous with the thieves? Could fate have drawn them together with Gunner when the Sea Lion never arrived?

Did Gunner's original client know? Had the Peruvians hired him? That's the thing about mercenaries, they'll change teams with the wind, so anything was possible. But how did they know I'd crashed here?

A car started and a moment later its lights lit the wood where I was hunkered down. I slid lower, became one with the shrubbery, and held my breath. Ray would be—

The car lights shifted hard to the right. The car drove up the road out of Puerto Esperanza, but the woods were too thick to see how many people were inside. I checked my watch again—time was running out. Maybe their hasty departure would provide the cover I needed.

I stood up slowly, wiped the sweat from my brow, and took a tentative step forward. Richard fucking Rostenkowski, a.k.a. Gunner, had been right here—

A stick cracked under my foot.

"*Halto!*" A voice shouted.

I stopped in my tracks, only yards from Betty. The remaining guard had his rifle pointed at my chest.

Shit!

He kept asking me questions, in Spanish, but I had no idea what he was saying.

I lifted my hands up. "I fell asleep back there. Where's Gunner?"

The guard jabbed his gun at me, then swung it to the side.

I got it. I moved forward slowly, kept my hands held high, and exited the woods next to Betty. She was dead and I was captured. Perfect.

"Americano?" he said.

He pointed the gun down toward the beach. I bent down slowly and got on my knees, keeping my arms up. The guard reached around his back, but I couldn't see what he—a bright light suddenly blinded me. He had a flashlight in my face.

"I don't remember another American with the big one," he said.

His English surprised me almost as much as Gunner and the Peruvians had.

"The Peruvians dropped me in the woods just up the road so I could keep watch," I said. "I sat down to rest and fell asleep. When are they coming back?"

"Not until morning."

He hadn't lowered the gun all the way but had taken a couple steps backward.

"And Gutierrez?" I said.

"What about him?"

"When will he be back?"

The guard lifted the rifle. "Show me some identification."

"Hold on, *compadre*, what's the—"

"The other American, the big one with the tattoos, he said he was looking for an American named Book Reilly. Colonel Gutierrez said the same thing. Neither of them mentioned—"

Just then a bright light from the road lit us up. The guard swung around. Headlights came toward us! The guard swung his rifle toward them and I sprang forward on my knees, grabbed him by the waist, and drove him into the ground, hard. The rifle flew out of his hands before he could fire a shot. I rabbit-punched the back of his head as the twin lights stopped in front of us, blinding me while I punched the man until he stopped squirming. Was it Gunner, or—

"Should I turn the lights off?"

It was Ray.

"Yes!"

He jumped out of the truck. "You kill him?"

"He's just unconscious. I don't kill people, Ray, jeez. Give me your belt."

I used both our belts to wrap his wrists and ankles together, then dragged him up in front of the plane.

"You'll never believe who I saw here, Ray."

"If they were in that car that sped past me up the street, tell me later. I want to get this over with."

"Right," I said. "Back the truck around then. Let's do it."

Ray positioned the bed of the truck under Betty's port wing. I jumped into the truck bed, tossed the tools over the side, and stacked the hay bales inside up under the engine. They didn't quite reach, but it was close enough.

"Here's your list," Ray said. "I'll take care of the wing."

I was glad it was night. Pillaging my girl would be a little easier if I couldn't see what I was doing. I had the first few items memorized, so I climbed inside the open hatch. It was open—and we'd locked it when we left with Señor Maceo.

What I saw inside hit me like a kick in the balls.

"Bastards!"

Whoever had done it—the guard, the fishermen, Gunner, the Peruvians—the gutting of Betty had already begun. Her seats were gone. My hands went numb and I wanted to punch someone, but in the back of my mind I knew this made the job ahead of me easier.

"Ready?" Ray said.

I forced my thoughts back to the task at hand. I checked the fuel gauges and found the dump valves open. The gauges showed empty. I remembered dumping the fuel when we crashed but needed to make sure.

"Go!" I said.

The sound of a hand saw cutting through Betty's metal was excruciating, but I checked off the first item on my list and moved to the next one. I cranked the wheels down, manually. Time flew by and I was only mildly surprised that none of the fishermen came to see what was going on. With the PNR sentry out here and the promise of more to come, they were keeping their distance. I periodically checked the bound guard and used some of the wire I'd stripped from the instrument panel to better secure his limbs so I could put my belt back on. I also jammed an old rag in his mouth.

Two thirds down my list, I suddenly felt the plane rock hard to the star-board side. A loud boom shook the darkness. I scurried out of the hatch, now angled toward the sand, and found Ray in the bed of the truck.

"Help me with this thing!"

He was hanging onto the raw edge of the wing, trying to shimmy it deeper into the truck's bed amongst the hay bales. I pressed with all my might against what had been Betty's port engine, and between the two of us, we finally got the job done. Once we'd repositioned the bales to provide as much support as possible, I threw the other items inside the bed. Wheel assemblies, electronics, brake cylinders, hydraulic pump, batteries, magnetos, starters, loose wiring, bolts and screws, alternators, circuit breakers, the transponder, radio, gauges, loose handles. I climbed back inside to retrieve some final items from the instrument panel.

"These sons of bitches won't have anything left to steal off you, girl," I said.

Maybe it was crazy, but since I'd convinced myself that I was saving her from Cuban looters, the process of gutting my beloved Betty became just a little bit easier.

I crawled under the panel and something caught my eye. I didn't have Ray's technical expertise, but I knew Betty's mechanical workings pretty damn well, and what I saw here . . . I reached up and felt the shaft, about four inches long, duct-taped behind the yoke. It peeled off easily. A tiny red light blinked on the end of the tube.

Son of a bitch.

"It's almost four a.m., Buck, we need to get out of here," Ray said.

I put the metal tube in my pocket and got up on my knees. I was down to the last item on my list.

"Ten more minutes."

"We don't need anything else—"

"I said ten minutes!"

Once the port wing was gone, the weight of the plane had rocked it onto its starboard wingtip, now bent at a 45-degree angle. Using the farmer's antique wrench, I nearly busted a gut removing the half-dozen bolts on the starboard float, which slipped off the lugs that held it in place.

"Give me a hand with this!"

Ray ran over and we each took one end, carried it over to the bed, lifted it, then laid it down at an angle on one of the hay bales. We stepped back and I noticed how low the bed was.

Uh-oh.

There was minimal clearance above the tires. Ray threw the tarp over the bed and tied it down. What if we blew out a leaf spring on this relic? Or got a flat tire? There was no choice but to give it a shot. If we had to jettison stuff as we went, so be it.

"Ready?" Ray said.

"I'll drive."

I put the truck in first gear and we lurched forward to the sound of gravel shooting out from behind the tires.

"Don't spin the wheels! You'll get us stuck," Ray said.

The truck felt like it weighed twice as much as before. The cargo had to exceed its capacity, but based on Ray's inventory of the Beast, we needed just about everything we'd taken. I let the clutch out slowly, and the transmission caught. We lumbered ahead to the grassy area past the beach, then onto the hard-packed dirt of the road.

"What about the guard?" Ray said.

"Screw him. He'll have a story for his grandchildren. That is if Gutierrez lets him live."

"I mean, what did he say that freaked you out?"

"Either my good friend Governor Raul Acosta of Panama got in bed with the Peruvians or they have the luck of the Irish, because they—"

"What's that have to do with the PNR guard?"

"He confirmed what I saw. Gunner and the Peruvians were in the woods by Betty, waiting for us."

"*Gunner!?* How could he—why would he—"

"Those were the same questions I kept asking myself, but when we were stripping Betty down, I found this."

I reached into my pocket and pulled out the four-inch metal tube. It looked just like the Lojack I used to keep on my Turbo Porsche, back in the day.

"It's a tracking device. That's how he followed us around the Bahamas and all the way to Panama," I said.

"And all the way to here," Ray said. "Why'd you bring it with us, won't he be able to follow it now?"

"I took the battery out."

"But I still don't see how he's connected with the Peruvians, or why he'd be waiting for us here, especially after he found Betty crashed on the beach."

"My guess is they think we took the treasure off the Sea Lion. I don't know why they'd think that, but it's the only thing I can come up with. Raul might have told them that if he was trying to get them out of Colón."

Ray was quiet for a moment. "If it was Gutierrez who unloaded half the treasure and he heard we intercepted the Sea Lion, it must be why he wants us so bad."

I didn't know which was the biggest shock, or who would want us worse. Gutierrez was bad enough, but the Peruvians would want our necks, and Gunner would be happy to hand over our heads on a bayonet if it meant getting some of the loot. The smell of blood was in the water, and unfortunately it was ours.

We drove on in darkness, but I could see the wingtip hanging over the roof of the truck's cab above the windshield. It was the hardest salvage job I'd ever done, cutting up my own plane. Once on the main road we drove at a modest speed, nothing like Nina's earlier. We didn't say much, exhausted from the work, the late hour, and the lack of sleep. I caught a whiff of something rancid and realized it was me. I'd give Ray's left arm for a shower. The thought made me laugh, and when I looked over at Ray I saw he was asleep.

I found the road south, turned off the coastal road, and headed toward farm country. A thought dawned on me that lifted my heart. Betty was an organ donor. She'd died in an accident but her parts would be used to restore the life of a distant cousin. Ray, her trusted mechanic, would perform the surgery, and I, her partner and pilot, would either fly the rejuvenated Beast back home or we'd die together in the process.

With that happy thought I turned up the old man's driveway, just as the sun appeared through the trees.

35

AWOKE TO THE NOISE OF A DISTANT YET STEADY POUNDING. I HAD TO REORIENT myself, having dreamed of flying low over Bahamian waters in search of an isolated beach and woken up on the floor of a Cuban farmhouse. I heard the squeak of the front door followed by voices that rose in volume and intensity.

Nina . . . and a male voice.

Was this it? Had they found us? I heard a crack in the man's voice—emotion, not accusation.

A few minutes later the door closed with a squeak and Nina rushed into the kitchen. I was still lying on the cool tile. Her face and neck were deep crimson, almost purple. Her fists were clenched, and she let loose a barrage of Spanish that sat me up straight.

"In English, *por favor*?"

She bit her upper lip, stopped, and took a deep breath.

"That was the fisherman from Puerto Esperanza. Juan Espedes, the one who took you in the night you crashed." She paced around the small room and waved her arms as she spoke. Then she spun and bent down to look directly in my eyes. "Colonel Gutierrez from MININT is in Puerto Esperanza and he's crazy with anger! He's furious that his man was attacked and your plane was taken apart with only a shell left behind!"

I imagined Manny Gutierrez as I last saw him, his slick little moustache, athletic build, incendiary eyes—and pictured him stomping up and down the beach in a tantrum. First the Peruvians and Gunner appear, then me, again. He must be incensed. Problem was, he'd be ruthless with the fishermen if he learned they'd rescued Ray and me.

"Is Juan still here?"

"And that's not all he said, either!"

"I know about the Peruvians—"

"The head of MININT, Director Sanchez, appeared in Puerto Esperanza to inspect your wreckage, too. And, yes, there were Peruvians too, and they asked many questions of the fishermen."

A spasm made me cringe at the sound of Sanchez's name. We'd crossed paths before, and his goons beat me senseless with rubber hoses. I'd rather have Gutierrez find me than Sanchez. Gutierrez may have provided the intel on the Atocha museum, but Sanchez was more likely the ringleader.

Why would he come out in the field, though?

"Did Gutierrez tell Sanchez about—"

She held up her palm.

"They weren't together. In fact, that is the strange part of what Juan said. Sanchez asked about you but he also asked if the fishermen had seen Manny Gutierrez, who had also been searching for the wreckage."

"Maybe they hadn't spoken?"

"Juan said it seemed like the director was concerned about Gutierrez, too. But not with worry, more like anger."

I swallowed a smile. Had Gutierrez double-crossed Sanchez? Maybe, maybe not, but something was awry between them. Who had been more surprised about the Peruvians showing up? And what about Gunner?

"Is Juan still here?"

"Are you crazy? I told him I hadn't seen you. I told him I'd given you a ride to Puerto Esperanza yesterday and dumped you out when you tried to steal my truck. But the PNR, the one you attacked last night, he said there was a vehicle, he thought it was a truck! They will find out sooner or later and come here! Damn you, Buck Reilly!"

Juan hadn't turned us in, or the Maceo's either. Yet. If he felt his family was in danger, wouldn't he?

Being sympathetic only goes so far. But whom would he tell?

Gutierrez? The Peruvians? Sanchez?

Were they all in this together, or what?

Would the other fishermen rat Juan out for taking us in?

I thought of his family and felt sick. Everywhere I turned, everything always turned to shit.

"You must leave here, today, now!"

A tear slid down Nina's cheek but I don't even think she realized it was there. When I tried to take her shoulders in my hands, she pushed me away.

"Nina! I can't tell you how sorry I am. Please to calm down—"

"Calm down! I'd call MININT myself if Papi didn't have that damned plane!"

She went on in Spanish, her rant directed at him, too. When she balled her fists on her hips and closed her eyes, I chanced a step forward and put my arms around her. The smell of her hair was fresh, with the delicate scent of a combination of fruits. I loosened my grip. She put her hands on my chest and pushed me back, then spun on her heel and stormed outside.

I followed after her to the barn, where Ray and Señor Maceo were already at work. We walked in silence and all I could feel was dread that I'd put their lives in jeopardy, along with Juan and Maria's in Puerto Esperanza. They would all be better off if I turned myself in, once and for all.

But again, to whom?

With Betty gone, Last Resort Charters and Salvage was history. I didn't have any prospects for income and nobody would miss me, so why risk all these people's lives? I could trade the waterproofed pouch with all the maps to Gutierrez for their safety. But was he acting on his own? Had he gone rogue? It only took another twenty feet of walking along the gravel path to catch myself: Gutierrez would never honor any deal I made with him. He'd take the maps *and* revenge on anyone who helped us. And if he or any of them believed what I assumed Raul Acosta told them, that I took the treasure aboard Betty, they'd never give up the search for us.

The late morning light lit the basement through the open barn doors. I was amazed at the progress. Betty's float was now on the starboard wing to replace the one on the Beast that had been crushed. The tires had been replaced, the old wing had been cut cleanly off, the engine was on a cart, and the crumpled wing leaned against the wall.

"Papi!"

Nina's recap of Juan's news was punctuated by fingers pointed at me, then Ray, then the Beast. I didn't need to speak Spanish to read Señor Maceo's reaction. He aged ten years, right before my eyes.

I looked at Ray. "We need to get out of here," I said.

He whipped a wrench into the dirt. It made a thud and gouged the earthen floor.

"This could've worked, damnit!" he said.

"Did the *pescadoro* think his people would talk?" Señor Maceo said.

Nina looked toward the ceiling and held both hands out.

"Will fishermen defy the Secret Police? Colonel Gutierrez, the Hero of the Revolucion? Director Sanchcz, the head of all the Secret Police? Please, Papi, enough of this fantasy."

The old man sighed. "Nina, I'm sorry. Your dreams have been jeopardized because I hid this old plane. For me, I don't care. I'm an old man, and I've kowtowed long enough to brutes who care only for their own power and nothing for Cuba's future, much less its past."

He turned his attention around the room and I followed his eyes. There were airplane parts strewn everywhere.

"The problem is that this plane, my Beauty, and all the pieces that came from the little Grumman, cannot be hidden," he said. "If the *pescadoros* talk, and depending on how badly Gutierrez wants the information, they will . . . then sooner or later, the Secret Police will arrive here. That we cannot change."

For a long moment nobody said anything.

"Sounds to me like the best way to get rid of the evidence is finish the job," Ray said.

He had a point. And the fact of the matter was that the old man had come to find us, not the other way around. He'd hidden this old Goose for fifty-plus years, and however she felt about it Nina had gone along with it her whole life.

She slumped onto the bottom ladder rung and put her head in her hands.

It was dangerous, but our best move here was to remove all evidence of our presence, including past and current sins, before Gutierrez and his goons figured out where we were, or hopefully, where we'd been.

36

THE BEAST HAD FAR MORE ROOM ON THE FLIGHT DECK THAN I WAS USED TO. I lay on the floor between the seats and pulled old wires that had been destroyed by mice, rats, and bullets. I replaced the bare necessities of the fifty-year-old electronic gear with items removed from Betty. We only had to make it ninety miles, but crossing the Florida straits could be tricky, especially if we had weather or had to go at night.

Sparks flew through the air outside the port window, and I could hear Ray shimmy around on top of the fuselage. We'd rigged the hoist he'd used to lift the plane onto its landing gear to hold Betty's port engine and wing in place for the welding operation. Ray was convinced the Widgeon's six-cylinder Lycoming engine on the port side would work fine in conjunction with the Goose's nine-cylinder radial engine on the starboard side. The weight differential between the two planes was dramatic, with the Widgeon at 3,200 pounds empty vs the Goose at 5,400 pounds empty, so finding the center of gravity was going to be tough. Had he not recently rebuilt Betty's port engine I'd have had zero confidence in this plan.

The batteries and magnetos were pretty interchangeable, along with the alternators and the brake cylinders. The fuses were the same, but all the wires leading into the fuse box needed to be changed out. Sweat ran through my hair and into my eyes, which made them burn. Exhaustion made me despondent, or maybe just realistic: it was insane to think we could get the Beast ready to fly by tomorrow morning.

"Take a look," Ray said from atop the plane.

I stepped back behind the tail.

"It looks ridiculous," I said. "Betty's engine looks tiny compared to the Beast's. And the wing looks shorter—"

"Not so. We'll use this gas tank for weight and leave the starboard side empty. I added metal from the old wing between the fuselage and the engine so both wings would be the same length. The Goose has a factory wingspan of forty-nine feet, and that's what we have here." He sighed. "Wish I had a decent rivet gun, though."

"You're worrying me, Ray."

"How you doing inside?"

"Still need to work on the hydraulics, and we're going to need brake fluid, not to mention aviation fuel—and what makes you think the starboard engine's going to work, anyway?"

"The prop rotates okay by hand," he said, "but I can't promise it'll fire up."

"So why are we wasting our time here if you're not sure of that?"

"It's next on my list," Ray said. " Where's Señor Maceo?"

"He went on a recon mission but promised to avoid Puerto Esperanza."

"Sounds questionable. What about the girl?"

"Brooding in the house, I guess. We've pretty much turned her world upside down."

"Your typical impact on women, then," Ray said.

The thought of 'women' hadn't entered my mind in—when had Karen left Key West? A week ago? It seemed forever. My mind turned to Nina when she ran up the driveway . . . when she climbed the ladder ahead of me . . . when I held her in the kitchen after the fisherman left. I was on the run for my life, my survival instincts dialed up to the max, trying to do an overnight rebuild of a plane that crashed fifty years ago with parts from my plane that crashed two days ago—combine their ages, and the two planes were over a hundred and twenty years old.

When things rush towards you at a hundred miles an hour, your senses jump up to another level. The highs are higher, the lows lower, and time just blows by. One second you feel invincible and run on pure adrenalin, the next you feel hopeless and count on dumb luck.

"I see the way you look at her," Ray said.

"What are you talking about?"

"You're attracted to the farm girl. It's like a bad joke. Admit it."

"I'm not even going to dignify—I've got work to do. And so do you, Dr. Frankenstein," I said. "Get back to work on your beast, we're running out of daylight."

I climbed back inside the hatch. I couldn't allow myself to think of Nina that way, nor would I risk all our lives just because she was. . . beautiful, smart, feisty, and . . . *focus*.

Down on my knees, I considered the dusty floor and wished I had a Shop Vac.

"Buck?"

I jumped up. Hit my head on the bulkhead. Saw stars.

"Are you okay?" Nina said.

She was leaning inside the hatch watching me rub my scalp.

"Awesome. What's up?"

The frightened look I'd seen in her eyes earlier was gone. Maybe she'd realized the best choice was for us to fly our collective problems out of here, or she had become resigned to the fact that it was the only choice. But she wouldn't meet my eyes, and she held her arms together as if she were cold. In fact, for the first time since I'd met her, she looked to be at a loss.

"I'm just . . . worried, Buck. What if the fisherman comes back? Or worse, what if the authorities come?"

"Any sign of your grandfather?"

She shook her head.

I wanted to console her, let her know everything would be fine, but I couldn't get the words out. I couldn't lie to her.

"I've been thinking, Nina. When we get the Beast ready, why don't you and your grandfather come with us? To America? For safety, that is. Once things settle down here in Cuba and the new government steps up, you can come back."

She shrugged. "We are meant to be here, no matter what. If we wanted to run, we would have long ago."

"But—"

"Ever since I was a girl, when I first found this plane, I always knew this time would come—"

"Nina!" Señor Maceo's voice boomed down from above. "Buck Reilly? Señor Ray?"

There was something about the tone of his voice that caused us all to drop what we were doing and get topside. In the light of the main floor, the old man's hands shook as he took hold of the railing.

He licked his lips. "They're burning the fishing boats, one every few hours until the men explain what happened to your plane."

"Which 'they' do you mean?"

"Colonel Gutierrez and his men. Once they run out of boats, he says they'll burn houses."

His face was ashen, his voice a whisper.

"This Gutierrez, he keeps yelling your name, Buck Reilly, over and over."

"How did you learn this?" I asked.

"Juan Espedes. He met me in San Vicente, at the gas station. He's terrified for his family, for his friends, he doesn't know what to do." He paused. "I lied and said I didn't know where you were."

"Did he say how many men are with Gutierrez?"

"He said two others," the old man said. "All with guns, all crazy. Juan says they don't act like *policia*, more like *pandilleros*, or hoodlums. Only one is in uniform."

"Uniforms or not, guns are what matter," Ray said.

If what Truck said about Gutierrez was accurate, then he clearly wasn't acting on official business. Wealth equates to power in the vacuum after a government implodes. Sanchez and Gutierrez might have planned to use the Atocha riches to build their strength. But with the Peruvians here, and with Gunner in the mix, all bets were off. Truck thought half the crates were gone when we rescued him, so where could they be?

"Did Juan say anything about where Gutierrez had based his search?"

"No, but he did say Sanchez left instructions that if you or Gutierrez returned to Puerto Esperanza, the fishermen were to contact him at the Hotel las Jasmines in Viñales. As for Gutierrez, only that he had a car and a truck, and the men stayed in the truck."

Based on his treatment of the fishermen, Gutierrez must have a lot more on his mind then revenge for when I sank his boat.

37

BACK ON THE FLOOR OF THE BEAST, UP TO MY ELBOWS IN THE SPAGHETTI OF wires behind the instrument panel, I couldn't shake the description of Gutierrez's men in Puerto Esperanza. Why would he have anyone besides uniformed PNR troops with him? What did the old man mean, they were 'staying in the truck?' Could they be guarding it? Was Gutierrez really in private enterprise with Sanchez but had gone AWOL? I couldn't imagine the Cuban government sanctioning an overseas theft of treasure—

What's that?

Lying on my back looking up behind the instrument panel I noticed a leather parcel. Too small to be the plane's log . . . I reached up and pulled it down through the wires. It was covered in dust, like everything else. I shimmied back out and climbed into the right seat.

There was a small lock on the parcel, which I now saw was more like a flat, letter-sized package. The leather was old, dry and brittle. I yanked the edge hard and it disintegrated. Inside there was another envelope, plain white with a red, waxed seal. In faded type above the seal were the words:

TOP SECRET.

Below the seal was a name:

PRESIDENT FIDEL CASTRO

Holy shit.

I tore the corner of the envelope open and pulled out the contents, a single sheet of paper. I unfolded it and was startled at the heading.

THE WHITE HOUSE

WASHINGTON

TOP SECRET

I read the letter through. It took a moment to realize I wasn't breathing. I sucked in a quick breath, then read it again, more slowly this time . . .

Dear President Castro, August 15, 1961

I apologize for the delay in responding to your proposal, which is why I have sent this in the most discreet yet expeditious manner given the deadline you set. Since the invasion force of former Cuban nationals destined for your country is imminent, time is, in fact, of the essence.

Per the confidential communiqué you sent through your emissary, I will agree to the following:

I will cancel all U.S. military assistance for the impending invasion;

We cannot control Cuban nationals, either inside Cuba or out, who will continue their aggression, but with our support terminated, your military will have little problem containing this challenge;

Once you have contained the uprising you will publically request that the President of the United States meet with you at a neutral location;

I will agree to that, and at this forum we shall mutually agree to the following:

The U.S. and Cuba will restore diplomatic relations;

The U.S. will restore our sugar subsidy, which prior to cancellation was approximately 700,000 tons per year;

Cuba will repatriate all U.S. or U.S. companies' assets, including oil refineries, banks, real estate holdings, etc., and we will agree to new tariffs or mutually agreeable profit-sharing to help provide greater assistance to the Cuban people;

Cuba will cease all trade with the U.S.S.R.;

You will reiterate your statements made in July 1959 that the new government is a "true democracy," and you will initiate democratic elections within seven years.

If you are in agreement, then return this to me with your signature and personal stamp via the same courier who brought it to you.

We are at a watershed moment in the relations of our countries, and the entire hemisphere, for that matter. On behalf of the United States, we will move forward in good faith to withdraw from the invasion, in anticipation of your agreement to these aforementioned parameters that your envoy proposed on your behalf. I am pleased to move beyond the initial confusion between our countries and look forward to a bright future of trade and cultural exchange.

Sincerely,

John F. Kennedy

John F. Kennedy

My mouth was dry. I checked the envelope again, scrutinized the wax seal, and sure enough the initials J.F.K. were melted into the wax.

Holy shit.

The letter from Kennedy to Castro was clear, concise, and outlined a deal they must have been working on through trusted middlemen to rectify a rapidly deteriorating situation. The Beast must have been en route to a secret location where Castro was awaiting Kennedy's response. When the plane never arrived, had Castro assumed Kennedy reneged? Or that he had declined the overture?

I checked the date again. It was the day The Bay of Pigs had commenced. When Kennedy withdrew U.S. military support at the last moment, he was castigated as a coward because he'd allowed the slaughter of Cuban nationals and because the effort had been an act of aggression designed to overthrow another sovereign nation's leader. The mess brought universal condemnation from around the world. Within a month, Castro declared Cuba a Socialist nation for the first time since taking power.

Good grief.

Could the Beast have been carrying men who, had they not been shot down and killed, might have changed the course of history? Kennedy's letter said he was withdrawing U.S. support for the invasion in good faith, so when the letter never came back countersigned, did he assume Castro had duped him? Wouldn't Kennedy have known the Beast crashed? Considering its importance, wouldn't he have had a U2 following them?

Based on the secrecy and gravity of the situation, maybe not.

And what about the crates of machine guns? A façade if they were captured? Or an escape route if things went awry?

If only my father were still alive. A career diplomat who'd been to Cuba several times and disagreed with the embargo and the mistakes that led up to it, he might have used this letter to expedite a catharsis between our nations today.

All very interesting, but what could I do with it all these years later?

I folded the letter carefully, reinserted it inside the envelope, placed the envelope inside the leather folder, then put the folder inside the waterproof pouch in my flight bag. Manny Gutierrez, Sanchez, or whoever the damn Peruvians were wouldn't give a damn about a historic letter between foes in the greatest grudge match of the last century. Nor would Gunner. And it wouldn't help us get out of Cuba, either.

"Knock, knock," Ray said.

With my reverie broken, I looked back between the seats through the fuselage to see him outside the hatch.

"Who's there?" I said.

"Bearer."

"Bearer *who*?"

"Bearer of bad news."

He looked pale, even in the low light of dusk that faintly lit the basement chamber through the open barn doors.

"Now what?"

"The Beast's starboard engine. Remember I said the prop was turning so I assumed the cylinders were okay?"

I just stared at him.

"It may not be that simple." He took a long breath. "It'll spin, but I removed the plugs, which look okay, but a few of the cylinder heads have metal shavings inside them. A lot of shavings."

I closed my eyes.

"When the plane hit the ground it must have jarred the crankshaft. I can't tell if there are some broken pushrods, lifts, a cracked head, or something else."

"What are you telling me, Ray?"

He rubbed a grease-covered palm over his face, which left a streak over his forehead, nose, and cheeks.

"I need access to a machine shop, or the Beauty ain't going anywhere."

I slumped back down on the floor. We'd captured the PNR guard, gutted Betty, made our presence known to Gutierrez and God knows who else, and put Señor Maceo and Nina at risk. All for nothing.

I dropped the flight bag on the floor, walked past Ray, climbed out of the Beast, up the ladder, and out into the evening.

"Buck, wait up!"

I walked in the farmhouse's back door to find Nina and Señor Maceo in the kitchen. The smell of chicken and herbs permeated the air. Tarragon, I think.

"I was just about to come find you," she said. Her eyes narrowed as she studied my face. "What's the matter?"

"The Beast's engine is shot—"

"We don't know that for sure," Ray said.

"Well, the cylinders have metal shavings in them, which means if we crank it over, whatever damage that exists will get worse."

I sat down next to Señor Maceo, whose expression had not changed since we entered the kitchen. He just stared from me to Ray and back again. I'd expected Nina to pepper us with another outburst of Spanish, but she turned back toward the stove and flipped the chicken.

"My brother's a mechanic," the old man said. "He can rebuild anything."

"*Tio* Luz?" Nina said.

"I don't think some amateur mechanic—"

"Amateur?" The old man laughed. "We've had the same American cars for fifty years, and Russian ones for thirty. Most Cubans are able to fix things out of necessity, but Luz is ingenious. He can make any part to fix any car."

"Does he have tools to hone out cylinders, or—"

The old man waved a backhanded wrist at Ray and made a "ppff" sound.

"One engine is the same as any other. Maybe the parts are bigger, but I tell you, Luz is a genius. People come from all over Cuba for him to make them parts for cars, and appliances too."

"He's in Havana, Papi. The Secret Police may be here at any time."

"So, you take the truck and lead these men to his shop." The old man gave his granddaughter a hard look. "Or we wait for Colonel Gutierrez."

We all looked at each other. Finally Nina shrugged. She was resigned to the worst, so this was just another step in that direction.

"We need hydraulic fluid, brake fluid, and aviation fuel, too," Ray said.

"If he doesn't have it, Luz can get it for you."

Sometimes you just have to keep going. When all is lost, whether as a result of being on the run and trying to fix an ancient plane to fly you out of a hostile country, or your wife has left you and taken your home and what little money you had left, or your parents are killed in an car accident in a foreign land and the police there suspect it was murder and think of you as the culprit, or your plane is shot down by your arch enemy who would love nothing more than to string you up by the nuts, there's nothing to do but keep going.

"Are the keys in the truck?" I said.

"I'll get started removing the engine," Ray said.

The old man stood up. "I'll help."

Nina turned the stove off.

"So much for dinner."

38

"Glad you called, Betty the Widgeon," Truck said. "Got some news for you."

I twisted the dial on the Maceo's radio a hair to the right to try and eliminate the crackle. "What news, Sea Lion? That you changed your mind and we'll see you soon?"

"No such luck, Betty." Truck paused and his voice sounded different. Something was wrong. "Got visitors on board. Came to take care of the dude with the booboo on his leg."

"What kind of visitors, Sea Lion?"

"Orange stripes—get the hell out of here! I'm still the captain of this ship, damnit!"

I heard rustling in the background, then a loud bang—the sound of a wood hatch slamming shut.

"Sons of bitches. Just cause they have orange damn stripes, they think they can run my ship."

The Coast Guard must have sent a crew to take care of the wounded Peruvians and to ensure Truck made it home.

"Have you mentioned anything about us to the orange stripes?" I said.

"No, man, but they sure been asking about *you*. Seems your old buddy from the FBI's in Key West raising hell. Says you must have been the ring-leader of the Atocha theft and run off with the rest of the shit. Got warrants out for you and everything."

"What's he basing that on?" I expected he'd mention the video, if he knew.

"Told Nardi he hid a tracking device on your plane so he could follow your every move. He thinks you went to the Bahamas, then threw away the phone he gave you and flew to Panama to recover the treasure on the Sea Lion, dove on Gutierrez's boat wreck to recover something else, then flew to Cuba."

The muscles in my neck stiffened. "You've got to be kidding me!"

"Wish I was, my brother."

"The orange stripes buy that?"

"My South American pals here are pretty good evidence that it ain't true, but only if they feel charitable. Considering how you left them, they might not be too helpful, and if they figure out the angle Booth's taking, they might just dump on you too."

My worst fears had been exceeded. I was a man with no country. Booth must be beside himself. That was *his* tracking device? Had he been feeding my location to Gunner?

"All right, Sea Lion. We're still working Plan B here, but it's a long shot. How long until you're back at home port?"

"Couple days, still. The orange stripes are keeping it quiet so there ain't no opportunists with crazy ideas coming at us. When we get back, I'll be on TV, man, and I'll tell the Feds they're wrong about you. Should be a helluva party, bro, so get your ass back here, 'cause there would have been nothing to celebrate without you. Hell, I'd probably be dead by now."

"I'm working on it, Bubba. Later."

THE ROAD WAS QUIET, BUT SINCE IT WAS NEARLY MIDNIGHT, THAT WASN'T A surprise. Nina drove, Ray was asleep in the bed of the truck on top of the tarp that covered the big radial engine with a pile of freshly cut tobacco plants as bedding. My mind drifted back to a time just after e-Antiquity had made its first big find. A cache of Mayan ruins in Guatemala, filled with artifacts, tools, and elements that shed new light on their customs and rituals. It made our company known worldwide, and as the president, founder, and point man, I was the toast of Wall Street and museums around the world.

That wasn't even ten years ago.

"Are you awake?" Nina said.

I nodded my head. "Just thinking. You okay?"

"That was nice, what you did for the fishermen."

"I hope they find it. I may never get the chance."

"Where did you get those maps? They looked very old."

"Some are over five hundred years old."

"Did you steal them?"

"What makes you ask that?"

"The Secret Police are after you, and Juan Espedes said your plane was shot down." She kept a straight face while eviscerating me. "And your presence at our farm will cause much bigger problems then Papi's silly plane."

My tongue felt paralyzed.

"I have a right to know, Buck."

I swallowed and thought of how I'd held out on Ray. She did have the right to know, but in order for it to have context, I went back to the e-Antiquity days and gave Nina a selective summary during the two-hour drive to Havana. Hitting it big, marrying the super model, losing it all when the market crashed. I even included the latest wrinkle, that I was adopted. It was the classic American success story, wiped out by classic capitalist greed. She listened patiently, asked the occasional question, and I could tell by her quick glances, sharp intakes of breath, moans, and even a shiver that she soaked it up. Karen was the only other person I'd shared all that with since the bankruptcy, and it took several months for her to squeeze it out of me, but that was romance. This was survival—I knew I'd never see Nina again once this was over, so I could spill my guts without recrimination. Plus I needed her help.

I studied her profile in the scant light off the truck's instruments. Her full lips, aquiline nose, dark brows, and a wave of sun- streaked hair made a striking combination. She wore no jewelry of any kind. I could still smell the fruit scent of her hair from when I held her in the kitchen.

"What are you looking at?" She kept her eyes on the road.

I felt like a teenager caught peeking at the neighbor girl through her window.

"Yeah, well, the U-Boat on that map for the fishermen was sunk not far off the northwestern coast, probably a little further west of Puerto Esperanza. I got the records from German naval files after I learned about the shipwreck in a Hemingway biography."

"He's still a hero here," she said.

"For hunting subs?"

"For accepting his Nobel Prize for Literature as a Cuban. *The Old Man and the Sea*. It's a part of our history now, mandatory in all the schools."

I knew that.

"How much gold is on the sunken submarine?" she said.

"The German records said it had five hundred pounds of gold, which in 1945 was worth a little over a quarter million dollars. It was supposed to be used to fund their espionage activities throughout South America, but the Nazis tried to hide it all in Argentina as the war came to a close."

I left out that it came from the teeth of Jews killed in concentration camps.

"Two hundred fifty thousand dollars back then would be worth—"

"Close to ten million today."

"And you just *gave* that to the fishermen?" She glanced over, her brows pushed low over her eyes. "Ten million dollars?"

"Don't you think they've earned it? It's worthless to me if we don't make it out of here. They needed some incentive to keep quiet as long as possible. If they lose their boats and homes, at least they'll have something else to fish for. Provided your Papi can get it to Juan before someone spills their guts to Gutierrez." A breath caught in my throat. "And my plane's gone anyway, so my salvage days are over."

She laughed and I could see the flash of teeth, and the crooked one in front. "But you'll have Papi's Beauty when we get her back together!"

"I think of her as the Beast."

"Beauty or Beast, it will depend on her heart," she said.

I bit my lip and stared at Nina for a long moment.

"A woman's heart is very complicated," I said. " A man is never quite sure what makes it tick."

"Tick?"

"Beat. What makes a woman's heart beat, or how to make it beat faster."

"My guess is you know how to make a woman's heart beat very fast, Buck Reilly."

I bit my lip again, but this time to hold back the smile.

39

A LOUD TAP ON THE BACK WINDOW NEARLY LAUNCHED ME THROUGH THE roof, but it was just Ray. He pointed to the side of the road, Nina pulled over, and we all got out.

"Be right back," Ray said as he headed into the dark pine forest next to the road. The moon had climbed into a sky full of brilliant stars.

"Do you ever look into the stars and wonder about the future?" Nina said.

"All the time," I paused. "See any answers up there?"

"Only mysteries. Quiet, peaceful, sparkling mysteries. I think of the stars as the souls of the dead." She pointed to one just below the Big Dipper. "I think of that one as my parents together. Their shared souls burn the brightest."

"That's Polaris, the north star," I said. "It's right above the North Pole. Sailors have used it to navigate for centuries."

I couldn't read her reaction in the darkness, but I thought I heard a sigh.

"Maybe that's why I look to it for guidance."

"What does it tell—"

"Whew!" Ray said. "I thought my bladder was going to explode."

Nina and I laughed.

"How much further to Havana?" Ray said.

She pointed to a distant glow on the horizon. "About forty-five minutes."

Ray joined us in the front of the truck this time, with me in the middle. When Nina shifted the gears her hand brushed my thigh. It was purely by accident, but I felt that touch of her fingers against my bare leg throughout my body. I renewed my vow not to flirt with her, but it was getting more difficult.

"So, Nina, how come you're not married?" Ray said as we approached the outskirts of the city.

"I have no interest in marriage."

"Ah, a Cuban feminist?"

"No, just a worker doing my part." Her lips puckered as if from a sour candy. "At least, that's the response we're expected to make." She glanced at Ray, then me. "I like men, and there are no shortage of interested ones, but marriage, children, these things would keep me from getting what I really want."

I looked at Ray, who seemed to have run out of questions.

"Your grandfather said you aspire to run the Ministry of Agriculture," I said.

"He told you that?"

"So you couldn't have a husband and still—"

"Papi is the only man in my life. At least, the only one I like being around for more than a weekend. Besides, with the farm I'm too busy for the distraction romance causes. Farmhands and jealous *vaqueros* are of no interest to me anyway."

Absorbed in the conversation, I hadn't noticed we were now on a city street. I sat up straight.

"Are we in Havana?" Ray said.

"Marianao, just a little west of the city. *Tio* Luz lives not far from here, near the Necropolis, Cristobal Colón."

"Necropolis?" Ray said.

"Graveyard," I said.

Ray shivered. "I hate cemeteries. They're full of dead people."

Nina and I laughed.

It was still dark when Nina turned down a narrow alley behind a decrepit old building in a block of gray, four-story structures. A dog scrambled from a recessed doorway and ran ahead of us with his tail between his legs. Nina pulled to a stop at the end of an alley facing a roll-up door.

"I hope Papi was able to reach *Tio* Luz—"

The garage door suddenly lifted, and a man stepped out.

"Nina!"

They hugged, already talking in rapid-fire Spanish.

"Hope you got some sleep, Ray." I said. "*Tio* Luz may be great at improvising parts for old cars, but I doubt he's ever seen a radial engine this big."

I was relieved when Ray smiled—it was a challenge he was excited to meet. Of course, working with another gear-head, they'd either be fast friends or disagree on everything.

Luz had Nina drive the truck in, then closed the roll-up door to the garage. He was a small and wiry, somewhere in his late sixties. Dark stains covered his palms and the old guayabara he wore, but he had an air of confidence that made the grease and oil stains seem irrelevant.

He held his hand out to Ray, then me.

"*Mucho gusto, mucho gusto.* Welcome to my garage. Antonio said you would be here at four a.m., and you were almost right on time."

"Antonio?" Ray said.

"That's Papi's first name," Nina said.

Luz and Ray stood close together, studying the engine and discussing how to proceed. To my delight, the older mechanic showed no trace of intimidation during the examination of the jumbo-sized patient. Nina and I drifted to the rear of the "shop," which seemed to be the gutted back area of what had been a café.

There were an amazing number of tools hanging from the floor joists, leaning in corners, or hung on the walls. I couldn't imagine that anyone other than Luz would know what each tool was for. I started to feel a sense of optimism but held it in check so the surely inevitable disappointment wouldn't be as painful.

Nina was at work in a dark corner of the garage, and the smell of strong coffee hit my nostrils just before she brought me a small cup of high-test brew. I savored the smell, but the taste was even better. Moments later, Ray and Luz came over, and I braced myself.

"Luz is the real deal, Buck. He has everything major we need to pull this off, and he's totally confident. He thinks we can make any parts we need. This guy's unreal!"

"How long will it take?"

"We're going to tear it apart right now. Depending on what we find, it could be done after lunch, so keep your fingers crossed."

Luz spoke with Nina, whose reaction wasn't anything like Ray's. In fact, she said something that caused Luz to take a step back, raise his palms, and launch into a calming voice, combined with some body language that bordered on dance moves. This elicited a "humph" from her before they turned to us.

"In the meantime," Ray said. "We made a list of things we need you and Nina to go pick up for us."

He held up a smudged piece of paper with several items listed.

"Oh sure, we'll just go to the local Sporty's Pilot Shop."

"My nephew, Ramón, he is very good at obtaining hard to find items," Luz said.

"That's because he's a thief," Nina said.

Luz flinched and resumed his verbal and full body gyrations. Nina flung her wrists toward him, snatched the list out of Ray's hand, and walked out toward the front of the building without looking back. Luz lifted his shoulders and gave me a what's-the-problem look.

With no idea, I followed after Nina and wondered what I was about to step in next.

40

WE STARTED OUT ON FOOT, THEN HOPPED ABOARD A STRANGE, HUMP-backed bus Nina called "the camel." She wouldn't explain what had her upset until we were seated.

"Do you know any languages besides English?" Nina said.

"I can get by on French, but just barely," I said. "Why?"

"Act French, or Canadian. Just not American."

"Any reason beyond the obvious?"

"My cousin Ramón can't be trusted. I hate him."

Her anger was as fresh as it had been at Luz's garage.

"He's five years younger than me, and when I was seventeen, he suggested I come to Havana to be a *jintera*!" Her whisper came out as sharply as compressed air in spurts from a narrow pipe. "Do you know what that is? A prostitute! He said he had friends in the tourist business at large hotels and they would take care of me! I was so pretty, I wouldn't have any problem at all—uggh!"

We got off the bus at a stop ten minutes after getting aboard. Nina said we were at Plaza de Armas, the oldest square in Havana. The sun had begun to peek over urban rooftops, and people were now on the streets in increasing numbers. We turned down a narrow street and walked two blocks until we stood in front of a short stairway that led to a red door. Nina hesitated.

I took her by both shoulders and she refocused her eyes on mine.

"Thank you for doing this, Nina. I'm sorry we dragged you into this mess, and sorry we're here. I know this'll be hard for you, and I can't tell you how much we appreciate it. How much *I* appreciate it."

She started to say something, stopped, then her eyes narrowed to a resigned glare of determination. It was the same expression she'd had when we first arrived at the farmhouse.

"Let's go," she said.

We entered the red door without a knock and found a stair with several other doors inside. At the top of the second flight of stairs she turned to the first door on the right and knocked three times, hard. It suddenly dawned on me that we hadn't established a story to explain who I—

The door swung open. The man who answered wore no shirt, offered no greeting, just stood appraising us while I did the same. Ramón was lean and muscular, handsome, his abdomen a classic washboard, his face closed.

He said something in Spanish, with Nina's name in the midst of it.

He nodded us in.

Nina said something, turned, and held her flat palm up in my face: stop. Just before she shut the door in my face, Ramón locked his eyes on mine for a split second. He looked to be the type who didn't need more than that to assess a person, or a situation.

The Ramón's of the world are at home in oppressive environments, the lubricants of weak economies. I hated what this one had tried to make of Nina, but the fact is, it was the Ramón's I had gravitated to in my pursuit of information, political favors, and strong backs to help line e-Antiquity's coffers.

They're never to be trusted, though, since their loyalty goes to the highest bidder. Problem here was, I had nothing left to buy loyalty with, so Ramón would be a loose end. I had no idea why Nina wanted to keep me outside, but I didn't like it.

The door opened and she walked out, followed closely by Ramón, who now wore a red shirt, buttoned halfway open. His eyes sought mine and he offered a quick rise of his eyebrows, which I returned with a quick nod. He smiled and led us down the steps, then lit a Marlboro as we stepped outside.

"Canadian collector, huh?"

His English had little accent, but I didn't respond, just held my stare.

"Ramón!" Nina launched a hiss of Spanish.

He pulled out Ray's list and said, "This will take a couple hours. Wait for me at the café on the square." Without awaiting a response he spun on his heel and strutted up the street.

"I told him you were a French Canadian collector restoring a rare car," Nina said. "I didn't tell him you were American."

"You didn't need to. The list was half in English, Ray's half."

"Ahh."

"And I'm a hundred percent gringo, remember?"

The café on the square was half full with customers about to start their day, or at the end of their night. I steered Nina toward a small table in the corner where I sat her with her back toward the street. If Ramón was more chickenshit than greedy, he'd send his local PNR contact our way, first thing. But my gut said he smelled a bigger score by helping his uncle Luz and cousin Nina's mysterious friend.

Once that was done, we'd see how Ramón played the game.

41

I**T TOOK A FULL TWO HOURS BEFORE RAMÓN SHOWED UP AT THE CAFÉ, AND** during the interim, Nina and I shared stories. She was surprised at how quickly I'd built a financial empire, but less surprised that e-Antiquity fell apart even faster. What astonished her, though, was my saying I had no interest in reacquiring wealth.

"Afraid you can't repeat the success?" she said. "Embarrassed at the doubt and insults that might dog you?"

Her grin made me wonder if she had a cruel streak, or was just trying to lighten the mood. "Hate to sound un-American, but having more money than I knew what to do with didn't make me happy. What about you?" I said.

"I'm a respected *Vaquera* at one of the most important farms in Cuba. My focus is on production." Her eyes got glossy. "And this year we expect the crop yield to—"

"Nina, really?" Her answer made me feel like an inspector from the Department of Agriculture getting a report on crop production. "Do you ever let your guard down? Ambition's a lonely existence, but success can be even worse. Trust me."

The interruption pushed her back in the chair. It took thirty seconds before she began to blink, then a few tears leaked.

I took one of her hands in both of mine.

"I'm sorry, I didn't mean to be insensitive, it's just—life's meant to be enjoyed, to be lived. Not alone amidst tobacco plants that come and go a few times each year—"

She brushed the tear away with her free hand. "This from the man who fled from his failures to a remote Floridian island?" She pulled her hand out of mine.

Ramón walked into the café. "Mission accomplished," he said.

"You found everything?" I said.

He smiled. No, he smirked.

"Great, can we carry it back on the camel to, ah, my garage?"

"Hah! Funny Canadian collector. And if these items are for a car, then it's like no car I've ever seen."

"Ramón!" Nina said. "Stop this—"

"Where is everything?" I said.

"In my car. Good thing it's a convertible, because it's full."

His car wasn't just any car, but a 1959 Cadillac convertible in mint condition. And it was *packed* with boxes. Ramón's status as an amateur scammer vaulted up several levels, which caused a tingle in my fingers.

He might be trouble yet.

"I had the aviation fuel sent to *Tio* Luz' garage," he said.

"*Tio* Luz?" Nina said.

He turned to look at her for the first time since he'd returned. His expression was totally blank. "The list was written on the same paper *Tio* Luz sends me to find him things, I don't know, maybe five times a week."

We all fit on the front bench seat, but Nina had to sit on my lap because there was a bag with several bottles in the middle. I noticed the caps peering out from the plastic.

"Havana Club rum?" I said.

Ramon pulled the list from his shirt pocket and pointed to the last item. It was in Ray's scrawl.

Good grief.

We lurched forward and my face was pressed into Nina's mane of hair. The smell of fruit had faded, diluted by her oils and the dust from the day's travel. It tickled my nose but I didn't want to push it away. I turned my head to the side to watch the city pass by. Ramón's car received a lot of attention, from envious *turistas* and even more envious Cubans. His high profile was more cause for concern, since that level of distinction came with complications, like officials he needed to keep greased.

I didn't want our little band of misfits to be the grease.

42

ONCE THE MATERIALS WERE UNLOADED BACK AT THE GARAGE, WE GAVE Ramón all the cash we had left. He said the cost was $700, but we only had $475. I offered to mail him a check, but he didn't laugh. For him to walk away angry was the last thing I—

"I'll take your coin necklace to cover the difference," he said.

"Ramón!" Nina's face flushed.

I felt the Spanish piece of eight hanging in front of my shirt. It was my last trinket from the e-Antiquity days, one I'd found on a three-hundred-and-fifty-year-old wreck off Cartagena, Colombia.

His extended hand didn't tremble in the least. With no leverage, what choice did I have? I unclasped the gold chain and dropped it in his open palm, which clamped shut like a mousetrap. Ramón never smiled, said thank you, nice doing business with you, or fuck off, he just said something in Spanish to Luz as he walked out.

"I'm sorry, Buck. I told you about Ramón," Nina said.

First Betty, now my necklace. I'd been stripped clean. Ray, of course, was like a kid on Christmas morning. He checked each box, read labels, smiled big, and hummed *California Girls*.

The Beast's engine was pulled apart, its entrails spread out across a large table. It was the scene of an autopsy.

"So, what's the diagnosis?" I said.

Ray didn't answer, but Luz flung a loose wrist at the table.

"Piece of cupcake."

"One of the pushrods had shattered on impact," Ray said. "It scored a couple of the pistons, but Luz has everything we needed." He paused, and then broke into song. "'*Well East Coast girls are hip, I really dig those styles they wear, and the northern girls—*'"

"Enough with the freaking Beach Boys already! Are you guys going to fix this thing, or what?"

"Was there ever any doubt?" Ray tipped his head toward Luz. "With the equivalent of Luz and Clark here, exploring new mechanical territories, using unheard of methods—"

"More like Laurel and Hardy." I held up a palm. "It looks like a scrap yard, so let's pick up the pace and put this bucket of bolts back together. Havana's not my favorite hang-out spot."

In the end, they used a belt and pulley to spin the motor, and there was no sound of scraping or signs of friction. The plugs had been cleaned, the cylinders were lubricated, and we had a truck bed full of fluids, fuel, and loose parts to put Humpty Dumpty back together again. All well and good, but . . .

Had Señor Maceo given the fishermen the map of the sunken U-boat?

Had Gutierrez broken one of them, or one of their wives or children?

What trouble had Gunner stirred up?

Was the farm now a trap?

I swallowed these thoughts like foul-tasting medicine. Why couldn't I ever just enjoy something good, like getting the Beast's engine rebuilt, without worrying about the next thing that could go wrong?

I waited in the truck with Nina while Ray said goodbye to Luz, his new soul mate, mechanical guru, and friend. When he got in the truck he was smiling and chuckling to himself.

"Don't take this the wrong way, Nina, but can we trust your uncle?" I said. "I mean we couldn't even pay him anything for all his work."

Her hands tightened on the steering wheel. "*Tio* Luz would never do anything to hurt me or Papi."

"Ahh, Buck?" Ray said.

"Because you said we couldn't trust Ramón," I said.

"Ramón is different." Nina's voice was a whisper.

"Buck?"

"What, Ray?"

"I kind of promised something to Luz."

I twisted over to look him in the face. "And what's that, Ray?"

"A Meineke franchise. You know, brakes and all that."

"And how—"

"Not until the country opens up, but hey, for all he did for us, that's cheap."

I inhaled a deep breath. Nina was actually giggling. "He won't forget, I can promise you that," she said.

Darkness provided the cover we needed to sneak out of town with our heap of cargo in the truck bed. We'd been on the go for days with little sleep, and I was out before we were out of town. I had no idea how long I'd slept until a sudden jolt launched me into the dashboard.

"What's the matter? Where—"

When I sat up, I saw that a dead horse blocked the road.

"What the heck's that?" Ray said.

"Horse. Let's see what we can do."

The banks on each side of the narrow road were too steep to drive around. The horse lay sideways, blocking the entire road.

"Grab its feet and—"

"Stop right there!" a voice shouted in English.

Two young men in uniform stepped out from behind dark bushes, one on either side of the road, both holding rifles trained on us. Why? How did they know we spoke—

"Put your hands in the air," one said. His accent was heavy.

The dead horse? It was an ambush.

Nina came out of the truck and started asking questions, but one of the men yelled at her in English.

"What is in the truck?"

"Tobacco," Nina said.

"And why is it that you bring tobacco *from* Havana *back* into the growing region?"

"It was being tested for quality. Cohiba is planning a new special reserve cigar."

The two men waved the barrels of their guns toward us and motioned toward the back of the truck. One of them lifted some of the tobacco and smelled it. He then dug his arm deeper in the bed, feeling one of the huge lumps in the middle.

"What's this?" he said.

The other guard, who had come to the same side of the truck, reached in and rapped on what by the sound of it was one of the fuel cans. They exchanged words, and then the first guard leaned his gun against the truck's front quarter panel and started to climb over the side of the bed.

I had to do—I leapt toward the guard with his gun trained toward us who was looking at his fellow PNR in the truck bed. He lifted his gun, but I was already on him. We smashed against the truck—which caused him to drop his weapon—then hit the ground hard with me on top. I could feel the wind burst out of his lungs.

A shout of Spanish followed as the other guard dove from the bed on top of me. Ray stood frozen, but Nina jumped for the rifle. The first guard tried to catch his breath while the other one worked his arm around my neck from behind.

I was hunched over with the man on top of me. I thrust my legs backward, pressing him into the truck, but he didn't let go.

"Stop, or I'll shoot!" Ray said.

The man's grip held, so I slammed backwards again into the truck and he slid to my side. He still had hold of my neck, but he'd lost his leverage. I dropped my left leg, spun in that direction, and shoved him up and off me. He landed on his feet, spun on his heel, and dove for his fallen comrade's rifle.

Ray jumped forward with the gun just as the man bent down to grab the rifle. He hesitated, his eyes on Ray, and I kicked him hard in the stomach, which sent him backwards to land with a thud on the ground.

"*Ay, mi madre,*" Nina said.

"Tell them to stay on the ground and have them put their backs against the truck, okay?" I said.

She told them and they obeyed, both breathing hard. I took the gun from Ray.

"Find something to tie them up with," I said.

"What are we going to do?" Nina said.

My eyes were fully adjusted to the darkness now, and I could see a vehicle down the road, parked on the side.

"Turn the truck off and kill the lights," I said.

Ray brought some of the rope we'd used to secure the contents in the truck bed. I motioned upward with the rifle and the men stood, but when I urged them down the hill into the ravine they just looked at each other, no doubt wondering whether this crazy American planned to execute them. I smashed the one who didn't speak English in the belly with the gun butt and he doubled over.

"Okay, we go," the other said.

Once at the bottom, we sat them back-to-back, bound their legs, and then tied their arms and torsos together. I removed their shoes and socks and stuffed the socks in their mouths. They struggled some, until I held the rifle butt toward one of their faces as if I'd smash that next.

"What are we going to do?" Ray said when we were back up at the road.

I took the rifle and said, "Wait here a few minutes, I'll be right back."

I kept my eye on the vehicle I'd seen, and indeed, it was a police car. In front of it was another vehicle, one I wasn't surprised to see. I crept close to the front car, whose driver was looking out his window. I stayed low, closed the distance, and pulled the passenger door open.

Ramón jumped at the sight of me with the rifle pointed in his face. He started to turn the key in the ignition.

"I wouldn't do that if I were you. Slide over into the passenger side here and get out of the car."

He got out, pulled a pack of Marlboros from his breast pocket, and stuck one in his mouth. It wasn't there a second before I smashed it with a knuckle sandwich that dropped him to his knees.

I shook my hand. His teeth had dug into my knuckles and a sharp pain shot up my arm. His body was limp on the ground. I shouldered the rifle, dragged him to the truck, tossed him inside the bed, and had Ray tie his legs and arms. Nina was so furious she couldn't speak. She spit on Ramón while he was unconscious.

"Nina, it's going to take the three of us to get the damn horse out of the way."

We nearly broke our backs dragging it by its forelegs to the side of the road and pushing it into the ravine, where it rolled once and stuck, about a third of the way down. I felt sticky goo on my hands and saw in the truck's headlights that they were covered in blood. Ramón's friends must have shot the horse and left him in the road to die. Traffic on these back roads at this hour was non-existent, which I assumed meant we were almost back to the farm. I'd slept longer than I thought.

I waved Nina ahead, and Ray and I ran to the other vehicles.

"What are we going to do? Push them down the hill?" he said.

"No, they'll be found too quickly. Who knows if Ramón or these junior PNR's told anyone else about us."

"Then *what?*"

"I always thought you looked like a Cadillac man, Ray."

"Seriously?"

With Nina in the lead, I followed behind her in the PNR's truck, and Ray followed me in the Cadillac. If an ambush awaited us at the farm, this might throw Gutierrez and his men off balance.

I had no idea, however, what we'd do then.

43

Down in the depths of the bank barn, candles burned to augment the few light bulbs that dangled from above. The conditions couldn't be worse for precision work, but there was no choice. What with Gutierrez, Sanchez, Gunner, and the Peruvians all on the frenzied hunt, Ramón's double-dealing, and *Tio* Luz's potential boasting, there were too many loose ends, any of which could lead directly to the farm.

Once back, the first thing we'd done was resurrect the impromptu hoist to lift the engine back into the mount. Even with Ray, me, and Nina, we were undermanned. We hadn't awakened Señor Maceo—Nina was afraid he'd have a heart attack over the Cadillac, the PNR vehicle, and his captive nephew Ramón—so we snuck into the farm, hid the vehicles, restrained Ramón, and set off to work. We could have used another set of hands to tighten bolts, add fluids, connect wires, and help prepare for what we hoped would be the sunrise flight of the Beast, but we made do.

Nina and I were bleeding the brake line to the port wheel assembly when a shriek from the pile of crates we'd been using for a scaffold shocked us to our feet. Ray had a hold of his crotch, and he half slid, half fell off the scaffold with a moan.

"What happened?" I said.

"My balls, I hurt my balls pulling too hard with the wrench on the final bolt."

"Hernia?"

His hand was down his pants to check his plumbing. He sat on one of the many hay bales on the floor.

"I don't think so, just a strain."

"Are you all right?" Nina said.

"No, I'm not all right. It's the middle of the night, I'm in a hole in the ground salvaging a dinosaur of an airplane, on the run for my life, I probably just ruined my rarely used testicles, and I'm beyond exhausted." He looked at Nina, then away quickly. "Sorry, I just . . . I need . . . sleep."

"Go ahead, take a break," I said. "Go lie on the couch up above. We'll finish the port and starboard brakes. There's not much more to do."

He rubbed his eyes.

"Sorry, guys."

He walked into the darkness and I could hear his feet shuffle up the ladder. I checked my watch. It was 3:27 a.m. At dawn we'd fly the Beast out of here or die trying. I was so tired I no longer cared which.

It took another forty-five minutes to bleed the lines, pump fluid into the cylinders (which now had pieces of rubber work gloves for gaskets), and close off the brake systems. Far from ideal, but hopefully sufficient to stop us if we made it far enough to need brakes.

When I ducked under the starboard wing to check on Nina, I found her asleep on the ground. The candle that flickered under the wing lit her face with a soft glow, and my delirious imagination thought of Mary in the manger after she'd given birth to the baby Jesus. Exhausted but content, and beautiful.

I bent down on one knee, slid my hands under her back, and carefully lifted and carried her outside the open barn doors. As I lowered her into the loose hay, her eyes opened and she whispered something in Spanish, then she took hold of my arm and wrapped it around her. We settled into the hay pile as if it were a featherbed. I felt the rise and fall of her chest next to mine, but I couldn't tell if she was awake or not. My own heart beat double, and the fatigue I'd felt just moments ago was forgotten.

A light from above caught my eye, and I watched the tail end of a bright piece of space debris skip through the atmosphere. The stars were brilliant, abundant, and silent. Here, outside the barn and in Nina's arms,

I felt at peace for the first time since we'd crashed into the waters of this wretched island. Nothing else mattered, and whatever came next, I'd have the fragrance of mystery fruits from her thick, wavy hair, and the memory of her arm around my waist to—

"Are you awake?" Nina said.

"I'm awake."

"I thought you fell asleep the moment we lay down," she said.

"My heart is beating too hard to sleep."

"I can feel it against my chest."

I swallowed. "I'm sorry for all this—"

She pressed her lips into mine with a force that made our front teeth click.

The moment extended to moments and I held her tightly as we kissed. I'd imagined what it would be like to kiss her since the first time I saw her. This was better. And soon her hands were caressing my shoulders, neck, arms, back and thighs, while I kissed her cheeks, eyes, ears, neck, and throat. She tasted sweet here, salty there—perspiration from the day's struggles—and I savored her like a luxurious nectar. I hadn't showered for days, but the scent of my body was no deterrent.

She pulled my shirt over my head and pressed her hands into my chest, then slipped off her blouse. We came together like a head-on collision. I could see our bodies connected as one, our limbs entwined, as if I were gazing down upon our union from an out- of- body experience, too enraptured to turn away.

I pulled her hips close and pressed deeply forward as she rolled me on by back and suspended herself momentarily above me. Convulsions led to an eruption of my senses, with smell giving in to taste, that succumbed to touch, and the sight of her pleasure cascaded into an emotional release and embrace that gradually abated as our limbs became limp, and the stars burned holes into the backs of my eyes.

DREAMS LED ME TO FULL ORCHARDS, WHERE ORANGES, LEMONS, CHERRIES and exotic fruits I didn't recognize grew in wild bunches. As I floated through them, I could taste and smell their bouquets, and the sky above was a brilliant cerulean blue. Then the sky darkened to copper, and through the thinning trees I spotted dark figures. I couldn't tell whether they were male or female, human or animal, but a sense of alertness replaced the euphoria.

I could hear one of the creatures whispering my name . . .

". . . Buck . . . *Buck!*"

My eyes fluttered and a light blinded me. It was sunlight.

"Buck, wake up!" Ray hovered over me. "Somebody's here!"

44

"**B**UCK!" RAY'S VOICE PIERCED THE FOG OF MY SLUMBER.

I blinked my eyes several times, then lurched to my feet.

The sun hadn't yet reached the horizon, but Nina was gone.

"Where's—"

"She's up with her grandfather. I heard a scream, then a bang . . . a crashing sound, not like a gunshot—"

A faint shout resonated across the tobacco field. I ran inside, past the Beast and up the ladder.

"Buck! No, Buck—wait!" Ray's voice was small down in the hole.

I stopped at the top of the ladder and listened, but all I heard was Ray huffing and puffing beneath me. Once at the top he bent over and put his hands on his knees.

"Don't go . . . running . . . in there." Ray gasped. "Nina said . . . she'd . . . handle it."

"I'm going to check it out."

I crossed over the road and cut into the woods. Ray scurried behind me, grumbling under his breath, no doubt ruing the day he agreed to help me dive on Gutierrez's speedboat. Fifty feet in and up the knoll through a thicket of bushes, an animal trail or erosion ditch cleared a narrow path toward the farmhouse at the top of the hill. As we drew closer, I stopped and listened. There were voices but no screaming or shouting. The trail continued around the back of the house, and once past I could see the driveway. There was a small Jeep-like police vehicle parked there.

Shit.

"What's that?" Ray said.

"It's not the pizza delivery man."

"What are we gonna do?"

Good question. If it *were* Gutierrez, he'd be armed and ready. I didn't know what to expect from Sanchez.

"I'll go take a look. Stay here."

The vegetation thinned toward the house. There were three windows spread evenly across the back, and with the exception of the kitchen window on the left, I had no idea which rooms they belonged to. There was a fifty-foot patch of dirt and weeds from the edge of the scrubby woods to there, which would leave me totally exposed if I crossed. The kitchen window was open. The side door was just around the corner. I bent down and scurried toward that corner of the house. It reminded me of when Ben and I spied on our parents when we were kids in Virginia.

The sudden sound of breaking glass brought me up short, halfway through the dirt patch. I expected to see a gun barrel protruding from a shattered window, but there was nothing. I crept to a stop under the kitchen window. There were voices, one of them Nina's, and though I couldn't understand what she was saying, her emotion was clear: anger and . . . sarcasm? My throat swelled with a sense of pride.

Kick some ass, girl.

I needed to find out if Gutierrez was there, but what would I do if it *were* him? The windowsill was just above my head. There was a bucket just past the corner of the house I could stand on.

I hesitated at the end of the wall, five feet from the bucket.

Was there anybody waiting outside? I peeked around the corner and saw no one. Just as I took a step forward, the side door flew open and a uniformed man backed out, shouting and pointing inside. I dove back behind the house.

The man wore the green uniform of MININT. I didn't see his face, but he was shorter and fatter than Gutierrez, and I doubted my old adversary had porked-up in the months since his glorious return.

The cascade of footsteps that stomped down the steps from the kitchen led me to estimate there were three men in the detail. But what were they looking for? Or who?

Like I didn't know.

The door reopened and the sound of Nina's voice rose again. It was less aggressive but still strong. She was no pushover, that one. My mind flashed back to our early morning beneath the stars. Did that really happen? Did I do something I shouldn't have? No, she had been the aggressor—not that I put up a fight.

The Jeep roared to life and moments later gravel was flung backward as they sped down the drive. I peered around the corner in time to see them round the first bend. There were three men in the cab, none of whom I recognized.

Inside the kitchen it felt like a wake. Problem was, I felt like it was for Ray and me. Old man Maceo sat crumpled in one of the chairs and didn't look up when I entered. Nina paced around the room, tidied, moved a pot from one counter to another, and acted as if I weren't there.

After a full minute of silence, I cleared my throat.

"What did they want?"

She smashed a coffee cup down on the table.

I winced, but the old man didn't budge.

"They killed the fisherman." She wouldn't look at me. "The one who helped you, who took you in for the night."

"Juan?"

I closed my eyes and stood there for a moment, swaying. Damn, damn, *damn*.

The side-door burst open and my heart stopped. Ray flew inside.

"Thank God they left," he said.

He searched my face, then Nina's, then Señor Maceo's.

"Trouble?" he said.

"One of the fishermen's wives told the police Juan helped you and you left with a farmer, but it seems they didn't know Papi's name," Nina said.

The old man rubbed the stubble on his cheeks with both hands at the same time.

"So now they're checking all the farms."

"Did Juan tell them anything else?" Ray said.

Nina pressed her lips tight and squeezed her eyes closed. A teardrop managed to escape, then another.

"We don't know," I said. "They killed him."

Ray listed toward the counter, and had it not been there, he might have kept falling.

"Those men that came in here . . . when Papi demanded to know what they wanted, they threw him to the floor. They said it was an old farmer who drove the two Americans away in a truck, and when they found him, he too would be strung up by his . . . personal parts."

Señor Maceo stood but didn't meet any of our eyes. "I'm a fool. An old fool," he said. "That silly plane . . . all these years . . . risking my family. Then your plane appears, so similar. It all seemed so clear to me then." He rubbed his eyes. "Now men are dead, my farm—my granddaughter at risk, and for what? A plane? Some crazy sense of duty to Cuba for a new future? Hah!"

He flung both wrists toward the wall and spit out a bitter, mirthless laugh. Then shuffled out of the room.

"It's time for you to go, Buck." Nina's voice was calm—remarkably so considering the circumstances. "I'm sorry, but there's no other choice."

"I agree. And the words I'm sorry can't express how I feel right now."

She put a hand to my cheek. In her eyes was a sparkle, a little dimmed, maybe, but not yet replaced with regret.

"Just take the truck," she said. "We need to be rid of it now that they're searching for one. If they catch you, say you stole it. Go to Bahia Honda. From there you can trade it for a boat, or steal one."

I nodded. Adrenalin seeped into my bloodstream that pushed the fatigue aside. It was time for action. Our presence here had already caused too much damage.

"Okay, we'll leave now. Ray?"

"But we can leave in the Beast—she's ready to go, Buck! We just need to fuel her up—I need to check the weight distribution one last time, but she's all set."

Nina and I met eyes.

She nodded once.

The three of us headed straight for the barn.

45

Nina helped me drag the twenty-gallon jugs over to fuel the Beast. Since Betty's old wing and engine were significantly lighter than that on the Beast's starboard side, only the port tank could be filled. The single tank held 75 gallons, which I estimated we'd use a third of to travel the ninety miles to Key West. Ray had hooked the fuel line to the port engine when we connected the wing so they'd draw from the single reservoir.

Señor Maceo started down the steps as we topped off the tank with the third jug. He stumbled off the bottom step, blinked again and again, took a step forward, then stopped. It was like he'd lost his direction. I could hear noises inside the plane, the scrape of metal and a thud.

"Nina?" Señor Maceo spoke in a small voice. "You didn't tell me Ramón came back with you from Havana."

Uh oh.

"He's not here for a visit, Papi. He ambushed us on the way home. He—"

"Did you let him out of the room?" I said.

Señor Maceo rubbed his chin. "Why was he tied to the chair? And with that tape over his—"

"Was?"

I checked my watch. How long had it been since the PNR were here?

"Papi, did you let Ramón out of the room?" Nina said.

"Yes, of course. He said—"

I tore up the steps through the barn, then up the gravel drive. I could see that the farmhouse's side door was half open. I continued to the front of the house and found that the Maceo's Lada was gone.

Damn!

Where would he go? Had he known the PNR was just here? His ears hadn't been covered, so he must have heard the conversation, including the part about the search for the Americans and the crashed plane.

The farm truck pulled up behind me, with Nina at the wheel.

"Get in!"

I was barely inside before she took off down the drive.

"Did the police mention Puerto Esperanza?" I said.

Nina didn't brake as she fishtailed out of the driveway.

"Yes, he must have heard everything!"

She smacked the top of the steering wheel as we accelerated up the road toward the coast.

"Damnit, *Papi!*" She shook her head. "No, it's my fault. He didn't know!"

Any sense of fear, regret, or concern in Nina had been replaced by sheer determination. She drove the old truck like we were on a Formula One road track.

"Would he run for home or go look for the police?"

"Are you kidding?" She gave a short gut-laugh. "Ramón has information that's worth something, worth a lot, in fact. He'll hunt for anyone who can reward him, especially those men who threw Papi to the floor!"

The old truck began to shimmy and I glanced at the speedometer, which lay flat on zero. Once to the coastal road, Nina swung a wide left and we hurtled west. A street sign giving the distance to Viñales sparked a thought. With Ramón on the loose and PNR troops already having been to the farm, we needed to change the game. Even if Ray and I got away, Nina and her grandfather would still be at risk.

"What'll we do with Ramón if we find him?" I said.

"I'll kill him!"

Nina clutched the steering wheel so tight, her hands were white.

A crazy thought hit me. "Nina, please slow down and let's talk about this."

She shook her head as if I was an irritating child.

"Technically, you haven't done anything illegal—"

"Oh, really?" she said. "You want to defend me when the Secret Police arrive to drag us to jail?"

"Ray and I coerced you. We found out about the plane that crashed on your farm back in the sixties and forced you and your grandfather to cooperate."

"Of course, now I feel safe." She gave me a sidelong glance. "Who would believe that after we went to Havana? Ramón will make it perfectly clear that I helped you."

"Even so, murder's a whole different story. Believe me, I'd like to strangle him with my bare hands too, but we need a better plan."

She shook her head once, and a moment later let her foot off the accelerator pedal. We slowed down to a moderate pace and Nina slumped in her seat.

"So what's the better plan?"

We drove for a while in silence, and I pulled together snippets of information we'd learned from the PNR guard who worked with Gutierrez, what Juan had said about Sanchez, and what this guard from MININT had inferred. It was clear that the search for the treasure hadn't abated, and that at least one of the groups had found the Maceo's farm in the Pinar del Rio. So others would too, and there'd be worse trouble the longer this went on.

From what I could deduce, Sanchez, Gutierrez, and the Peruvians had some sort of partnership that, given their separate searches, seemed to have gone sour. Good news. I had no idea where Gunner fit in—he could have forced himself in like he tried to with Ray and me—but I hoped his being an outsider would keep him from rallying the resources to find us. Honor amongst thieves and all that, but considering the power vacuum in Cuba, and the brewing revolution in Peru, and the greed of the thieves, it wasn't hard to imagine these groups being at each other's throats.

The question was, how could I manipulate that situation to our benefit and still provide the Maceo's protection after Ray and I were gone?

The answer came to me and I flinched.

It was either extremely foolish, or very bold.

But my entire life had been defined that way, so why should this be different?

"Take me to Viñales," I said.

"What?" She looked at me. "*Why?*"

"I'm going to surprise Sanchez and try to get the wolves focused more on each other, rather than us chickens."

She stared at me over her shoulder as she drove. "The Director of the Secret Police? You're crazy, Buck. Why would you do that?"

"I'm betting Sanchez was in on the Atocha theft with Gutierrez and the Peruvians. He has connections Gutierrez would have needed."

"Sanchez is a monster—ask any Cuban."

"I never won a fight clinging to the ropes, Nina. Nobody would expect this approach, which gives me the benefit of surprise, and hopefully, sincerity."

She wasn't happy about it, had what seemed a few choice words in Spanish, in fact, but she turned south, toward Viñales.

46

THE APPROACH TO VIÑALES WOUND THROUGH A BREATHTAKING VALLEY. Mango fields and guava farms lined the road and filled the air with their delightful fragrance. The horizon was dominated by giant karst plateaus, known locally as mogotes, which rose as high as a thousand feet and were flat on top like mesas. We wound through forests as the road crisscrossed up out of the valley toward the town.

At the top we found the village of Viñales, with its lovely colonial buildings that dated back into the early 1800's. Nina drove slowly through the town and parked the truck on a side street.

"Hotel Las Jasmines is on top of that hill." She nodded toward a driveway up a steep incline. "I'll wait for you there." She pointed to a small restaurant on the corner.

"If I'm gone more than an hour, go home, get your grandfather, and drive to Havana. If they catch up with you, claim ignorance, or say we stole your truck, or held you hostage and forced you to help us."

Our eyes locked for several seconds, then I turned to go. I felt her hand grab my shoulder. She leaned into the passenger seat and pressed her lips against mine. She held her arm tight around my neck.

"Be safe. I'll be waiting."

The climb up the hill in the wet heat produced sweat blossoms all over my back and chest. At the top, I stopped to catch my breath. The view was spectacular.

Why couldn't I be here for a romantic holiday with Nina?

I wiped the sweat off my brow, brushed my fingers through my hair, and tried to make myself presentable. The simple, elegant three-story building looked like it belonged in Provence, France. There were only a few vehicles parked outside, two of which had Havana license plates.

Once inside the lobby, I saw a large pool through the back windows, flanked by large chairs and white umbrellas. I continued on as if I belonged there and headed straight into the bar. Every surface was a dark stained wood except for the wall behind the bar, which was red brick. Had I spoken passable Spanish, this desperate play might not have felt so much like a *really* long shot. I had to be that much more cautious.

Now that I was here, my heart pounded double, and I had a sudden epiphany that this might be the most foolish move of my life. Guts were one thing, boldness another, but to walk into the lion's den without so much as a chair and whip was just plain idiotic. I sat on one of the yellow cane stools and the bartender stood patiently in front of me.

"Havana Club, *siete años, y Coke.*"

I did know how to order a drink, at least.

I took a napkin off the bar, borrowed the bartender's pen, and wrote a note. I folded the note in half, wrote Sanchez's name on the front, and asked the bartender to have a bellhop take it to Señor Sanchez's room. He disappeared toward the front desk. He returned a moment later and nodded.

Crap. He must really be here.

I wanted to guzzle the rum to steady my nerves, but it was more important to keep my head as clear as possible.

It took only seven minutes until Sanchez strode into the room with two goons in tow. Dressed in white linen pants and shirt, he stopped as soon as he entered and put both hands on his hips. I held my glass up to salute him and held my breath.

A slow smile creased his face. He waved his men back, and when they stayed inside the door, he flung his wrist at them and growled something that made them scamper into the lobby.

"Buck Reilly. I can't believe my eyes."

"Can I buy you a drink, Sanchez?"

The bartender had already poured him something, which Sanchez carried to a table in the back corner of the room, where we took seats across from each other.

"Social call?" he said.

"Let's cut to the chase, all right? You know my plane crashed on your lovely island, but my guess is you don't know all the details. I'll tell you everything I know, in exchange for two favors."

"Really, Buck. Favors?" The smile on his lips did not match his eyes.

"I came to you, that should be worth something. You've been looking for me, but you've also been looking for Manny Gutierrez."

At the mention of Gutierrez's name, Sanchez's right brow arched.

"And so have the Peruvians," I said.

Sanchez glanced over his shoulder, then scooted his chair closer to the table and leaned forward.

"You're well informed, Reilly. Perhaps you really are CIA."

"No, just a guy that got double-crossed by your Hero of the Revolution. A guy whose only remaining possession is now a crumpled heap of metal on a desolate beach, ninety miles from home."

"Tell me what you want and I'll decide what to do with you," Sanchez said.

"I want you to arrange a boat to get me out of here tomorrow—"

"Hah! Certainly! I'll have the *Guardia Frontera* take you anywhere you'd like to go." He glared at me. "Don't test my patience."

"My second request is that you find Gutierrez and let him rot indefinitely in a piss-coated cell, with no hope for a trial."

"Now *that* we agree on."

The waiter appeared with two more drinks. Sanchez's appeared to be sparkling water. I took a gulp of rum to finish my first drink and handed it to the waiter. Sanchez's eyes glistened as he smoothed his hand over his close-cropped silver beard.

"As you already know, the *Atocha* treasure was stolen in Key West, nearly a week ago," I said. "The thieves also stole a schooner called the Sea Lion and kidnapped its captain, who happens to be a friend of mine. The police unfortunately thought my friend was one of the thieves, so I set out to find and rescue him. I started in the Bahamas, on gut instinct, but then found out that was a waste of time."

"What made you realize the ship was not in the Bahamas?"

"That's where the story will start to interest you. I got a phone call from a familiar voice with a slight Spanish accent, who told me the Sea Lion was headed for Panama, and from there to Peru."

"And who was this tipster?" Sanchez said.

"He didn't give me his name, but I'd bet my life it was Manny Gutierrez."

"So you have." He let his statement sink in. "What makes you so certain?"

"I wasn't, at first, but when I went to Panama, an old friend who's an official in the Canal Zone confirmed that the Sea Lion was awaiting passage through the canal and directed me to its coordinates. An American merce-nary-type had been following me around the Bahamas in a nice Gulfstream jet, and he showed up in Panama too."

Sanchez sat forward in his chair.

"In fact, I had to elude him there, but as you're undoubtedly aware, he's shown up here and brought the Peruvians with him."

"Who is this man?"

"He goes by Gunner, but his name is Richard Rostenkowski." I took a deep breath. "He's a mercenary. In fact, he's so ruthless he was kicked out of Iraq. My guess is that he's tied in with Gutierrez too, but he's obviously connected with the Peruvians."

Sanchez massaged his beard long enough to put pieces together. "So what happened in Panama?"

"I was able to capture the vessel, but my friend on the Sea Lion was wounded during the battle and died shortly afterwards. But not before I spoke with him."

"And what did you do with the . . . cargo?"

"I loaded it on my plane, scuttled the Sea Lion with those murdering bastards on board, and headed back toward Key West. But there was one important detail my friend told me before he died." I waited, but Sanchez just stared at me. "He said that several hours after they set sail from Key West, the Sea Lion rendezvoused with another boat and transferred half the treasure to them. Gutierrez was on the boat they met."

I gambled that if Gutierrez had disappeared on him it would confirm his suspicions about being double-crossed. The information about Gunner spiced that up nicely, too. Sanchez had a hell of a poker face, but I sensed a slow boil beneath the surface.

He sat back in his chair.

"Congratulations on finding the boat, and too bad about your friend." He sipped his sparkling water. "But if you were headed to Key West, how did you crash your plane on the shore near Puerto Esperanza?"

"Before I ever left Key West—before I even knew about the theft of the *Atocha* treasure—a friend in the Coast Guard tipped me off that a group of Cuban divers had been searching the Florida straits for Gutierrez's boat. The one I sank when he was on the run back to Cuba."

"I'm well aware of your involvement in that, but why would you care any more about that boat?"

"By asking that, you've just confirmed that Gutierrez has been holding out on you since he returned to Cuba."

"I'm growing tired of this, Reilly. What are you saying?"

"Gutierrez had stolen some very valuable maps from me before he took off in that boat. Archeological maps and letters I'd obtained while at my former company. He knew there was tremendous value to—some would call them treasure maps—either to sell or pursue treasures himself. So when I got the tip that Cuban divers were searching for that boat, I knew it had to be Gutierrez, and I decided I'd do my damndest to beat him to it."

"But first you had to rescue your friend?" Sanchez shook his head. "You're a fool, Reilly. No wonder your business failed."

"It was *because* my business failed that my priorities have changed."

"Then what?" His voice had an edge to it now. Sanchez was not the type of man who tolerates being double-crossed, lied to, or out-smarted.

"Gunner and the Peruvians got to my contact in Colón, so they knew I'd found the boat. Before I left Panama, Gunner invited me onto his G-IV and showed me all his fancy tracking equipment to let me know how he'd been following me." I lowered my voice. "He also showed me a secret panel inside the plane that held automatic weapons and rocket launchers."

Sanchez touched the cell phone on his belt like it was a six-shooter.

"How did you elude this Gunner to get to the Sea Lion, then?"

"Slashed his tires as I got out of his plane, then hauled ass."

Sanchez actually smiled at that.

"By the time I intercepted the Sea Lion, got the treasure, and headed north, Gunner and the Peruvians were on my tail again but a couple steps behind. When I got up here Gutierrez was waiting for me at the wreck site with a rocket launcher and shot my plane down. I was able to glide toward the closest land, which happened to be western Cuba, and crash-land in the water. Some local fishermen towed me to shore."

Sanchez had the decency to look a tad uncomfortable. His charade was over.

"So where's the treasure?"

"I had to dump the weight out over the wreck site in order to remain airborne after Gutierrez blasted my plane—"

"While still flying the plane?"

"I had no choice," I paused to stare into Sanchez's narrow eyes. "My guess is Gutierrez either marked the location or dove down and collected the boxes I dumped after I went down in flames."

He stood and walked around the table. After two complete circuits, he stopped and bent toward me.

"This is all very fantastic, Reilly. Why should I believe you?"

"Because I just want to get the hell off this island and go home. If you get me a boat and take me back into U.S. waters, you'll know I left empty-handed."

"Or perhaps you know exactly where the treasure was dumped and will return to collect it yourself," he said.

"I was after my friend, Sanchez, not treasure I couldn't do anything with." I shrugged. "Sure, I might have been given a reward, but if I can get my maps back off that wreck—"

I stopped mid-sentence. Both of Sanchez's eyebrows lifted this time. Greed is such a fine motivator for most men. I'd gambled that it would be for him.

"The fishermen who rescued me could vouch for the fact that my plane was empty. In fact, one of them, his name was Juan, let me sleep in his house that night."

"His last name?"

"Doesn't matter. Gutierrez and his men killed him yesterday. I guess he's trying to clean up his trail, which is why he's been looking for me—and why I came to tell you the whole story. Even if he gets me before I find a way home, you'll catch up to him, sooner or later."

Sanchez stood tall. He glanced to the restaurant door, where I assumed his goons were just outside.

"And why should I let you go, Reilly? I could make you take me to the location where your plane was hit by the rocket."

"Three reasons, Sanchez. First, our countries are moving toward normalized relations and I radioed my friend in the Coast Guard, Ensign Frank Nardi, to tell him I was coming to meet you. Second, you want me gone before the Peruvians find out I met with you. And third . . ."

I pulled a piece of paper out of my pocket, unfolded it, and placed it on the table.

"These are the coordinates my friend at the Coast Guard gave me where Gutierrez's boat sank, where he nailed my plane, where I dumped the treasure."

The coordinates were written on a piece of personalized stationary emblazoned across the top with: 'Ensign Frank Nardi, United States Coast Guard, Officer of the Deck, Cutter Mohawk.'

"I just want to get home," I said.

Sanchez rubbed his palms together and a slow smile came over his face.

"Where have you been hiding and how are you getting around?"

"I stole a car. It's parked in Viñales. I've been sleeping in fields and abandoned barns. Just smell me."

I lifted my arm and leaned my armpit in his direction. He stepped back with a sour expression.

"You're a pathetic loser, Reilly. But this is too fantastic not to be true. It fits with . . . some of the pieces I have deduced. Meet me at the public pier in Bahia Honda, tomorrow morning at eight. I'll have a boat meet us there, and we'll tow another boat behind it for you to return to Florida, once we confirm the location of Gutierrez's sunken boat."

No handshake marked my departure, and the goons watched me closely as I passed through the lobby.

If Gunner's G-IV was still in Havana, my guess was that it would be seized within the hour. I still hadn't figured out how he'd connected with the Peruvians, but I didn't care anymore.

Sanchez could have followed me or kept me captive and forced me to cooperate, but my visit was so freaking crazy I think he believed me. Lies work best when wound around enough truth to be plausible. My days of hustling Wall Street analysts still served me well, even with my rehabbed sense of values. And if he bought my story, Sanchez would call off his hounds.

No matter what happened now, at least Gutierrez was in deep kaka here at home.

When it All Falls Down

47

N INA'S TRUCK WAS UP ON THE CORNER. SHE'D WAITED—
"Buck Reilly, what a coincidence."

I spun hard toward the male voice—but a sudden blow buckled my knees. I remained upright but wobbled back a couple steps.

Gunner stood in front of me, arms cocked, ready to launch another punch.

"That was for slicing the tires on my plane," he said.

He moved toward me and the stars cleared just in time to deflect the next right jab. His blue reflective sunglasses made it seem like a giant insect was descending on me. He pressed forward with his bulk and switched from single shot to rapid fire. I deflected a few more blows until an uppercut to my belly expelled every bit of oxygen from my body.

A small voice in the back of my head reminded me I wanted to avoid fighting Gunner, but that was no longer an option. With a feint to my left, I ducked and pushed off to the right, dodging two more shots. I swung back hard with a left hook to his ear that sent the mirrored glasses flying.

Gunner, however, didn't budge.

Crap.

His eyes were even more menacing without the glasses.

Once a Golden Gloves middleweight champion (regional), I was an adroit fighter, but against a heavyweight mercenary like Gunner, the odds were—

He came at me again, faster this time, like a whirling dervish with hands and feet kicking and jabbing, and the next thing I knew he kicked the back of my legs and I was falling backwards, only to feel a chop on my nose and—

I AWOKE IN AN ALLEY, SURROUNDED BY REFUSE, MY LEGS TIED TOGETHER with one of those plastic straps police use instead of handcuffs. Sitting on a crate next to me was Gunner. The blue shades were back on, but one of the lenses was cracked.

"I knew if I watched the driveway to that hotel long enough, one of my quarries would show up. When I saw you earlier I was going to grab you then but figured if you made it out you'd have more to tell me," Gunner said.

"Why should I tell you anything?"

I'd forgotten about his square teeth.

"I laughed when I saw your old junker washed ashore like a dead whale," he said.

"What do you want, Gunner? Or should I call you Rostenkowski?"

"Very good, Reilly. I'm impressed."

I hoped Nina wouldn't come searching for me.

"So how did you meet the Peruvians?" I said.

"Easy, really. Your friend at the Canal Zone tipped them off when the boat and their men disappeared. We met at the airport because I captured the limo driver who made the mistake of hanging around after he dropped you off." Gunner smiled. "Your friend arranged the introduction to the Peruvians in exchange for his driver. He didn't have anything good to say about you either."

Raul. Nice.

"And why did the Peruvians agree to get you involved?" I said.

"We had mutual interests and were able to help each other on an impromptu basis. I needed two new tires—nice move, by the way—and they needed a plane to go out and find their merchandise."

"Merchandise, huh? Who are you working for anyway?"

"Myself. Thought you'd have figured that out by now."

"And that's *your* G-IV?"

"I was hired by Standard Mutual Insurance to find the Sea Lion—"

"Hence the SM on the plane's tail."

"But like any good soldier of fortune," he said, "or at least one that wants to prosper, you sometimes have to roll with the punches. When you evaded me, fate brought me the Peruvians who were hotter than an artillery barrel after a daylong barrage. I had the tracking gear, so—"

"You followed the signal from the transmitter inside my plane?"

He smiled. Lots of small, square teeth.

"Before either of us left Key West," he said, "you were punching out such a strong signal, following you was a breeze. I figured the police or maybe the Feds were watching you."

Booth's transmitter. He almost got me killed—still might.

"So Standard Mutual covers the Sea Lion?" I said. "Pretty expensive plane for—"

"They insure the Atocha Museum."

That made sense. I wondered if Donny Pogue knew SM had this bastard on the prowl.

I said, "As the insurer, I imagine Standard Mutual had some access to police reports, the Coast Guard's and Treasure Salvors' people. They feed that to you?"

Another smile. "Took me less than an hour to figure out you were on the hunt for the same boat I was, and the captain was a friend of yours, thanks to their intel."

"What about the pilots for your plane? How'd they feel about switching teams?"

He cracked his knuckles. "Like they had a choice? They weren't too happy about landing in Havana either, let me tell you."

"What makes you think they haven't left you?"

He reached inside a thigh pocket on his black cargo pants and removed a circuit board the size of a playing card.

"Nice thing about modern airplanes, Reilly, they're just big computers. You remove the hard drive, they're just worthless boxes of shit."

"So what do you want, Gunner?"

He took the sunglasses off and leaned in close. His dung-brown eyes betrayed no emotion or insight.

"I want the treasure you took off the Sea Lion. What the hell do you think?"

I shook my head the way you do when you feel sorry for somebody, even though it made my jaw hurt.

"The Peruvians made at least two mistakes, so far. The first was thinking I scuttled the Sea Lion—"

"They had that from Governor Raul Acosta, said he was getting even for you ripping him off—"

"He helped me ambush the Peruvians, Gunner. The Sea Lion sailed back toward Cuba all by its lonesome. Treasure intact, with the Peruvian thieves as captives."

He clamped his square teeth together and I saw the muscle in his jaw twitch. "What was their second mistake?"

"Trusting you."

He sat back on his heels, closed his eyes for a few seconds, then I heard a long exhale followed by a sigh.

"Then what's your angle in all this, Reilly?"

Gunner, bless him, was like Gutierrez and Sanchez, his needs and desires universal and totally transparent. With all of them, it was all about greed. Which made improvising simpler.

"The police in Key West were right," I said. "I *am* partners with Gutierrez and Sanchez."

"You're a pirate, after all." He smiled. "I knew I liked you."

"Problem is, Gutierrez double-crossed us and had the Sea Lion rendezvous with him in Cuban waters where he removed half the treasure. I flew around the Bahamas to lure the Coast Guard east, then double-backed to help Truck Lewis get rid of our other partners, the Peruvians aboard the Sea Lion."

"What the fuck are you talking about, Reilly?"

"Truck doesn't realize the partnership has fallen apart. He's sailing back here expecting to meet me, Gutierrez, and Sanchez in Bahia Honda tomorrow morning to divvy up the goods."

Gunner squinted at me as if I were an alien. "You shitting me with all this? What about your plane?"

"When I flew to Cuba to meet Gutierrez, the greedy bastard shot my ass down."

Gunner hacked out a laugh that had him coughing, then alternated laughing and coughing for maybe thirty seconds.

"Now what?"

"I'll be at Bahia Honda tomorrow morning to intercept the Sea Lion before Gutierrez can get to it first. With Sanchez at my side."

"And me at your other side," he said.

I shut my mouth, rubbed my face, and felt the fresh lumps administered by Gunner.

"Sanchez just told me they've commandeered your plane," I said.

"Fuck it, who cares. If I can get some of this—"

"He's also furious that you brought the Peruvians here. He's issued orders to shoot you on sight."

Gunner bit his lip. "Not with you as my shield."

"Oh, really? You think Sanchez won't try and take me out, too? You think there's any honor left amongst this bunch?" I spit on the ground and saw blood mixed in with mucus.

"So what're you saying, Reilly?"

I smiled. "I'm saying we double-cross them first."

Another slow laugh rumbled out of him and his eyes crinkled at the edges. He was having a great time.

"I like the way you think. But, how?"

I leaned forward. "I stay out in the open so Sanchez doesn't suspect anything. You do what you do best and set up an ambush—"

"Oh, no, I'm not letting you out of my sight."

"Won't work, Gunner. We won't get anywhere near Bahia Honda if they see us together—"

"So how will I find you? How can I trust—"

"Because I need you too, damnit! I'll be on the main dock there at eight a.m. tomorrow. I hope you still have access to some of that fancy weaponry you showed me in Panama. Get yourself in position by seven and don't be late."

His eyes narrowed for a moment. Given his line of work he had to consider it might be a trap, but I was counting on greed and a lack of options and his perfectly reasonable belief that I needed him to trump his suspicions. He took a knife out of his pocket, hesitated, and I nearly went into cardiac arrest as he leaned toward me.

He sliced the plastic clasp on my ankles.

"You double-cross me, Reilly, I'll find you."

"I know you would, I'm not stupid. And think about it. My plane's been shot down, I'm wanted back home, my partners here have double-crossed me and I'm totally expendable to them. My job was to stake out the museum and run the operation there. I'll never get my share of that treasure and I've got no way off this island. I need you as much as you need me, Gunner."

I held out my hand. He grabbed it and squeezed hard.

"Just remember, you screw me, I'll get you, one way or another."

I walked out of the alley, got my bearings, and went the opposite way down the street to make sure the coast was clear before I circled the block to meet Nina. My mouth was dry, my head was pounding and my mind was spinning.

Oh what a tangled web we weave when trying to save our asses.

48

BEHIND THE BARN, A FRESH SWATH WAS CUT THROUGH THE TOBACCO FIELD as far as the eye could see. It was about sixty-feet wide and dropped slowly in elevation. Señor Maceo was atop his tractor and driving fast toward the barn.

"Papi's cleared you a runway," Nina said.

"He's a pretty amazing man, Nina. And unbelievable as it may be, it looks as though we may actually get the plane off your farm. It all seems to be coming together."

"For you, yes. For us, what will happen when Ramón comes back with the authorities?"

She said it with no malice in her voice, the way she might have asked a question about the weather. I didn't have an answer. I wished we'd found Ramón but wasn't sure what we'd have done with him if we had. I explained what I'd told Sanchez.

"Very clever, Buck Reilly," she said. "That should buy you and Ray enough time to try the Beast."

But what would happen when I didn't show up at Bahia Honda? And Gutierrez was still out there. How could we just take off and leave Nina and her grandfather to face Gutierrez, or Sanchez once he realized I double-crossed him? Or what if CNN announced the treasure was safe aboard the Sea Lion, under escort by the Coast Guard, before my scheduled meeting with Sanchez tomorrow?

It was still a mess, and nobody was safe.

"Come with us, Nina." I nodded out to the field, where Señor Maceo pulled the tractor off to the side of the dirt runway up next to the barn. "You and your grandfather should leave Cuba, once and for all."

He held a fist up, and then Ray emerged from the barn and held his fist up too.

Nina sighed.

"Look at him. At least he's recovered from this morning's humiliation." She turned toward me and put her hand on my leg. "We can't come with you, Buck. Our lives are here, with roots as deep as these tobacco fields we've tended for generations."

"But what if you're right? What if Ramón returns with the police and they make a thorough search of the property? Remember the PNR truck and Ramón's Cadillac? There are airplane parts all over the barn. There's no way to hide all that, and look."

I pointed to the fresh cut path.

"It's a trail right to you. They'll know you helped us, Nina. They'll . . . they'll . . ."

She raised her palm to my cheek.

"Papi will never leave, and I could never leave him. We can't run from our lives, no matter what will come. Cuba is on the brink of freedom, and perhaps thugs like Gutierrez will finally be brought to justice." She popped the door open. "Come, let's see what those two have done."

"But what will *you* do?" I said.

"Once you leave, I'll get on the radio to the Ministry of Agriculture. Remember, our fields produce some of the premier tobacco in the world. Cuba survives on tourism, sugar, nickel, and cigar exports. Calls can be made to those who oversee MININT. If Gutierrez and even Sanchez are pursuing their own interests, maybe they can be stopped."

Her eyes and smile were steady, as if she believed what she was saying.

I leaned over and took her in my arms. We held each other close and she buried her face in my neck. I bent lower to kiss her, and this morning's dream of making love under the stars was no longer a fantasy. My mind raced along with my heart, but Nina pulled back to look at me, with moist eyes.

"Come, Buck, we need to get you out of here."

I felt lighter than air as we walked towards the barn, my arm around her waist. She went straight down the steps and into the pit where the Beast lay ready. I felt like David descending into the lion's den. Would the Beast kill us or deliver us to the Promised Land?

Hah, never thought of Key West as that before.

"Papi!" Nina said.

Ray and Señor Maceo rushed toward us with broad smiles on their faces.

"Did you see that?" Ray pointed out the barn door and the broad runway easing down a gradual slope. "A couple thousand Cohibas just bit the dust to make way for our departure."

Nina hugged her grandfather and he laughed like a mischievous young man, a completely different person from the one the police had left earlier.

"A man can be crushed but never broken," he said. "I've waited for this day for most of my life. The Beauty will rise from the field where she crashed, where the insurrection her pilots were sent to lead failed."

I thought of the letter from Kennedy to Fidel Castro and how different a half-century of relations between our two countries might have been. Ray and I had placed the pilot's remains in a box to bring home.

"You, my friends," Señor Maceo said, "Ray Floyd and Buck Reilly, you will take my Beauty home, to America."

I doubted he'd consider my appeal for him and Nina to leave with us, but I still had to try. "Why not experience the Beauty with us? Come to Florida, there's danger for you both if you stay. Our fault, so please accept our invitation."

His eyes lit up and he looked from me to Ray, who looked surprised but quickly got my drift.

"Buck's right, come with us."

"No, no, you boys are kind, but the harvest comes soon. Nina and I have a responsibility to the workers, and to our history," he paused. "But Nina, you should go with these men. Your grandmother would be overjoyed to see you."

A tear ran down her cheek. "No, Papi, I will never leave you, no matter what you say. Once Buck goes, I'll radio the ministry and get them to help us." She looked to us, her expression resolute. "It's time, my American friends. You should leave so we can all continue with our lives."

Ray hugged both our hosts and climbed aboard the Beast without a word. Moments later, Betty's valiant port engine turned over, caught, and roared to life. From the flight deck, Ray pushed his hand out the side window and gave us a thumbs-up.

Seconds passed and the starboard propeller started to rotate, slowly. A backfire spit black smoke out the exhaust, and the engine coughed and sputtered. It had been five decades since she last ran, and our hopes were pinned to a Cuban mechanic accustomed to keeping vintage Chevys, Fords, and Ladas running on bubble gum and homemade parts. She chugged, spit more smoke, gasped, and just when I began to fear our plan was poised to fail, the engine caught with a loud backfire and settled into a purr.

Ray's up-turned thumb shook like mad and I could hear him howl from the cockpit. The plane pulled slowly out of the barn, with dirt, dust, tobacco, and rocks flying in all directions. The holes in the fuselage had been sealed with burlap, canvas, and tar. She had a patchwork skin but appeared to be airworthy.

What about *seaworthy*?

Nina, her grandfather and I took several steps back.

The old man was laughing and doing a victory jig.

Nina was looking at the ground, and I realized we were standing on the exact spot where we'd held each other during the early morning hours.

I took her in my arms and pulled her close. "Come with us!"

I couldn't hear her reply, but I read her lips when she said: "What?"

I placed my mouth next to her ear and shouted the request again.

When I pulled back she was shaking her head. She stood on her tiptoes and kissed my cheek just as I was looking at Señor Maceo, who gave me a deep nod. I spun her around and backed her over for a real kiss, undistracted by the roar of the Beast and the spray of debris that peppered us. When Ray let go of the brakes and the Beast lurched forward, I broke away and dashed for the open hatch.

Once aboard, I immediately noticed the difference of the cabin in direct sunlight. It was dusty and bare, with four seats and little else aside from the boxes used to offset the weight discrepancy from the port and starboard engines. I pulled myself forward and navigated my way into the right seat, where I strapped in and donned the headset we had taken from Betty.

Ray ran down a mental pre-flight checklist. He moved the flaps, rudder, and checked the various antiquated gauges on the instrument panel, batteries, and magnetos. My eyes were locked on Nina, who'd backed inside the barn and continued to stare out at us. She was beautiful in all conditions—wind-blown, sleep-deprived, hunted by the Secret Police . . .

My heart pitched again: what would Gutierrez do if he learned she'd helped us?

"Based on the wind, we're going to have to taxi to the end of the runway and take off back up hill," Ray shouted over the noise of the engines.

I tried to focus. We were about to take off in an ancient pieced-together plane with operating concerns that could result in our facing the same fate as the Goose's last flight crew. As we tumbled down the dirt path, the tires crunched over stalks of fresh-cut plants that jostled us in an irregular line. I watched the port wing, cut from Betty and welded to the three-foot stub that remained after we removed the crumpled wing from the Beast. The wing bounced with each bump but looked solid, and the flaps were working just fine, so far. I searched for sparks under the instrument panel, checked the brake and hydraulic lines for leaks, the gauges for erratic behavior, but everything looked, sounded, and felt secure.

There was a slight dip to the dirt runway, then it began a gentle climb up a low rise. When we got to the end, Ray used the throttles to maneuver the Beast around to face into the wind. As we turned, I noticed that the end of the runway was perpendicular to the road that led to the farmhouse, and that a long straightaway to the south could be seen from our vantage point. I wondered how far—

Lights flashed in the distance. They were moving fast, headed our way.

"All right, Buck, you ready?" Ray said.

The lights headed toward us were mounted on top of a truck.

Could it be?

"I wish they'd come with us," I said.

"Tradition is the cathedral of the poor," Ray said. "Cross your fingers, here we go!"

He pressed the throttles forward and the plane began to vibrate with anticipation.

49

RAY RELEASED THE BRAKE AND THE BEAST JUMPED FORWARD.
"Stop!" I yelled.

He flinched, then yanked up the brake and whipped the throttles back. "What's wrong?"

He looked around the cockpit as if he expected a malfunction.

"Look." I pointed to the truck speeding up the road toward us.

"What the hell'd you stop me for? A truck? We gotta get outta here!"

I swallowed hard and looked up the hill. Nina and her grandfather would be waiting to see us take off. But there was no way to avoid the truck with the flashing lights seeing us, too. Ray grabbed the throttles.

I undid my safety belt and jumped out of the seat.

"Where the hell are you going?"

When I told him, he said I was insane. There was no time for debate. I cracked open the hatch, jumped out, slammed it shut, and dove into the uncut tobacco. The engines revved loudly—and unevenly, one having six and the other nine cylinders—and I said a quick prayer for Ray's safety.

The Beast rolled forward at what seemed an impossibly slow pace. I lost it for a couple of seconds in the dip between hills, then heard rifle shots from the road. The Beast appeared from the gully and was going much faster. Finally she lifted off, and from my angle appeared to just clear the barn.

Ray kept her on a straight course as she ascended, listing heavily to starboard, and I could almost hear the sound change as he calibrated the

RPM's on the engines until there was a harmonious balance between them. The Beast leveled off and continued north at a low altitude until she vanished on the horizon. The rifle fire stopped, replaced by the sound of the truck roaring up the road. I took off through the tobacco, whose broad leaves slapped my chest and legs. The ground was uneven but the rows ran parallel to the runway, so I found a groove and picked up the pace.

Would the truck stop at the farmhouse? Given the rifle fire, that seemed certain.

Had Ramón found Gutierrez, or his people? The truck was different from the one that had come earlier. Was there more than one? I couldn't tell from the angle on the road, as it had been headed straight toward us. The rough ground kept me from doing much more than concentrating on not twisting my ankle, and I had no plan other than to get to the top and see what was going on.

Sweat soaked my shirt. My lungs, quads, and calves were aflame as I reached the end of the tobacco field. The barn lay ahead, but the large doors that led into the basement were now closed. I listened, and heard nothing inside. I worked my way up the steep hill, stopped periodically to listen for any sounds but heard nothing beyond the birds buzzing, singing and cackling, unconcerned with my predicament or the Maceo's fate.

Once across the gravel drive I was back on the animal trail toward the house. I snaked my way up and at the peak spotted the same truck that had been coming up the road now parked across the driveway to block any other vehicles from leaving.

Damn!

Inside the truck were two men, at least, but I couldn't tell if there were any troops in the back. Time was of the essence. If Gutierrez was inside, he'd assume that Ray and I had escaped. His vengeance would be swift and brutal.

I crouched in the woods, my shirt stuck to my skin, and my hands and pockets were empty. With no weapon and outnumbered at least three-to-one, the odds sucked. I'd been on the Beast at the end of the runway, seconds away from being airborne and on my way back to Key West.

And now here I was.

Son-of-a-bitch.

But damnit, what choice did I have? I couldn't just leave these people alone to face the consequences of helping us. If my end were to be at the hands of Gutierrez and his goons, then I'd rather go with my guns blazing.

If I only had a gun, that is . . ..

I hurried around the to back of the house, beyond where I'd stopped before on the trail. It ended in a copse of trees and brush. I kept pushing my way through toward the road, then curved back toward the driveway. I crossed to the other side of the drive, crept to the top—and saw the truck. It was more like a van, the back enclosed. I didn't see any other police or troops, and my guess was the two guys up front were alone. I glanced around but saw nothing I could use as a weapon. I continued ahead until I was just off the back corner of the truck. Sweat dripped from my face, or was it adrenalin seeping from my pores?

Now what?

A minute passed and just as I was about to blunder out and make a bare-fisted frontal assault, the passenger door opened and a man dressed in khaki got out. He said something over his shoulder, slammed the door, and stepped into the trees. He was six feet away from me. I remained as still as the forest. The man unzipped his trousers and began to urinate. He lit a cigarette and started humming a tune.

I launched toward him in one swift move. He froze for an instant, unable to see what was coming through the trees, and held his hands out as I burst through the bushes with a roundhouse that caught him on the side of the jaw. It wasn't a very solid connection, but he fell to the side, probably more off balance than hurt, but he didn't make a sound, which was the best break I could have hoped for. His feet caught and he was off balance when I connected with a stiff jab that dropped him onto his face.

No movement.

Whether his friend saw us from the side mirror or heard the sound of bone on bone I couldn't tell, but I grabbed the man by his ankles and dragged him into the trees. I used the drawstring from my pants to tie his wrists together, my belt to secure his legs. He started to moan, so I tilted his face toward the sky, rubbed my knuckles, and nailed him again from the side. A loud crack sounded, which based on the sharp pain that shot up my arm, could have been his jaw or my knuckles. Either way, he was out cold.

I tried to catch my breath, but my heart rate made it impossible.

I felt around his pockets but found no weapons.

Great. Now what? I heard the driver's door open and the man shouted something in Spanish.

Crap.

He repeated himself, then called out: "Enrique!"

Crouched down, I watched his feet as he stepped out of the truck.

"Enrique?" He said again.

Silence.

I crawled under the truck, slowly and quietly. I was three feet away from his boots. I saw the flash of a rifle butt as he pulled it from the cab and shut the door softly. He didn't call Enrique's name again.

I watched his boots move toward the back of the truck, where he paused, then jumped around the end. Definitely ready to shoot first and ask questions later.

I grabbed a handful of gravel and threw the largest pebble toward where Enrique was tied up in the woods.

The soldier jumped around the corner again but this time hurried along the passenger side, heading toward the woods. When he ran past me I reached out and grabbed his foot, which caused him to pitch forward.

I held on tight.

His forward momentum pulled me out from under the truck, and whether he tried to use the gun to try and break his fall or not, its barrel ended up stabbed in the dirt. He hit the ground and rolled toward it, I crawled on all fours at high speed and dove toward him.

He was young and muscular. There was no fear on his face, only the expression of one predator evaluating another. In the split second I was in the air, he coiled his leg back and kicked out, catching me square in the chest, which knocked me to the ground.

When he tried to slide out to the side, my high school wrestling moves came back to me in a flash. I lunged again and hooked him in the armpit, spinning him back the other way. He tried to roll and swung a roundhouse left that caught me in the ear and launched a loud ringing in the depths of my brain.

No words had been spoken. Maybe he instinctively knew I couldn't understand him or felt confident he wouldn't need help from inside the farmhouse, which caused me a stab of doubt.

He coiled on a knee, then pounced.

I rolled away and heard him hit the ground, hard. I flung myself backwards, threw all my weight onto my elbow, and thrust down hard. It hit something soft that made a crunching sound, and we collapsed together.

He writhed wildly beneath me, which felt odd, not like he was trying to counter-attack but like he was squirming for . . . what? I spun, ready to deflect his next blow, but found him clutching his throat with both hands and rolling from side to side.

A gurgle from his mouth and eyes bugged halfway out of their sockets told me he couldn't breathe. I bent down and pulled his hands away.

His throat looked concave.

My elbow had crushed his larynx.

I watched him, horrified, until he went still.

Oh my God, I'd killed him.

Oh my God! I jumped to my feet, weaving, and swallowed a rush of bile.

My hands shook as I dragged him into the woods and placed him next to Enrique, who was moaning and starting to move. I knew I should hit Enrique again, but I couldn't. My legs trembled, my throat burned. I knew I wasn't finished yet, either.

Back on the driveway, I picked up the rifle and hurried toward the side door.

From inside the house I heard a scream that sounded like an enraged animal.

It was Señor Maceo.

50

FROM THE WINDOW I SAW SEÑOR MACEO WITH HIS ARMS WRAPPED AROUND a man he held from behind. In the moment it took me to get to the door I heard a gunshot inside.

I kicked the door open and lifted the rifle toward the crush of three people just as Señor Maceo dropped to the floor.

Manny Gutierrez was standing over the kitchen table, and Nina was prone on top of it, her blouse torn open and her jeans partially pulled down. I hesitated, the urge to shoot him put off because he was so close to Nina.

"Freeze, Gutierrez!"

His face went from bunched tight to wide eyes and an open mouth, then back to slit eyes in less than a second. He lowered the pistol to Nina's head. She hadn't moved. Face down, Señor Maceo hadn't stirred either, but a stream of blood flowed out from under him along a groove in the wood floor. The room smelled of burnt cordite, and faint smoke lingered around the light.

"Buck Reilly. I thought you'd escaped me, again."

"Drop the gun, Gutierrez." I shouldered the rifle. "I should have killed you last time I had the chance."

He laughed, and I saw his teeth were still as white, his moustache as perfectly groomed, and his skin as brown and buffed as it had been when he lived in Key West. He was still as cocky, too.

"No, Reilly, you drop the rifle or this beautiful young lady gets a bullet to the head. Which would be a shame, since I haven't finished with her yet."

"Leave her alone!"

"Ahh, touched a nerve, eh? It seems I'm always taking what you want." He shoved the pistol into her throat and she flinched for the first time. "Drop the rifle, NOW!"

Shit. I lowered the rifle and leaned it against the counter.

"Kick it to the floor!"

I tapped it with my foot and it fell with a crash.

Señor Maceo hadn't moved. Nina covered her chest with one arm and struggled to pull her pants up with the other. Gutierrez took a step away from her, turned the gun on me, and kicked one of the chairs forward.

"Sit," he said. "How did you get in here? What happened to my men?"

"Those two outside? *Siesta* time."

Nina rolled off the table. Her left eye was swollen and her cheek had begun to turn purple. Gutierrez hadn't wasted any time exacting his revenge. She pulled what was left of her blouse around her and knelt over her grandfather. She put her hand on the side of his neck.

I turned the chair backwards and sat facing Gutierrez so the chair back protected me.

"He's dead." Nina's voice was a whisper.

My heart broke for her—

A loud crack preceded excruciating pain and blackness.

I CAME TO ON THE FLOOR. GUTIERREZ HAD COLD-COCKED ME WITH HIS handgun.

"Get up!"

I rubbed the side of my face, which had gone numb. There was blood in my palm.

"Back in the chair!"

He gave a sidelong glance at Nina, but she was hugging her grandfather and crying quietly.

"I want the treasure you stole in Panama, Reilly. You should have crashed in the water—my men were ready to dive on your plane and my former speedboat to get the treasure and maps all at once. But somehow, you made it to land." He jerked the gun toward me. "So where is it?"

"You better worry about your boss, Director Sanchez. He wants to know where you stashed the *other* half of the treasure."

The look on his face was priceless.

"What are you talking about?" His voice was barely a whisper.

"I met Sanchez this morning, at the Hotel Las Jasmines. You know, the one in Viñales where he set up camp to look for you?"

"You're lying! He'd shoot you on site."

"We had a couple drinks together. He was most interested in what I had to tell him."

"He'd never let you go!"

"I have no value to him, Gutierrez. You have all the treasure. At least, that's what I told him. If I were you, I'd quit worrying about the other half, go to Viñales, and make peace with your boss. You'll never be able to enjoy it if you run."

Gutierrez bit his lip. "The treasure was on that plane that just left, wasn't it? Where did that come from? There's an old local legend that an amphibian plane crashed somewhere in western Cuba during the Bay of Pigs. Was it here? Is that what you did with the parts you took from your plane?"

I again looked at Nina. Sorry that fate had brought us all together.

An evil smile curled Gutierrez's lip. "Now your beloved Betty's just another hunk of garbage on the beach."

"I never had the treasure, Gutierrez. It's still on the Sea Lion, now safe under the Coast Guard's wing. Along with the captured Peruvian thieves who've already given your name as the man they delivered half the loot to. Should be on the news by tonight. Worldwide."

His eyes opened wide and his nostrils flared. "What about the maps you took from my boat?"

"You mean *my* maps? The ones you stole from me?"

"Semantics. You stole them from others first." He pointed the pistol toward my face. "Where are they?!"

"A place that would welcome you with open arms. And leg irons."

It was my turn to smile. Nina started to get up, and sensing her movement, Gutierrez kicked back and caught her on the shoulder, which sent her into the wall.

He turned the gun toward Nina. "Now, Reilly!"

"Should be in Key West by now too. Come back with me and I'll be happy to bring you copies in jail."

He raised the gun—

"Why do you care about old maps, Gutierrez?" I said.

He held the gun straight toward me.

"You have half the Atocha treasure," I said. "Reconcile with Sanchez and you'll get your cut. Otherwise, either he or the Peruvians will find you. Both think you double-crossed them. Then there's the half-crazed mercenary who brought the Peruvians along from Panama. Sanchez has confiscated his thirty-million-dollar G-IV and he's desperate."

His eyes opened wide and I knew I'd scored multiple hits. He started to nod his head, then glanced toward Nina, who had inched across the floor toward us.

He swung the gun toward her.

I launched forward on the balls of my feet and jammed the back of the chair into Gutierrez's chest, sending him backwards but he didn't go down.

He spun on a heel and hit me with a kick to the side of my head.

I crashed into the counter, but the momentum of his kick threw him sideways, off balance. The room became a blur of motion.

I lunged and caught him by the waist and tried to flip him over.

My grip didn't hold and I rolled over top of him, then he swung the gun and connected with the side of my head. A kaleidoscope of colors flashed behind my eyes.

Gutierrez shoved my legs off him and I fell onto my shoulder, still dizzy from getting gun-whipped. He easily rolled on top of me and pinned my arms with his knees.

He gritted his teeth and held the gun aloft.

My ears rang, my head swam, the side of my face felt flayed.

"If power's what you're after, an international thief and murderer will be a tough sell, even here in Cuba," I said. With his weight on my chest, my voice didn't sound nearly as tough as my words.

Gutierrez shoved the pistol in my face.

"Damn you, Buck Reilly!" He stared straight down the barrel. "At least I'll have the pleasure of killing you."

I tried to squirm left but he jammed his knees into my chest. There was nothing I could do—I closed my eyes.

BOOM!

The gunshot was so loud. I didn't feel—

His body suddenly fell on top of me.

Gutierrez groaned and squirmed, blood from his chest dripping onto mine.

Nina stood in the middle of the room, rifle to her shoulder, one eye closed and the other still looking down the sight now aimed at us on the floor.

"Nina! You got him!"

For a split second I wondered if she was going to shoot me next—after all she'd been through, who would blame her?

The rifle clattered on the floor, and Nina covered her face with both hands.

I pushed the now semi-conscious Gutierrez aside. Based on the blood pouring out of him, I decided he was beyond help. Nina fell into my arms and I held her tight.

Now what?

51

NINA WASN'T IN SHOCK, BUT SHE WAS PRETTY CLOSE.
Based on what I found in the back of Gutierrez's truck, he'd been well on his way to funding his power base or living in splendor until Ray and I showed up and jammed a broom in his spokes. Shame about that.

We hurtled at high speed in Gutierrez's truck down the coastal road I'd come to know oh too well. Nina was quiet, but her tears had stopped. There hadn't been time to move her grandfather, and my suggestion that she come with me back to Key West was again rebuffed, but she couldn't stand to be alone at the farm with dead and bleeding bodies in her kitchen, so she came with me. I hadn't told her about the body in the woods. The thought of that sickened me, but if I hadn't made it past those men, Gutierrez would have not only killed her grandfather, he'd have raped and killed Nina too. The term justifiable homicide had never registered with me until now.

There was no way to know whether Gutierrez had allies in the police, PNR, or Secret Police. But based on the cargo in the back of the truck, along with his reaction when I mentioned my meeting with Sanchez—

I'd forgotten something.

"What about your cousin, Ramón?" I said.

"That bastard."

She made a spitting sound toward the floor.

"It's his fault Papi's dead," she said. "*Tío* Luz and I will hunt him down—"

"The problem is, there's no way to know who else he's told," I said. "He might have been in the bushes the whole time for all we know. He can profit from any scenario, especially now."

She bit her lip and shook her head.

"Please come with me, Nina. It's too risky here now, especially if—"

She made a fist and pressed it against her lips. She didn't break down, but her face turned red holding the rush of emotion back.

I wiped a sudden tear away from my cheek.

"My family has run the farm for generations," she said. "I will bury Papi and appeal to my contacts at the Ministry of Agriculture. Nobody knows about the airplane, or you, aside from Ramón, and he's a criminal. I'm a respected *Vaqeura . . ..*" Her voice cracked.

Her profile was beautiful, even in anguish. The wave of her hair, the almond color of her skin, the inner strength that . . . I realized there was more than a concern for her safety driving my appeal for her to come to Key West.

I kept quiet for the last few miles to Puerto Esperanza. When we rounded the corner into the small fishing village, the sight of Gutierrez's truck sent women, children, and men alike running to their homes. Gutierrez's reign of terror here had peaked when he had Juan killed, but on the beach there was further evidence of his rampage. The remains of several fishing boats were piled in a heap of charred wood and ashes. A few boats remained intact on the shore. Would they be enough to sustain the village? Had Señor Maceo given the map of the sunken U-boat to Juan? I hoped someone still had it.

I checked my watch. It was 7:45. Sanchez and Gunner should be intersecting in Bahia Honda soon, so our escape from here should be clean.

I backed the truck in next to the remains of Betty. She too had been burned and was now completely destroyed, almost beyond recognition.

I'd thought my heart couldn't sink any further, but I was wrong.

The Beast had survived its take-off, but how had it held up in flight? I prayed that plane and pilot were okay.

"What's the point of coming here, Buck?" Nina said. "If there was a way back to Florida from Puerto Esperanza you'd have already taken it, right?"

"Come on, let's check Juan's family."

Once out of the truck, I went to the back and opened the gate. I took a gold ingot from one of the crates and placed it in my pocket. Faces appeared in windows. Once people could see it was me, and not Gutierrez, a few children emerged from their homes. There was no movement at Juan's house and the windows were drawn shut.

Inside, I found Maria lying in her bed. Her face was bruised and her eyes black.

"I'm so sorry, Maria. Your husband was a very good man."

Nina translated. When we asked about her children, she waved her wrist—they were outside. She had not uttered a word, and based on the swelling, I worried that her jaw was broken.

"Tell her Gutierrez will not be back to hurt them any more."

Based on Maria's wide eyes and the time Nina it took to explain, I assumed she went into detail as to Gutierrez's fate. Tears came, and maybe a sigh of what I hoped was relief.

I took the gold bar from my pocket.

"Tell her that while this will never replace Juan, it will help her family survive."

Nina placed the gold bar on the bed next to Maria, who looked bewildered.

"Where did that come from?" Nina asked.

I heard a distant clamor—a vehicle? It was getting louder by the second.

"What's that?" Nina said.

"Let's go."

52

WE HURRIED OUTSIDE AND FOUND THE VILLAGERS ON THE RUN TOWARD their homes. The noise of the vehicle, ever louder, was coming from the road leading into town.

"Come on!"

We ran toward the truck. Were there any weapons inside? I couldn't remember. Halfway there, the source of the sound appeared around the corner of the mangroves, palm trees and casuarina pines.

"Oh my God!" Nina said.

The Beast banked hard around the shoreline, maybe a hundred feet off the water. Her engines sounded in perfect cadence, which considering their difference in size was an amazing tribute to Ray Floyd's mechanical and piloting abilities. He banked out over the water and leveled off.

"So that's why you wanted to come here," Nina said.

I checked my watch. Ray was right on time.

When I turned to see Nina's expression, I was surprised to see many of the villagers back out on the narrow beach. They watched in amazement as Ray lowered the Beast into the water where the channel led to shore. The wind was light, as were the waves, so she settled in gently. The wing and engine from Betty looked solid, and it appeared as though Ray had worked out the weight difference in flight.

Now, if all the patches on the fuselage held, we'd be fine.

Nina's cheeks glistened with tears. She didn't need to say what was on her mind. Her grandfather would have been thrilled to see his Beauty on the water. I squeezed her close, she put her arm around my waist, and we locked in a tight embrace. Her tears were wet against my neck. I kissed them off her cheeks.

"Come with us, Nina. The farm will be fine. When the new government settles down, you can come back. I'll bring you in the Beast."

She shook her head. The answer was still no.

I could see the smile on Ray's face as he taxied up to the beach. I ran a finger across my throat, signaling for him to kill the engines, then waved him to shore. While he waded the fifty feet from where the Beast had come to rest, I opened the back of the truck.

"You see that?" Ray's grin was wider than I'd ever seen on him before. "She runs like a dream!"

Ray scanned down the beach. "Where's Señor Maceo? He's got to see this!"

His expression soured when he focused on me. "What happened to your face? And Nina's eye?"

Nina covered her eyes when Ray started to ask another question.

He finally saw me shaking my head. His brow furrowed, and he looked past me.

"Where'd you get that truck?"

I gave him a thirty-second rundown on what happened after he left. Ray deflated totally after about ten seconds. He hugged Nina, tears streaming down his cheeks, and then looked at me.

"What about Gutierrez?" he said.

Nina lifted her chin. "I shot the bastard."

One of the villagers must have spoken English, because that began a chain of Spanish that ran up the beach, and each time one person conveyed the news to the next, their eyes lit up and they hugged, or snapped their fingers, or clapped and hooted. It reminded me of *The Wizard of Oz*.

The wicked witch was dead.

"Help me with these, Ray." I pointed into the back of the truck.

He stared for a long few seconds. "Where have I seen those boxes before?"

"On the Sea Lion."

He looked confused. "Did Truck come—"

"Gutierrez and his boss, Director Sanchez, were behind it all. He admitted it before—" I looked at Nina. "He's been driving around with them in this truck because he double-crossed Sanchez and had nowhere safe to hide. It's the other half the Peruvians dropped off en route to the canal."

I climbed inside the truck bed and pushed the first crate out to the edge. Ray and I horsed it through the surf and hefted it up into the Beast's hatch. We did this three more times, and when we were finished, the once voluminous fuselage was heavily laden. No water was evident inside, so the patches had held, so far.

"This is going to play hell with the center of gravity I worked out," Ray said.

From the water, I scanned the beach. Hopefully these people's lives could be restored to a sense of normalcy. My gaze stopped on Nina. She was sitting on the truck's open tailgate watching us.

"Fire up the Beast, Ray. Let's get the hell out of here."

He disappeared between the crates and I waded back to shore. The sound of the engines starting got everyone's attention. I was amazed that the old Goose was airworthy, but then again, it wouldn't be by FAA standards. If and when we made it back to Key West, we'd see if she was really worth salvaging.

As I walked toward Nina there was a commotion amongst the villagers. They began to hurry toward their shacks again, just as they had when Nina and I arrived. She hopped off the truck and I was about to hug her goodbye when I saw what the others had seen.

A truck flew into the small compound.

It was the Maceo's farm truck.

53

I GRABBED NINA'S HAND AND PULLED HER INTO THE SURF.

"What are you doing?"

She followed my gaze toward the road and didn't miss a beat when she saw her truck. We high-stepped into the water until a rifle shot stopped us cold.

The Beast was fifty feet away, but we'd never make it.

To my amazement, Gutierrez stepped out onto the beach, followed by the guard I'd knocked out and tied up in the woods, who now had a rifle aimed at us.

We held up our hands.

There was a makeshift bandage around Gutierrez's shoulder and upper part of his chest, stained dark. He wavered as he stood and said something to the guard, who kept the rifle trained on us while Gutierrez tumbled over to peer into the back of the truck.

All his precious crates were gone.

I studied the men and saw no weapons other than the rifle. If I could disarm the guard we'd have a chance, but I was ten feet into the water, and thirty feet away from them. Gutierrez leaned on the truck's open tailgate and waved his hand toward us.

"Just stay behind me and move slowly," I said.

We shuffled toward shore when a loud roar behind us caused Nina and me to dive into the water.

What the hell?

Another continuous burst sounded. Water and sand flew into the air in front of us. The guard threw the rifle down and held his hands aloft.

Over my shoulder, I saw Ray in the Beast's open hatch aiming a Thompson submachine gun toward the shore.

Holy shit! *Ray?*

The guard backed up toward the road—then with no warning, close to a dozen villagers appeared from the brush and blocked his path to the truck. Maria, Juan's widow, walked forward from behind them and said something that sounded menacing. The villagers were holding machetes and fishing knives. One held a gaff.

The guard stood frozen. A machine gun on one end, or retribution on the other. He dropped to his knees and started to plead with the villagers who encircled him.

Good luck with that, amigo.

Gutierrez hadn't budged. I walked toward him. He was pale and held the arm on his wounded side with his good arm. His shirt was soggy with blood and he didn't look like he'd last long without medical attention.

"Reilly," he whispered. "The Bay of Pigs plane . . . There's supposed to be a letter . . ."

Letter? Did he—was it that well known?

Nina, now next to me, stared at Gutierrez as if he were a leper.

Maria walked toward us, speaking in Spanish.

"She says these are two of the men who tortured and hung Juan," Nina said.

I could see in Maria's eyes that she had a plan. She said something else and motioned toward Gutierrez.

"She said they'll take care of them and that you should get going before the others come too," Nina said.

Gutierrez stared into the sand. Wounded, defeated, dying on this shabby little beach in western Cuba, his stash of riches gone, and estranged from the power base that had allowed him to act brutally and without consequences. He'd been a thief/murderer while living in Key West pretending to be an art dealer, a thief/murderer while living in Cuba pretending to be a hero of the revolution.

As one of the conspirators behind the Atocha theft, though, he could also prove Truck's innocence—and mine.

"Ask Maria if I can take Gutierrez with me back to Florida. He's wanted there for murder."

"He murdered here, too, my Papi—"

"Nina, would you rather have him rot in jail the rest of his life for murder and treason, or meet a swift and merciful death here on this beach?"

She stared at me, her lips quivered, and her eyes were hot embers. Nina balled her hands into fists and spoke in a hushed yet determined tone with Maria. Finally, Maria nodded, gave Nina a hug, me a quick nod, and returned to her people.

"What's the deal?" I said.

"They keep that one, and we get Gutierrez," she said.

"We?"

Ray slogged to shore, holding the Thompson like he was Rambo. When he stopped next to me I saw he was grinning.

"Nice job, partner," I said.

"I kept a couple crates of guns and ammo for ballast to help with the center of gravity. Never thought I'd need to use one!" He grinned. "This is way better than video games."

The guard cried and pleaded as the villagers dragged him. I didn't know where Juan had been hung, but my guess was they would take him to that exact spot.

For the next few minutes Nina held the gun on Gutierrez, who lay on the beach while Ray and I organized the crates to balance the weight. The village had gone quiet, and Gutierrez had slipped back to a semi-conscience state.

I walked back to the shore. "All right, time to take this criminal back to Key West," I said.

Nina stood up, still holding the Thompson.

"I'm coming too."

A tingle passed through my back that stood me up straight.

"You were right, Buck. There's nothing left for me here." She nodded back toward the village. "I don't want to live for vengeance, and I don't want to live at the farm with Papi dead."

She started toward the plane, but I grabbed her and pulled her into my arms. She hugged me—with the gun between us.

"Don't take this the wrong way, Buck, but I'm leaving Cuba with you, not *for* you. Do you understand?"

A tinge of hurt cut through me, but just for a moment. I understood. Nina had to do things on her terms. I could live with that, but it didn't mean I'd leave her at the Key West airport like some kind of charter. And it didn't mean I wouldn't help her integrate into American culture or help her find her relatives.

"I understand, Nina. And I'll be there for you any way you need me."

A hint of a smile pulled at the corners of her mouth.

Gutierrez, now delirious, had to be carried, and once we were all on board, Ray gave me a you've-got-to-be-kidding look. Then he sighed, threw a weapons crate into the water to reduce the weight, closed the hatch, and helped me secure Gutierrez between the crates of Atocha treasure. Nina watched him from the jump seat.

"Okay, Captain," Ray said. "We're green to go."

The statement caused a reflexive glance back at Betty, now a charred, skeletal heap on the narrow beach. I knew the villagers would tell stories about her until she rusted into oblivion, and the thought made me choke up.

After a few seconds, a deep breath drew a mixture of adrenaline, joy, and trepidation into my system. A quick prayer and an accelerated pre-flight check led to a bumpy takeoff—listing heavily to starboard, and out over the Florida straits. Ray fine-tuned the weight distribution and Nina crawled forward, which helped, but it still wasn't perfect.

"How much fuel do we have left?" I said.

"A little more than half a tank," Ray said. "Flying around waiting for you took its toll."

"You're in charge of planning our escape if we have to ditch," I said.

"I already called the Coast Guard to let them know we're headed their way," Ray said. "Just in case."

Crap. I needed to call my favorite FBI agent, T. Edward Booth. His accusations about our disappearance could have been hard to defend if we weren't flying home in what I thought was a government-owned airplane that had been missing for fifty years. The Beast had no registration numbers, but the documents I found behind the instrument panel told quite the story.

And not only did we have the treasure, we had one of the thieves and an escaped spy.

That'll shut Booth up.

I realized I was smiling like an idiot. I'd never admit it, but my arrangement with Booth did have its upside.

What was I thinking?

Postscript

54

CONFUSION, JUBILATION, AND AMAZEMENT GREETED US AT KEY WEST Airport. Booth's accusations fell silent at the sight of Gutierrez, who was whisked into a waiting ambulance. No doubt torn as to where he'd get the most credit, Booth elected to dive in with the paramedics before they shrieked off the tarmac.

The news that followed over the next few days was nothing short of fantastic. Given that Gutierrez was a captured spy, albeit kidnapped from his home country, Booth had enough leverage to keep a tight lid on the facts that led up to the capture and the rescue of the missing antiquities. The lack of details had the news hounds crazy, and with Booth at the center of the storm, it looked like he'd been the one calling the shots.

Anonymity for me was just fine.

Gutierrez was airlifted to Miami-Dade Hospital where he faded in and out of life, finally stabilizing and regaining full consciousness. Booth told me Gutierrez had no recollection of coming to Puerto Esperanza to intercept us and would not believe for days that he was in a Miami hospital. His next stop would be an FBI safe house, then a federal penitentiary.

Truck's greeting upon his return to Key West was not what he'd envisioned. Yes, there were television crews, but they were there to witness his arrest for the theft of the *Atocha* treasure. He remained in jail until Booth had confirmation from Treasure Salvors that the treasure was intact and

Gutierrez's identification was verified. My constant pressure and insistence that Truck was innocent did nothing but irritate Booth.

Dismay is the only word that could describe how the Beast was viewed, both at the airport by those who knew Ray and me, and by the FAA, who after a careful review and investigation into her long-forgotten existence tried to claim she was government property. I filed a salvage claim, which under Florida and national maritime law gave me ownership. With challenges and threats by bureaucrats in Washington, the case promised to be complicated, high profile, and far more expensive than I could afford—until I had an epiphany and offered Booth the letter from Kennedy to Castro in exchange.

The government challenge was dropped the next day.

The Beast was now officially mine, which was sort of like winning a mold-infested houseboat in a poker game, but tickled the daylights out of Ray and me anyway.

Fully engaged in the restoration project, Ray had called known amphibian hotspots around the country. After six days, he hit the jackpot in Sitka, Alaska. There was a charter company there that had winnowed its fleet of amphibians to switch over to more dependable sea planes like Cessna Caravans and de Havilland Beavers, but they had one Widgeon they felt was worth repair. The good news was they also had a Goose they were parting-out, and our luck held as their Goose had an intact port wing assembly and original radial engine they agreed to trade for Betty's Lycoming engine and wing that we'd fashioned onto the Beast. Arrangements were made, trucks chartered, and the dismantling of the Beast was commenced. Ray and I did the work after hours since I couldn't afford to pay him and he had an understandable fondness for the Beast, having brought her back to life. She would be out of commission for a few weeks, at best, but there was a slight chance that Last Resort Charters and Salvage would fly again.

The full recovery of the Atocha treasure made headlines all over the country. Donny, the General Manager of Treasure Salvors, was euphoric since much of their operation was fueled by the museum exhibit and store that provided a steady income and occasional investors for new salvage activities.

The missing gold ingot caused a brief stir until I explained the sacrifice Juan's family had made to keep Ray and me safe, which ultimately led to the treasure's rescue. Donny muttered that as much of a pain in the ass as Standard Mutual Insurance had been, they could cover one three-pound gold bar. I decided against mentioning his insurance company's rent-a-mercenary, Gunner, as that would only exacerbate Donny's situation, and he wouldn't have known about him anyway. He promised a grand celebration to coincide with the climax of Fantasy Fest, with me and Ray to be the guests of honor.

In a rare quiet moment in my suite at the La Concha, I read a letter that had arrived while I was gone. It was from my brother.

> Buck,
> Sorry for the way things went down in Geneva. We may not see eye to eye, and we may have never been close, but adopted or not, you're my brother. I don't agree with everything you've done in your life, and the investigations into your activities at the end of e-Antiquity remain a concern, but if you ever need my help —badly— then call me. See you ...
> —B

His words made me smile. Not exactly a proclamation of brotherly love, but I wouldn't expect that from him. It was a start.

I suddenly remembered another letter; the one Karen had left the morning she took off. I took a deep breath, tore the envelope open and read the single paragraph once, then read it again.

"I'll always remember you too, Karen," I said.

With the two letters folded and placed with the note from my father saying I was adopted—news I still hadn't had the chance to process—my heart felt lighter. I spent some quiet time alone, thought of the souls that had come and gone from my life, and treasured their memories.

The night had finally come and Key West was in the throes of another wild climax to Fantasy Fest. Women whose outfits consisted of colorful paint adorning their otherwise naked bodies roamed the Old Town streets, bars, and restaurants in the local version of Mardi Gras or Carnival. Hotels and jails were packed, the line of cars extended halfway up the Keys for day-trippers hoping for some quick memories, and Duval Street was closed to all vehicular traffic. The weather cooperated and I watched what promised to be another memorable fête from The Top, the rooftop lounge above the La Concha Hotel.

I had lived through a few of these parties and braced myself for any surprise that might come, knowing none would be more welcome than the lovely lady to my right.

Nina Maceo had been welcomed into Key West like the hero she was—after all, she'd disabled the Atocha thief and saved my life. So many people viewed her with awe and respect. The rest just marveled at her beauty. I had respected what she'd told me on the beach at Puerto Esperanza and waited for a sign from her, which took all of half of the first evening to come. Since then we'd been inseparable. I had delighted in showing her around my island home and helping her connect with her grandmother and other relatives who'd prospered in the sugar industry mid-state. She was set to go see them tomorrow, but for tonight, she was all mine.

"Are you ready?" I said.

Her smile was brilliant. Incandescent. Irresistible.

"I feel so overdressed," she said.

She was wearing a slinky, cream-colored silk dress that offset her almond skin and glorious hair, and accentuated her shapely, athletic build.

"We can go get you painted up, if you'd prefer."

She took my arm and we made our way down the elevator and through the back of the La Concha lobby, where every eye turned to watch her pass. We took our time and walked arm in arm up Whitehead, past ancient banyan trees, government buildings, and small inns. The noise and energy a block over on Duval was palpable, and horns, fireworks, and sweet and musty aromas filled the air. But it was all background to the purr of Nina's voice and her rich laughter, meant only for me.

We arrived at the Treasure Salvors museum at the same time as Ray, who'd taken a cab.

"Fancy meeting you two here." Ray pulled the door open for Nina and shook his head as he watched her pass.

"What's the matter?" I said.

"How come you always get the girl?"

"Sorry old pal, but this time it's special."

"Sure, Buck, it's always special."

The crowd inside erupted a second later as Nina walked in. Ray and I followed and found the museum full of friends, officials, and one person I could have done without, Special Agent T. Edward Booth—who joined the cheers for our entry. Yes, even Booth. But he wasted no time taking me by the arm and steering me to a quiet corner.

"One last piece of official business before your little party starts," he said.

"I lost your phone if that's—"

"Forget the phone, Reilly, I'll get you another one next time I need you." He glanced around, then leaned closer to me. "Do you know a Richard Rostenkowski, a.k.a. Gunner?"

I scratched my chin. "Doesn't sound familiar, why?"

"He was a hired gun for Standard Mutual, the insurance company that covers these criminals." This with a nod toward the Treasure Salvors crowd. "The Cuban Secret Police have him in custody. He says he knows you and that you were supposed to get him out of Cuba but double-crossed him."

I took a step back.

"Would I do such a thing?" I smiled. "And that reminds me, Booth, when we were salvaging Betty we found a transponder on board. I understand you planted that there."

A rare smile puckered his lips. "I knew you'd lead me to that treasure one way or another, Reilly, but I wasn't sure you'd come home."

"Such trust." I noticed a crowd forming around Nina. "Go have yourself a Shirley Temple, Booth. I'm headed to the rum bar."

Donny Pogue, Truck Lewis and I all converged upon Ray and Nina at the same time. Donny gave Nina a tentative peck on the cheek and me a bear hug.

"We're going to have a quick ceremony to honor and thank you, Nina, Truck, and Ray before we kick off the party."

"That's not nec—"

"And when I give you the reward check, act pleasantly surprised and don't let your eyes bug out of your head, all right?" Donny dug into his pocket. "But first, this is from me."

He held his clenched hand out and I placed mine below it.

When I saw what he'd dropped in my palm, I couldn't speak.

It was a beautiful gold chain with a handsomely mounted gold doubloon.

"It's from the Atocha. Whether you found it at the bottom of the ocean, at the Panama Canal, or on a Cuban tobacco farm, you earned this one, friend. But the real reward is the check, so thanks again."

I found my voice. "Thanks, Donny, you shouldn't have."

"Yeah, right. Now you better catch up to Nina with all those drooling buzzards around her."

He gave me a slap on the back and I couldn't help but smile.

Life was finally starting to look up.

The End

Read on for a preview of *Crystal Blue*, the next Buck Reilly adventure...

CRYSTAL BLUE

by John H. Cunningham

1

THE AIR WAS TURBULENT OVER THE LOWER KEYS, BOTH IN AND OUTSIDE THE Beast. Towering cumulus clouds had built throughout the day, and now squalls caused me to zig and zag my way toward my charter customer Goodspeed's destination of Fort Lauderdale.

"When I heard you were running a charter service in Key West," Goodspeed said, "I expected something first class. With as much money as you ripped off at e-Antiquity, I figured you'd be living large."

I bit my lip.

He'd started the verbal attack right after we took off out of Key West. Rather than watching the turquoise water and islands pass under us like most charter customers, he stared right at me.

"Hell, the engines don't even match the wings. What'd you do, build this thing out of scrap?"

He was a big man, probably a former high school or university sports star who'd gone soft but still had the big frame. A bully all his life, I'd bet on it. He had money—or at least he dressed to make sure you thought he did—and wore his generation's symbols of prosperity: golfer's tan and a bulky gold watch. Judging by the wrinkles around his downturned mouth he'd never had a kind word for anybody, certainly not me.

I gripped the wheel and glanced down to my left. The seven-mile bridge was below. On and on he yapped.

"Are you going to keep this up the whole way to Fort Lauderdale?" I said.

Goodspeed smiled. "I've only just got started, boy. You cost me several hundred thousand—"

I shoved the wheel forward and added 20 degrees of flap. The Beast nose-dived toward the thin strip of land below.

"What the hell're you doing, Reilly? We're going down—"

I flicked off the intercom.

Halfway up Marathon Key was the small airport where I set the Beast down hard on the tarmac, military style, which bounced Goodspeed in his seat. His arms were crossed now, his mouth a thin line. We taxied to the small terminal, a hundred miles from his destination, where I reduced the RPMs and pulled off my headset. He stared at me, squint-eyed.

"This is your stop, *Mr.* Goodspeed."

"I paid for a round-trip flight—"

"You should have read the fine print in the contract."

He just stared at me. I took off my sunglasses and quoted from it word for word. "'*The pilot has the authority to deviate from, or alter the flight plan at any time, for any reason, if in his sole judgment the aircraft is in danger, in which case the pilot can terminate the charter.*'"

I unclipped his seatbelt, pulled him up, and all but tossed him out of the hatch.

"This charter's terminated."

Once he had both feet on the ground, he scurried to the wing tip, turned and shook a fist at me. "You'll regret this, Buck Reilly!" Something else about how he had a contract this time and he'd have my ass, but I didn't hear the next threat because I'd slammed the hatch shut.

Airborne and headed south, I envisioned the deserted island out in the Marquesas. I'd be there tomorrow, alone, camping for as many days as my water would last, or at least until Lenny Jackson's first political debate next week.

I was done with charters. Time for some snorkeling, spear fishing, and solitude under the starry skies above the little no-name Key out in the Marquesas.

As I flew over the old Bahia Honda bridge, I remembered jumping off the lower section as a teenager when my family vacationed here. We'd rent old conch houses in Key West and drive the thirty-odd miles north to picnic at Bahia Honda. Legend had it that a fifteen-foot hammerhead shark cruised the channel. My brother and I would walk out along the bridge's old rusted spans, twenty feet above the waterline, and jump in. We convinced ourselves there was safety in numbers. Until the time, a couple hundred yards from shore, when we counted to three and jumped into the gin-clear waters and I surfaced to find myself alone. I searched a terrified few seconds before Ben's laughter sounded above me.

"Better get your ass moving before that hammerhead eats you!"

I swam as hard as I could, convinced the shark would rise from the depths and rip me in half. With what strength I had left I chased Ben down the shore and throughout the campsites until I caught and pinned him in a patch of briars. He was still laughing, and before long I was too. But I never again trusted him to jump with me below that bridge.

A noise my engine shouldn't have been making brought me back to Goodspeed's bad-mouthing my old amphibious Grumman. Yes, this 1946 era Goose was a work in progress, and no, maybe I shouldn't have agreed to the roundtrip flight—the first since the Beast was deemed airworthy—but dammit, I needed the money. It didn't happen often, but every now and then a former investor in e-Antiquity, my bankrupt former treasure hunting business, showed up and dug at my scar tissue.

Nearly back to Key West, a familiar voice sounded in my headset and called out my N-number.

"What are you doing in the tower?" I said.

"Got an important message for you," Ray Floyd said. As the head mechanic at Key West International Airport, he was usually banished from Air Traffic Control, but Donny the controller was a friend known to bend a rule.

"Such as?"

"How does your customer like the Beauty?" Ray said.

"He didn't."

"*Didn't?* You can't even be to Miami yet—"

"Let's just say he was a little too critical of the Beast's comforts. I dropped him at Marathon."

I imagined Ray's shoulders sagging. He'd worked hard to get the Goose back into condition, and even with the new seats, the in-depth aesthetical renovation had yet to commence, thanks largely to the fact that I was broke.

"There goes the money for the paint job," Ray said. "How's Last Resort Charter and Salvage ever supposed to be profitable if you leave customers stranded?"

"I'm done with charters, Ray. Pompous assholes like Goodspeed are too hard to swallow. I just want to go—"

"Done with charters? What, you're now just Last Resort Salvage? How will you afford—"

"What's so important, Ray?"

He was silent a moment, then cleared his throat.

"There was a beautiful woman here just now, looking for a multi-day charter to the Virgin Islands."

"The only reason I'll end my camping trip will be to witness the release of Lenny Jackson's political aspirations on his unwitting competitors in next week's debate." The thought made me smile. Conch Man was primed to give them hell. "When I get back, I'm heading to the La Concha to get my stuff together. I'll be back at the airport bright and early tomorrow, just like we agreed."

"She was sexy."

"I don't care—"

"Even her name's sexy—Crystal. Said a famous musician referred her to you and that it was for a charity—"

"No charters and no charities!"

Mechanical genius, social philosopher, and video game ace, Ray had become a close friend in the time I'd been living in Key West. Eccentricities aside, he didn't give a rat's ass about my past, and he provided ballast to my occasional overly aggressive endeavors. But he could also be a pain.

I'd made a plan and I was sticking to it, even if I couldn't afford to blow off a call for a multi-day charter. I deserved a break. The stress of pouring my energies into fixing up the Beast had taken its toll. I needed a deserted island—alone with my snorkel gear, a Hawaiian sling, and hammock—a lot more than another charter customer.

Even a beautiful one.

Buy the rest of **CRYSTAL BLUE** at WWW.JHCUNNINGHAM.COM
Available in print and e-book formats

CPSIA information can be obtained at www.ICGtesting.com
Printed in the USA
BVOW08s2039300915

420346BV00003B/286/P